'A SERIOUSLY creepy thriller. I may never venture into the loft again'

MARK BILLINGHAM

'A mind-blowing, head-rattling, whirlwind of a thriller'

JOANNA CANNON

'A brilliantly chilling story with tension on every page. A razor-sharp thriller'

T.M. LOGAN

'Disturbing, blackly funny and completely compulsive, Jackson wrings every bit of possible tension from his deliciously chilling premise'

ALEX NORTH

'Brilliant. So twisted, clever and funny. Highly recommended if you like your crime novels pitch black with a splash of humour'

MARK EDWARDS

'Dark and disturbing yet so absorbing. Jackson knows how to reel you in with emotion and yet shock you with the darkness. Creepy as hell'

MEL SHERRATT

'Utterly compelling and impossible to put down. A terrifying glimpse into a fractured mind. Incredible'

LUCA VESTE

THE
RESIDENT

DAVID JACKSON

This paperback edition first published in 2021
First published in Great Britain in 2020 by
VIPER, part of Serpent's Tail,
an imprint of Profile Books Ltd
29 Cloth Fair
London
ECIA 7JQ
www.serpentstail.com

1 3 5 7 9 10 8 6 4 2

Printed and bound in Great Britain by
CPI Group (UK) Ltd, Croydon, CR0 4YY

A CIP catalogue record for this book is available from the British Library.

ISBN 978 1 78816 4368
eISBN 978 1 78283 6513

For Lisa

They're here! They've come for us!

Not possible. How could they know?

Who cares? They know. What else could this be?

Brogan stared wide-eyed at the flashes of blue light bouncing crazily off the windows of the houses. No sirens, just the lights. They wanted to catch him by surprise.

We have to go. NOW!

Brogan raced back to the dining room. He grabbed his backpack and turned to the couple seated at the table.

'It's been a pleasure staying with you,' he told them. 'Thank you for your hospitality.'

He didn't wait for a response. He moved swiftly to the kitchen, slid open the patio door and stepped into the night's embrace.

He could hear urgent whispers and footsteps in the neighbouring garden to his left. He went right, hopped up onto a wheelie bin, then swung over the fence.

A torch beam sliced through the blackness and picked him out.

'He's here!' yelled a voice. And then: 'Police! Stay where

you are! Down on the ground!'

Brogan knew that the copper was expecting him either to obey or flee. He did neither.

He ran straight at the approaching police officer, who yelped in surprise. Brogan kicked out, slamming his foot into the man's chest, sending him hurtling into the wall of the house behind. As the officer rebounded, Brogan drew back his fist. He did not pause to think, *This is a policeman, and if I hurt him I will be in deep trouble.* He didn't worry that the man might have a wife or kids. He knew only that the uniform in front of him represented an obstacle to freedom.

And so Brogan let his fist fly, right into his opponent's throat. Hit it so hard that it seemed the man's windpipe was crushed against his spine.

As the officer collapsed to the ground, clutching his neck and spluttering, Brogan set off again. The voices were growing louder, closer. A noose was tightening around him.

He scaled the next fence with ease. Then the next, and the one after that. Lights came on. Dogs began barking. At one house, a man in pyjamas came out to see what the commotion was. He took one astonished look at Brogan and scurried back indoors.

Brogan kept going. He was fit and he was strong, and he didn't worry about consequences. They would catch him one day, he knew that.

But perhaps luck wasn't ready to abandon him just yet.

TUESDAY 4 JUNE, 1.46 AM

He stayed away from the main roads, knowing that they carried the most risk. But he also knew he couldn't keep roving through the city's capillaries for much longer. The police would be out in force, armed with his description and now a grudge for the harm done against a fellow officer.

The problem was where to hide. The Carter house had been perfect. They didn't get any visitors – hardly any phone calls, for that matter. He was able to keep them company for days. Not that they appreciated it. A lodger like Brogan was the last thing any sane person wanted.

He wondered how the police had cottoned on to his presence. What error had he made?

I think it was the noise. You had that music system turned up really loud, you know.

Yeah, well, there was a good reason for that.

The stutter of helicopter blades yanked him back to the present. He looked skywards and saw the machine hovering overhead.

They're looking for us.

Yes, yes, I know.

We need to find cover. Once they spot us, it's over.

I know, damn it! Let me think.

He changed direction, seeking an escape from the centre of police activity. He didn't know where he was. All the houses looked the same: row after row of small terraced properties, sleeping while swirls of rubbish danced on the pavement in front of them. The occasional shuttered pub or corner shop. Graffiti on the walls.

And then he saw it.

The abandoned end house, its windows and doors boarded up as if to reassure Brogan that it was willing to turn a blind eye and say nothing.

Brogan crossed the street and entered the alleyway adjoining the house. He scanned the area to make sure nobody was observing him from a window, then he leaped, clamped his hands onto the top of the wall and pulled himself up.

He dropped down into a yard that had been concreted over many years ago. Now the surface was marbled with cracks, and waist-high weeds had shouldered their way up through them.

He made his way to the back door of the house and studied it in the weak moonlight. The boards covering it were made of plywood that had been screwed to the frame.

He slipped off his backpack and felt around inside. He had items in here that most people would never dream of toting around with them. He rejected a crowbar as being too noisy, and instead brought out a screwdriver. He spent the next few minutes carefully unscrewing the board covering the lower half of the door, dropping each screw into his pocket in case anyone should search the area. He liked to be thorough.

When he moved the board aside, he saw that the door itself looked sturdy enough, but that its lock was cheap and primitive. He took out his set of picks and had the door open in no time.

He left the upper boards in place, and ducked under them to enter the house. When he was inside, he pulled the lowermost board back into position and closed the door.

The darkness was total. Brogan slipped his hand once more into his pack, and pulled out his torch. He flicked it on and played its light over the door. He saw that it had hefty bolts at the top and bottom, and he slid both into place.

He turned, and saw that he was in a bare kitchen. There were no appliances here now. Just a sink, a few battered units, and a single wooden chair. He tried the light switch, but nothing happened. No surprise there. No gas either, probably. But what about water?

He walked to the sink and turned on both taps. Nothing, not even a single explosive spurt.

He searched the cupboards and drawers, and found some scouring pads, a half-empty bottle of bleach, a plastic jug with a crack running down its side, a rusty can opener and a tin of nails and screws.

Great. All the things a man could ever want.

He found the stopcock beneath the sink and tried opening it up, but his efforts were in vain. The water had obviously been disconnected at the mains in the street.

He did a quick survey of the rest of the house. He found a

living room, dining room, bathroom and two bedrooms. The only thing to get excited about was an old mattress left on one of the bedroom floors. Somewhere he could get some sleep. He suddenly realised how exhausted he was.

You can't sleep yet.

Why not?

Your arms. Look at your arms.

Brogan rolled back his sleeves, then sighed.

He headed back downstairs. In the kitchen he turned off his torch, then opened the back door and moved away the board so he could clamber outside.

The air smelled sweet. In the distance he could hear the helicopter hunting for him. He would be safe here for a while. The danger would come when he needed to go in search of food and drink.

He followed the wall to the rear corner of the house. There was a rainwater barrel here – he had noticed it when he arrived. He leaned over and peered inside. The disc of the pale moon stared back at him from the still surface of the water. He doubted it would be safe to drink: the stagnant smell told him that much. But that wasn't why he had come out here.

He plunged his arms into the water. Dark tendrils curled away from his flesh and swirled across the face of the moon as he washed off the blood of the couple he had murdered.

TUESDAY 4 JUNE, 8.07 AM

He didn't know what made him wake up, or even whether it was a time he wanted to be awake. It was so black in here.

He reached out an arm and swept it across the carpet, which felt distastefully hard and sticky. His fingers found the torch, and he grabbed it and turned it on. The blaze of light blinded him, and it was a while before his eyes could adjust enough to read his watch. He saw that it wasn't long after eight. He debated whether to get more sleep, but he started to notice how musty the mattress smelled, and his mind began to race with thoughts of what tiny creatures might be living in its damp, fungus-ridden interior.

He sat up, shone his torch around the room. In several places the flowery wallpaper had peeled away, revealing in one corner a patch of mould in the shape of a smiley face, beaming happily at him.

'Morning to you, too,' said Brogan. 'What's for breakfast?'

Who're you talking to?

You, I suppose.

I don't look like that. Is that how you imagine me?

Well . . .

Don't answer that. And in response to your question, the answer is nothing. There is nothing for breakfast. You should have been better prepared. I told you to fill the bag with food for this kind of emergency. But would you listen?

Brogan's stomach issued an angry growl.

See? Even your internal organs agree with me.

Brogan's mouth was dry, too. He needed water even more than he needed food. A cup of freshly ground coffee would hit the spot nicely. That, and a full English breakfast.

His stomach rumbled more loudly.

He stood up. Was it sunny outside? Overcast? It didn't sound like it was raining.

He couldn't live like this for long. Not in permanent darkness with no food. He would either starve or go insane.

Insane. Some would say he had ticked that box a long time ago.

Maybe they're right.

It's all relative. One man's normal is another man's looney tunes.

But that's what makes the world go around, right? Variety is the spice of life. And death. Yup, a death or two certainly relieves the boredom.

The police would have discovered that for themselves in the past few hours. Their night would not have been without a substantial amount of stimulation. They would have looked down at the lifeless, blood-drenched bodies of the Carters and wondered what the hell had gone through the mind of their killer.

Let them wonder. We don't owe them any explanations. We do what we do, and that's that.

Brogan went on another tour of the house, hoping that he'd missed something of value the previous night. On the landing, a wooden ladder lay along the wall. He wondered why the previous occupants hadn't taken it with them, but on closer inspection he realised it was old and rotten. It would probably snap as soon as anyone put a foot on it.

He went into the front bedroom. Just a wicker chair here with a huge hole in the seat. In the bathroom, a cabinet fixed to the wall contained a manky toothbrush and a half-empty bottle of Listerine.

Back downstairs, he realised that the living room and dining room had been completely stripped. Not even carpets left.

Sullenly, he walked to the kitchen. He switched off his torch and stared into the blackness while trying to imagine the humming of a fridge, the sizzling of sausages in a pan, the bubbling of a kettle coming to the boil.

Don't torture yourself. We'll get through this. We always do.

Yeah, sure.

He switched the torch back on, then sat down on the only chair. He knew he couldn't go out yet, not in broad daylight. He'd be easy pickings. He'd have to wait until nightfall. Swap one darkness for another. And that was a long time off.

Let's play a game.

What kind of game?

Celebrity kill-off. We each choose a celebrity we'd most like to kill, and how they should die. The most fitting ending wins.

Nah, I don't want to play that.

Suit yourself. Just trying to pass the time.

He turned the torch off again to save battery, then sat

there for what seemed like a whole morning. When he finally checked his watch, he found that less than an hour had passed.

Shit.

He went upstairs to the bathroom and voided his bladder noisily but didn't bother to flush. In the unlikely event there was still water in the cistern, it would be worth saving.

He went back out onto the landing. His torch alighted on the ladder again.

Why the hell was it here anyway?

Hey, genius, what do you think a ladder's for? You go up them, stupid.

Brogan raised the beam of light. There, in the ceiling. A hatch.

What the hell. Anything to pass the time.

The ladder creaked and shifted in his hands, as if it was about to fall apart. He carried it to the alcove behind the banister overlooking the stairwell, then used its upper end to poke the hatch cover open before levering it into position.

He shone the torch up through the hatch. Little to see but rafters and the underside of the roof tiles.

Here goes nothing.

He started climbing. One rung, then a second. Pausing, he rocked the ladder from side to side to check it would hold his weight. It felt rickety, but it stayed in one piece.

He kept going. Up and up, until his head and shoulders were in the roof space. He scanned the attic with the torch, and realised he had almost certainly wasted his time. The only thing up here was a single cardboard box.

In for a penny . . .

He climbed to the top of the ladder and stepped into the loft. Moving around wouldn't be easy: there were no floorboards, so he'd have to keep his feet on the joists if he didn't want to go crashing through the plaster into the room below.

Carefully, he made his way across to the cardboard box. He so wanted the box to be heavy, and when he reached out a hand and pushed it, he willed it to offer some resistance.

It moved easily. Too easily. It was just an empty box.

What did you expect? The crown jewels?

I don't know. Just . . . something. Anything.

Life doesn't work like that. The only stuff people leave behind is the crap they can't be bothered to carry. Unless they die, that is.

Brogan's shoulders slumped. Sometimes, he thought, it would be nice to have a pleasant surprise.

A few more of those might have convinced us to spare a life or two.

He sighed, then took a final look around before heading back to the ladder.

And that's when he realised something.

Well, will you look at that?

At the far end of the attic, the wall separating this house from the adjoining one wasn't whole. Presumably to save on bricks, the builders hadn't taken it all the way up to the roof's ridge, and through the gap he could see the neighbouring space beyond.

Brogan felt a surge of excitement. It wouldn't be too difficult to climb through that gap and make his way into the attic of the next house.

What are you waiting for? Get yourself in there.

He stepped from joist to joist until he reached the wall. The bricks stopped at chest height, and although his torch revealed that the next attic was as empty as this one, he didn't despair. Below that attic was a house, and in that house could be all manner of interesting things. Perhaps even people. Someone to play with.

He put the torch down on top of the wall, then clambered over. Once on the other side, he retrieved his torch and made a fuller examination. The layout seemed very much like the previous one, but what made it even more thrilling was that it also allowed passage into the next house in the terrace.

Jesus, this is a goldmine. Looks like we can get into every house on the street!

We're in no hurry. One house at a time. Spread the fun out a little.

He made his way to the ceiling hatch, then lay down across the joists and put his ear to the wooden cover. No sounds reached him.

He opened the cover a fraction, to test the quietness of its hinges. When they didn't complain, he raised it a little further, then inched forward and peered down.

As in the first house, the hatch was situated above an alcove overlooking the staircase. There was no loft ladder here, but a chest of drawers stood in the alcove, providing him with a handy stepping stone.

He listened some more. Heard only the ticking of a loud clock. He began to think the house was empty. Perhaps the occupants had gone to work.

He started to raise the cover to its full extent . . .

And nearly dropped it when he heard his own name.

'Thomas Brogan was last seen in the Mayhill area of the city, and police are advising that he should be regarded as extremely dangerous.'

Brogan smiled, partly in relief at the realisation that the voice was coming from a radio, but also from pride at his new-found fame. It was amusing to have achieved celebrity status due to multiple homicides.

'Although police officials have not explicitly identified Thomas Brogan as their chief suspect in the murders of Mr and Mrs Carter, it is clear that he is linked to the killings. Mr Brogan was already on their wanted list following the discovery of the dead bodies of his parents over two weeks ago. There are also reports that he may have been involved in a series of similar murders across the city, although police have refused to confirm this.'

Brogan's smile broadened. It was clear that the police were panicking, while simultaneously trying not to alarm the public.

The cops know exactly what you did.

I know.

They know who, and how many.

I know.

Took them a while, though, the stupid bastards. They probably still wouldn't have a clue if you hadn't killed your parents.

Yeah. Wait – are you trying to blame me for something?

No. Not at all.

Because it was your idea, as I recall.

Absolutely. I wasn't trying to pass the buck. Your parents' card was always marked. It was just a question of when.

Brogan suddenly became aware of another voice – a real one this time, almost drowned out by the radio.

'Elsie! Elsie!' A woman's voice, coming up the stairs.

Brogan lowered the hatch cover into position, then scooted across to where the sound of the radio was loudest beneath him.

'Elsie! Turn that down. You'll disturb the neighbours.'

Brogan heard another voice, weaker and more croaky than the first, but couldn't make out the words.

The radio was suddenly silenced, and then the first voice spoke again. 'What were you saying, Elsie? I couldn't hear you with that racket.'

'What?'

'I said— Never mind. Here, let's sort you out.'

The conversation stopped for a minute. Then: 'There. Can you hear me now?'

'I could hear fine before.'

'Only because the radio was at full volume. You can't keep doing that, Elsie. You'll annoy the neighbours.'

'They're miserable buggers, anyway.'

'I'm not surprised. I'd be miserable if the lady next door to me kept making so much noise. Why don't you put your hearing aid in when you wake up?'

'I told you. It keeps whistling at me.'

'You should be grateful. I can't remember the last time anyone whistled at me.'

She broke out into raucous laughter at her own joke, but Elsie didn't seem to appreciate the humour.

'All right,' said Elsie's visitor. 'Come on, let's get you washed and dressed. What do you fancy for breakfast?'

'Cornflakes.'

'Okay. Have you got any?'

'No.'

Brogan smiled again. He was taking a liking to this old dear. He followed the voices to the bathroom, then back to the bedroom. He delighted in the fact that he could spy on them so easily, and yet remain completely invisible. Less detectable even than the proverbial fly on the wall.

He learned much from the conversation. Elsie was eighty-nine years old and lived alone. The visitor's name was Kerry, and she was Elsie's carer. She came twice a day, morning and evening. The only other regular caller was Reg, the Meals on Wheels man. He was, according to Elsie, another miserable bugger.

Brogan heard the front door shutting when Kerry left the house. A minute later, a car was started up and driven away. Elsie was alone again. Or so she thought.

What do you think? Shall we go down there?

No. Not yet. It's too soon.

The woman's eighty-nine. It's not too soon for her. She might prefer to go at the hands of a virile young serial killer rather than wasting away with dementia and diarrhoea and all those other features of decrepitude.

If I kill Elsie, we'll have to leave.

So what do we do now, then?

In response, Brogan shone his torch towards the attic of the third house in the terrace.

He stood up and made his way to the wall, once again careful to put his feet only on the wooden joists. He scaled the wall as easily as he had the first, then dropped lightly to the other side.

Another dismal void. No floorboards or lighting. Not even a cardboard box. But what of the home below?

As he had done in Elsie's house, he spread his weight across the joists and put his ear to the hatch. He could hear two voices, a male and a female, and it sounded like they were bickering.

He raised the hatch cover slightly and peered down. No sign of a ladder or even a piece of furniture below. Getting in and out of this house could prove tricky.

The voices were loud. Brogan could tell the couple were downstairs, but even from this distance he could make out the conversation.

'She's a bloody nutcase,' the male was saying. 'I don't know why you listen to her. She's not a doctor. The closest she's ever come to medical training is putting on a plaster.'

'She looked it up on the internet,' said the woman.

'Oh, the internet. Well, she must be right, then. We all know how reliable the information is on the internet.'

'She said it could be a ruptured disc, and that you should go back for a second opinion.'

'Barbara Lewis has given me enough opinions to last me a bloody lifetime. Do you know who her latest target is?'

'No. Who?'

'Ralph.'

'Ralph? What's wrong with Ralph?'

'Exactly. According to Barbara, he's severely obese and in danger of having a coronary.'

'He's not overweight. He's just . . . big-boned.'

'That's what I said, and that's why I don't trust the advice of Barbara bloody Lewis. I don't need to go bothering the doctor again. I've put my back out, that's all. It'll be better in a few days.'

'Well, I hope so. It's hard enough getting all the house-work done without having you under my feet all the time. But anyway, to be on the safe side I've made you an appointment.'

'An appointment? Who with?'

'What have we just been talking about? The doctor, of course.'

'Pam! I've just told you, I don't need—'

'I don't care. You're going.'

'When?'

'Tomorrow. Three o'clock.'

'Well, you'll have to take me. With this back, I can't—'

'Yes, Jack, I know all about your flipping back. I'm sick of hearing about it.'

'Charming. Word of advice, Pam: don't go into the nursing profession, will you?'

Brogan continued to listen. He learnt eventually that Jack worked for the city council. Pam had long ago abandoned her job as a dental receptionist, and now occasionally helped out at a charity shop. They'd had kids – at least two – who were grown up and had fled the nest. Brogan guessed the ages of Jack and Pam to be about fifty.

He closed the hatch again and considered his next move.

I don't like it up here. It's stuffy and uncomfortable, and those insulation fibres stick in the back of the throat. They can probably give you cancer, you know.

One more house, and then we'll go back.

As it turned out, the fourth house was the last one he could get to. As he dropped into it, he saw that the far wall had been built up to the roofline, making further passage impossible.

This attic looked more promising, though. Loose wooden boards had been laid across half the floor space, making it easier to traverse, although most were covered with boxes, suitcases and items tightly wrapped in bin bags. Brogan decided he would rummage through them at some point, but of far more interest now was the fact that a proper collapsible loft ladder had been installed. Getting in and out of the house below would be a breeze.

Yet again, Brogan listened for a while at the hatch, then lifted the cover slightly to take a peek at what might await him.

The hall and stairwell below had been recently decorated in bright, neutral colours. In the corner of the alcove rested a pole for opening the hatch and pulling down the ladder.

It's like everything has been laid on for our personal convenience. It would be rude to disappoint them.

The house was deathly quiet. No voices, no animals, not even a ticking clock. Didn't mean it was empty, though. It would be safer to gather more information before descending. Forewarned is forearmed, and all that.

He closed the hatch again, then sat up and pulled his knees into his chest.

So, which one's it going to be? Who's our first customer? Eeny-meeny-miny-mo . . .

TUESDAY 4 JUNE, 10.26 PM

The final house was calling to him. Something told him it was the one.

But his stomach demanded to be filled. He couldn't blame it. Over twelve hours had elapsed since he'd discovered the attics, and over twenty-four since he'd last eaten. He'd spent the day in the abandoned property, waiting for nightfall to descend before he ventured back up the ladder.

He tried Elsie's house first, and knew instantly it would be his saviour. Elsie's snoring came rumbling through the ceiling, while the occupants of the other houses would probably still be wide awake; and since Elsie would undoubtedly have taken out her despised hearing aid, she wouldn't even know he was there.

He opened her loft hatch. Lowered himself carefully onto the dark mahogany dresser on the landing. For a brief moment he feared it might collapse under his weight, but it was solid enough. It didn't emit even a squeak of protest.

He eased himself onto the landing, then immediately switched off his torch. It wasn't so much Elsie that worried him as people on the street outside spotting the moving light.

Besides, there was enough of a glow coming through the window at the front of the house to enable him to see what he was doing.

At Elsie's door he paused for a few seconds, but didn't go in. He wondered what wild events were befalling her as she journeyed noisily through her dreams.

Probably nothing as terrifying as the idea of a killer loitering outside her bedroom door at night.

He descended the staircase, not caring about the occasional creak underfoot.

When he reached the hallway, he took a quick look around. In the dim light he could make out a small table supporting a telephone. On the walls were some cheap landscapes and a row of painted plates.

He went into the kitchen. It smelt of cabbage, old cooking oil and fly spray. On the counter were some boxes of cereal. He held one up to the moonlight.

Corn Flakes!

Ha! She told Kerry—

Yeah. Looks like the old girl hasn't lost her sense of humour.

Brogan opened the box, grabbed a handful of cereal and stuffed it into his mouth. After so long without food, the slightly stale flakes were heavenly.

He ate another handful before replacing the box, then went to the fridge and opened it. The nauseating stench of sourness and decay almost made him gag, but he wasn't about to let that put him off. On one of the shelves he found an opened packet of ham. In a pine bread bin were two loaves: one brown and one white. Clearly, Elsie liked her bread.

He hurriedly put together a ham sandwich and wolfed it down. Still hungry, he found a pack of mini sausage rolls, from which he ate two, plus a box of strawberries, of which he ate three. Although sorely tempted by a cheesecake in the fridge, he decided that any further depletion in Elsie's provisions might become obvious. He washed it all down with two glasses of water.

It was time to move on.

He went back upstairs. Elsie was still dead to the world, and still refusing to keep quiet about it.

'Thanks for the food, Elsie,' he whispered. He climbed back up into the attic and closed the hatch. It was almost as if he had never been there.

Minutes later he was in the fourth house once more. He hadn't even bothered stopping in Jack and Pam's. They had been arguing again – this time about what to get their niece for her birthday – and Brogan could not summon up the interest to loiter.

But as for the fourth house . . .

Woo-hoo! They're home. And they're my kind of people.

In what way?

Listen to them. They're young! Mid-twenties, max. Fresh meat. Even younger than the Derwents. Remember them? How amazing they were?

Yeah, they were pretty special.

'Athletic' is the word you're looking for. I bet she never imagined she could fold that far backwards. Certainly took her husband by surprise.

Brogan listened. Heard how the pair below joked and

laughed and flirted and traded jibes in a way that more jaded couples had forgotten how to.

I hope they don't have a baby. You're not great with babies.

Fuck you.

I'm just saying. With your history—

Shut it. I'm trying to listen.

'Have you set the alarm?' said the woman.

'Why do you always ask me that?' said the man, amusement in his voice. 'I don't have to set the alarm. It's permanently set. It comes on at the same time every morning, as well you know.'

'Best to check. I wouldn't want you being late for work.'

'What are you talking about? I'm always up before you are.'

Incredulity in her voice now: 'You are not! Who made you that coffee this morning?'

'That was an aberration. And it was your fault for making me drink all that wine last night.'

'My fault?'

'Yes. You always do that when you want to take advantage of me.'

A tinkle of laughter. 'I don't need alcohol to get you into bed, mister. All I have to do is this . . .'

A few seconds of silence, and then: 'Oh my God, Colette. Don't do that to me. You've just been saying how you want me to get up in the morning.'

She emitted a throaty laugh. 'You're up now, by the looks of things.'

Jesus, this must be what a porno movie is like for a blind person. It's killing me.

Yeah. What do you think they look like?

Like Venus and Adonis. If they turn out to be more like Jabba the Hutt, I'm putting in a complaint.

'Are you ever getting into this bed?' the man said.

'What's your hurry?' said Colette. 'Need someone to warm your feet?'

'It's not my feet I'm concerned about at the minute.'

'Ooh. Well, you'd better stop hogging the bed, then. Move over.'

The conversation stopped. Words replaced by actions, Brogan guessed. A minute later came giggles, murmurs, moans.

Brogan moved crab-like along the joists, trying to find a position from which he could hear better. He took hold of the insulation material and started to peel it back, so that all that remained between him and the couple was a thin layer of plasterboard.

And then he saw it.

A chink of light.

Brogan blinked, not understanding at first. He reasoned that his torch beam must be bouncing off something reflective. But when he switched off his torch, the light remained.

He inched further forward. Like a moth, he was drawn hypnotically to the light. And even when he discovered its origin, he decided it could just as easily have been the glow from a fairy. Because his wish had come true.

A wooden batten had been nailed between the joists. It had originally been used to support the weight of a ceiling light beneath, but Brogan saw that the white electricity cable pinned to the joist now fed into a junction box, handing off its power to a second cable that ran to another part of the room. Someone – perhaps the couple below – had decided to move the light, but they had not filled in the hole at the original ceiling position. By lowering his eye close to the batten, Brogan could see . . .

Everything.

It was a view so perfect and unexpected that Brogan let out an involuntary gasp.

On the king-sized bed below, Colette opened her eyes and looked in Brogan's direction.

'Martyn,' she said to the muscular man writhing on top of her. And when he ignored her, she prodded him in the ribs. 'Martyn!'

'What's up? I'm a little busy.'

'Did you hear something?'

'What kind of something?'

'I . . . nothing. I thought . . . never mind. As you were.'

Martyn didn't need the prompt to return to work. He was already hard at it, his back undulating, his hips grinding.

But Colette's eyes remained open, and it seemed to Brogan as though she had locked her gaze with his.

Colette. Beautiful Colette. Strawberry-blonde hair fanned out across the pillow. Firm, pale breasts jiggling with each thrust of the man who had now become an irrelevant plaything in this scenario, because all the while she was looking directly into the eye of another.

It was as if she were saying, *This is for you, Thomas Brogan. This is all for you.*

Her face had stayed with him all night.

She had joined him in his dreams. Walked silent and naked into his room, and then somehow insinuated herself between him and his filthy mattress. She didn't care about the hovel she was in. Her eyes were only for Brogan. Those huge, round, captivating eyes. She stared into his soul, willed him to move his body in time with hers. He obeyed without question, and felt their heartbeats synchronise, their pulses surge together as if part of one conjoined network. Their flesh became slick with perspiration, their muscles taut, their breathing hot and rapid.

And then it all changed. The badness found its way in and exerted its control. He watched objectively as his hand reached for the soft curve of her throat. He saw his fingers begin to tighten of their own volition. Colette's eyes bulged. Her full lips parted and allowed a gentle croak to escape. He continued to squeeze. The engorged purple fruit of her tongue sprouted into view. Tears of blood ran down her cheeks. Crimson fountains burst from her nostrils, her ears and her mouth. And still those massive eyes continued to burn through into his brain.

He awoke with screams ringing in his ears, and he wasn't sure if they belonged to himself or to Colette or to all his past victims. He searched frantically on the floor for his torch, and when he found it, he shone it on his hands.

They were not covered in Colette's blood.

Colette was still alive. For the moment.

What time is it?

Brogan checked his watch and cursed when he saw how late in the morning it was. He had wanted to study the couple's morning rituals. He had hoped to catch a glimpse of Colette in the revealing glare of full sunshine, her hair unkempt, her eyes half-closed and her lips in a dreamy smile as she crossed the divide to awareness.

You do realise they've probably left for work now, don't you?

I realise.

Doesn't have to ruin our day, though. While the cat's away . . .

Brogan rolled off the mattress. Paid a quick visit to the toilet. Then he was up the ladder once more. Elsie had her radio booming again. Jack was yelling instructions to Pam on how to work the microwave. And in the young couple's house – silence.

He waited a good half hour with the hatch open before making a move. The previous night the couple had discussed setting an alarm to get them up for work, but it was always possible that one of them carried out their business from home.

But he heard nothing. He was as certain as he could be that the house was empty.

He lowered the loft ladder, making quite a racket, but the fact that nobody came to investigate confirmed that he was alone.

Right, let's poke around a bit.

Not yet. We need to eat first.

You're such a killjoy.

The first thing he did was to search the hall, porch and cloak cupboard for any sign of an alarm control box. Finding none, he opened the kitchen door slightly and peered through the gap. He could not see any alarm sensors. Taking a breath, he stepped inside, then relaxed again when no bells or sirens blasted his eardrums.

The kitchen was bigger than that of the abandoned house, having been extended at the rear. Brogan checked the windows to make sure that the room wasn't overlooked by any of the neighbours, and saw that one of them had been left slightly open.

That's careless. Don't they know there are undesirables out there who might want to get into their house?

Brogan closed the window and turned his mind to breakfast.

He helped himself to a bowl of cereal with a splash of milk, a mug of black instant coffee and two rounds of toast – one spread thinly with jam and the other with marmalade. He would have loved some bacon, sausage and eggs, but decided that they were all items whose disappearance would be too noticeable. He washed his dishes and cutlery, then dried them and put them back exactly where he had found them.

You know, one day you'll make someone the perfect wife.

Be quiet.

It's true. A real domestic goddess.

That's not only insulting, it's sexist. There's nothing wrong with a man wielding a mop.

Or a carving knife.

In the recycling bin Brogan found an empty plastic lemonade bottle. He rinsed it out and filled it with water to take back to his temporary accommodation.

And then he began exploring.

He poked his head into the dining room first, but decided to venture no further into it. It was at the front of the house, and since there was no garden distancing it from the pavement, there was a risk that he would be seen by passers-by. Besides, the room contained little other than a table and chairs, a couple of bookcases and a two-seater sofa.

The living room had more to tell him. In an alcove next to the chimney breast stood a beech-coloured sideboard. Brogan went through each of its drawers in turn. Much of the content was the junk that people hide away because they can't think of anywhere else to put it – batteries, drawing pins, birthday cards and phone chargers – but there was also a lot of paperwork here. Some of the documents were just user manuals and warranties for appliances, but there were also bills and other personalised letters. Brogan was able to discover that the surname of the couple was Fairbright, that they had been married for almost three years, and living in this house for slightly less time than that. He learnt also that Colette worked in marketing for a healthcare firm, and that Martyn was a sales consultant for a kitchen company. Neither of them had a huge salary.

Bored, Brogan went back upstairs. In the bathroom he looked through the cabinets and the airing cupboard. Colette was on the pill; Martyn wore disposable contact lenses; both used sonic toothbrushes.

You should make the most of your presence here.

What do you mean?

You're sweaty and grubby, and that mattress back in our little shit-heap is the most disgusting thing ever. You should take a shower.

I can't do that.

Why not? Who's going to know? Even if they come home and think that something doesn't seem quite right, why would it even cross their minds that somebody would break into their house, get cleaned up, and then leave? Burglars take lots of things, but showers aren't usually on the list.

Brogan needed no further persuasion. He stripped off, turned on the shower above the bathtub, then climbed in. It felt wonderful, as though he were sloughing off a thick layer of dirt and decay and blood and sin. He lathered himself with coconut shower gel. Washed his hair with shampoo that smelled of crisp green apples. When he was done, he shook his body and squeezed his hair to rid himself of as much water as possible, then stepped out and dabbed himself dry with a used towel. He folded the towel and replaced it in its precise position on the rail.

Before he left, he took a look behind him to make sure nothing would scream intruder alert to the Fairbrights. His eye picked out what at first he thought was a crack in one of the white wall tiles. Craning forward, he realised it was a hair. One of his own hairs.

Maybe we should just leave it there.

Why?

For the hell of it. See if they notice. And if they do, what will they think? Will they make something of it, or just dismiss it? It'd be interesting to find out.

Brogan smiled. It would indeed be interesting. But the games could begin later, when he'd given them more contemplation. For now he decided to play safe and flush the hair down the plughole.

He didn't immediately dress. He was relishing the feeling of being clean, and his clothes were anything but that. Instead, he gathered the pile of garments in his arms and padded through into the bedroom.

Ah, yes. The bedroom. The place where Colette and Martyn believed they could act out their erotic fantasies in private. The one place they would not expect the eyes of another to be upon them.

And yet, it was not a difficult feat for Brogan to convince himself that Colette had been somehow aware of his presence. Was that her guilty secret? Her ultimate fantasy? Did she get a kick out of the idea of being watched by a stranger while she made love?

He dropped his clothes to the carpet. Naked, he wandered round to Colette's side of the bed. The duvet had been thrown back untidily. He could see the impression that Colette's body had made in the mattress and the pillow. He reached out and allowed his hand to follow its contours. In his mind he could see his rough palm travelling almost without friction along her smooth skin.

He climbed onto the bed, face down. He sucked in as much air as he could manage through the pillow, and experienced the aroma of her touching him inside. He stayed like that for some time, imagining her beneath him, waiting in exquisite expectancy for him.

He flipped over and looked up. He could see the hole in the ceiling, the light fixture having been moved to a position more central. This was her view last night. This was how she had stared back at him. From this distance the hole was just a dot – it would not be possible to see an eyeball through that hole – but Brogan was not about to allow irksome truth to get in the way. What ran through his mind now was a story in which Colette craved his presence above her. She wanted him to see, wanted him to enjoy the show she was putting on for him. His pleasure was her pleasure.

And then the story changed. This was no longer a bed but a chilly stone floor. Instead of bright sunshine outside, the window panes trembled in a howling gale. Colette became harder to picture, her features twisting to take on the face of another. Attractive became ugly, innocent became guilty, loyalty became betrayal.

The story ended as it always did, drowned in blood. Hot, gushing, arterial blood. Gallons of it. The ultimate, but unrepeatable, climax. It was inevitable, and the delay in achieving it was always worth it, but with the ending came a sadness, an acceptance of what he was and what he could never be.

He rose from the bed, then scrutinised it to ensure no trace of him remained. When he dressed, the clothes felt stiff and scratchy; his cleanliness had been short-lived. He assumed once more the mantle of death and decay.

Then, like a spectre, he disappeared through his portal into the eternal darkness above.

It was a relief when noon came and went. He had killed some of the morning with exercise. Hundreds of push-ups and sit-ups. Afterwards, in the darkness of the abandoned house, he thought, but was not sure, that he had drifted off a couple of times. The sensory deprivation was torturing him. He suspected this was worse than being a prisoner in solitary isolation. He needed human contact. He needed more food. He needed...

Colette.

She filled his mind. Bloated his brain to the extent that it felt it might burst out of his skull. In the brief time since he had first caught sight of her, she had become an obsession. He wasn't even sure why. There was something different about her – something he couldn't quite put a finger on. Something that made her a cut above the average victim.

Ha, that's funny.

What is?

A cut above the average victim. Very amusing.

She'll need special attention.

Of course. And we know why, don't we?

No. What are you talking about?

She reminds you of someone.

Don't even go there, all right? This isn't about her.

It is. It's always about her. Her and all the others.

The storm building in Brogan's mind prompted him to go and sit by the back door. He opened it and slid the plywood aside, allowing in some precious light and air. He knew he was running the risk that someone at an upstairs window of one of the surrounding houses might notice, but he was beyond caring. He was suffocating in here.

He sat like that for about half an hour, staring out at the weeds and the insects. At one point, a tabby cat came strolling soundlessly past. Sensing Brogan's presence, it froze and locked eyes with him through the gap in the doorway.

Hey, this is like Mitzy.

Are you blind? She looks nothing like Mitzy. Not even the same colour.

This is how it started, though. Staring at each other through a doorway.

Brogan closed his eyes while memories both pleasant and painful were replayed in his head. When he opened them again the cat had disappeared.

What is it with you today? Why are you so determined to open up old wounds?

Those wounds have never healed, my friend.

Yeah, well, I'd appreciate it if you'd stop rubbing salt in them, okay?

Don't be a cry baby. I'm the only thing that keeps you going.

Don't flatter yourself. I could manage without you.

You would die without me. Show some gratitude.

Irritated, Brogan slid the wooden panel back into place and closed the door. Darkness returned. He had the torch, but it didn't seem worth switching it on. He turned around and leaned back against the kitchen door, willing time to speed up. He could still hear the noises from outside: birds, aircraft, road traffic, children. Occasionally he detected the discordant wail of sirens, and wondered if he might be their cause. False alarms as people reported sightings of the killer in their midst.

I'm starving.

You're always starving.

Yeah, well, I'm speaking for both of us. Sometimes it would pay you to listen.

We'll have to wait.

We can't wait. You've already burned off all the calories from breakfast.

I have to stay fit, and that means I have to exercise.

That'll go on your gravestone. Here lies the fittest skeleton on earth.

Look, what do you want me to do about it? We can't take any more food from the Fairbrights. They'll notice. And people will be up and about in the other houses now.

So, then, when are we eating again?

Tonight. We'll go back to Elsie's.

We can't last that long.

We'll have to.

Brogan's other voice went quiet, but thoughts still danced

36

in his head. Images, sounds and snatches of conversation toyed with him.

He checked his watch.

What is it?

The people next door to Elsie. Jack and Pam.

What about them?

They mentioned a doctor's appointment. Wasn't it today?

Yes. Yes! Three o'clock, they said. What time is it now?

Almost two.

And then Brogan was on his feet, clicking on his torch, running upstairs. He climbed the ladder into the attic, then stealthily made his way across Elsie's house and into the home of her neighbours. He could hear voices, but they were faint, suggesting they were coming from the ground floor. Brogan slipped his knife from his waistband, then carefully raised the hatch cover and pushed the hilt of the weapon under it, propping it open by about an inch.

Jack and Pam were engaged in their typically robust conversation. Brogan didn't catch all of it, but it seemed to involve complaints about everything from a leaky tap to the state of the government.

Then, at about twenty minutes to three, Pam's voice grew louder as she entered the hallway.

'Are you coming, then? The clinic will be closed by the time you get out of that chair.'

'Give us a break, woman,' Jack retorted. 'Can't you see I'm suffering here?'

'Not half as much as I am. Get a move on.'

There followed much groaning and swearing.

'Finally,' Pam said. 'And don't try to put a brave face on when we get there. I know you. You'll just say it's nothing serious.'

'I hate doctors.'

'Well, I don't think they're overly fond of you, either.'

Brogan heard the front door being opened, a yelp of pain from Jack, and then the slam of the door. A minute later, they got into a car and drove away.

Food time! Get down there!

Brogan retrieved his knife and raised the hatch cover fully. He peered down onto the landing.

One problem.

What's that?

How will I get back up?

Duh! That's what ladders are for, stupid.

Elsie might hear.

Not if you're careful. But hurry up, will you? We don't know how long we've got.

Brogan made his way back to the first house. He pulled up the battered wooden ladder, then carried it across the attic space. Getting it over the separating wall and across Elsie's house took him a lot more time. He was worried about knocking the ladder against something that might alert her to his presence, and he still had to take the utmost care about where he placed his feet.

Hurry up!

I'm doing the best I can.

When he eventually managed to get the ladder into the adjoining attic, he took a moment to rest.

Like Pam said: Get a move on!

Brogan shook his head and muttered, 'No rest for the wicked.'

If that's true, we'll always be on the go.

Brogan slid the ladder through the hole and made his way down.

The house seemed eerily quiet without the bickering couple, as if it was making the most of the opportunity to get some sleep. Its smells were very different from those of its neighbours. The atmosphere was heavy with air freshener and the scents of polish and bathroom cleaners. There was something else, too, that he couldn't quite put his finger on.

You can breathe later, after we've got the food.

Brogan descended the staircase, moving past a line of photographs of two chubby children at various ages. When he reached the hall, he saw that the kitchen door was closed. Next to it, a dark wooden clock wagged its brass pendulum at him and gently tutted, as if warning him not to approach.

How far away do you think the clinic is?

Why?

It's nearly three o'clock now. What if they were seen early and are almost home again?

Early? When have you ever known a GP to run to time, let alone early? We've got ages. Just get in there, grab something to eat, and then we'll go.

Brogan nodded. Stepped up to the door. Opened it.

He was greeted by the colossal figure of Ralph.

He knew it was Ralph, because that's how he introduced himself.

'Ralph!' he said.

At least, that's what it sounded like. Difficult to tell. It was more of a bark than a word. Which is only natural, seeing as it was coming from a dog.

Well, not just a dog. A beast, really. A fucking huge, slavering, demonic, red-eyed monster. A single-headed Cerberus, undiminished in its ferocity by the reduced quantity of biting apparatus.

The clock chimed three o'clock, as if announcing the start of a fight.

Brogan turned tail and ran. This was no time to find out whether this animal's bark was worse than its bite – not when the slightest nip from this Hound of the Baskervilles was capable of leaving him with fewer than the desired number of limbs.

So he ran, faster than he had ever run before. And Ralph – whom Barbara Lewis had reportedly assessed as being far too obese to be capable of vigorous exercise – ran too. Despite having the proportions of a beer barrel, it lumbered after

Brogan with a velocity that seemed to match his own. It was like Indiana Jones trying to outrun the boulder.

Brogan hit the stairs. Took them two, three at a time, knowing that any misjudgement, any slip on a step could lead to his doom. He knew the beast was at his heels. He could almost feel its breath, its slobber soaking his legs. Just one more leap to the landing . . .

And then Ralph got him.

The dog's jaws clamped down with an alligator-like snap. The razor-sharp incisors pierced the leg of Brogan's jeans. He felt them scrape against his skin.

And then he was being dragged downstairs. He turned and looked into the incandescent eyes of the behemoth as it pulled him backwards. He wrapped his arms around the bannister post. Sensing the resistance, Ralph responded with a growl and then a series of yanks, its massive frame rippling with each insanely powerful jerk.

He's going to eat your flesh and bury your bones in the garden if you don't do something, so do something!

Brogan felt his own grip loosening, and knew he couldn't win this tug of war. He raised his free leg and kicked out at the dog's face. It seemed only to make Ralph's eyes glow brighter, and the animal raised the side of its mouth in a sneer, as if to say, *Is that all you've got?*

Brogan remembered his knife, but reaching for it would mean losing his anchor to the bannister post. He was also less than confident that his single sharp implement would be adequate opposition for the many owned by his assailant. He kicked out again, and again. When a particularly savage blow struck the end of Ralph's snout, the dog released him with a yelp. Brogan scrambled to his feet and bounded back up to the landing.

He sprinted for the ladder, conscious of the hulking animal immediately behind him, convinced that it was about to sink its teeth into his calf. He leaped up the ladder, hitting the highest rung he could, and as he did so he heard a cracking, splintering sound, and he thought, *No, don't break, please don't break*, but his legs were now a whirlwind, spinning with a force that could probably elevate him even without a ladder.

He reached the top, springing through the hatch opening like a jack-in-the-box. Panting, he gazed down at his pursuer, at the saliva-dripping fangs and the incendiary gaze.

Get the ladder! Get the fucking ladder!

Brogan took hold of the ladder and began sliding it up into the attic. As if sensing that his prey was about to escape, Ralph jumped and grabbed the bottom rung in his teeth.

Get it off him!

I'm trying to, damn it!

Brogan pulled, but the dog was too strong and heavy. He was in danger of losing the ladder altogether. In one last desperate effort, he dragged it upwards until the dog was on its back paws, then shoved suddenly downwards, forcing the wooden rung into the back of Ralph's jaw. The dog loosened its grip just long enough for Brogan to yank the ladder beyond its reach.

When the ladder was safely back in the attic, Brogan sank to his knees and stared down at the animal. Ralph growled – a deep-throated rumble that seemed to be focused in a beam that caused Brogan's whole body to shudder.

Close the hatch. We need to get out of here.

I wasn't planning on staying, but what's the hurry?

The Happy Snapper down there. We need him to get bored and move away. If he's still there, staring up at the ceiling when Pam and Jack get back home . . .

That's a good point. Wait! Shit!

What?

They're going to know anyway, as soon as they see that Ralph isn't in the kitchen.

You'll just have to hope they think they forgot to shut him in.

I don't think they'd forget something like that.

Well, if you want to lead Ralph back to his kitchen, be my guest. Maybe you could tempt him with a juicy arm or two.

Brogan thought about it, then slowly closed the hatch.

WEDNESDAY 5 JUNE, 4.07 PM

He expected sirens, footsteps, voices, banging on the doors.

Truth be told, he didn't know what to expect. Jack and Pam had to be back home by now. What would they have seen? Ralph, still growling up at the hatch in their ceiling? They'd have to think someone was up there, right? With Ralph released from his kitchen prison, wouldn't they reason that someone had been in their house?

Brogan had spent the last hour sitting in the blackness of the abandoned house, waiting to be discovered. He sat on the rickety wooden chair, clutching his knife and staring in the direction of the back door.

He waited.

A part of him wanted to go back up and investigate. He wanted to listen in on Jack and Pam, to be washed by the relief of hearing mundane conversation, proof that they didn't suspect anything.

You need to stay away. Give them time.

Time for what?

Time for that stupid mutt to get bored or hungry. Time for his meagre brain to forget about what led him upstairs in the first place.

It's not the dog I'm worried about. It's his owners.

You're overthinking it. Do you really think they came home, found the dog on the landing and thought, Hey, there must be a serial killer up there, call the cops? *No. As soon as they opened the front door, Ralph would have rushed straight downstairs to greet them, and they would immediately have started accusing each other of leaving the kitchen door open, because arguing is what they do.*

Yes. You're right. That's probably how it went.

But it took another couple of hours before Brogan could allow himself to believe that. At six o'clock he gave himself leave to abandon his vigil.

Thank Christ for that! I thought we were going to sit here all night.

I had to be sure.

Great. Now you're sure. I told you there was nothing to worry about. So what now?

We make a final check.

Brogan made his way upstairs. He found himself moving quietly and stealthily even here, two houses away from the dog. He kept his movements cautious as he ascended the ladder, and even more so as he traversed Elsie's attic. When he reached the boundary wall, he paused and found his breath again.

He climbed over the low wall, then moved at an agonisingly slow rate towards the hatch, each footfall pressed lightly home as he stepped from joist to joist. Once at the hatch, he

45

lay down, spreading his weight across the joists. He put his ear to the cover. He could hear the voices of Jack and Pam. They were on the ground floor, squabbling as usual. Brogan brought his fingers to the edge of the hatch cover.

What are you doing?

I need to know.

No. We know enough already. Do you see cops swarming around? No, you don't.

I just need to be sure.

You know that dogs have incredible hearing, right? That thing is already spooked. If he hears you opening the hatch, he will lead his owners right to us. There's a reason people say to let sleeping dogs lie.

Brogan pressed on nonetheless. He began to lift the cover, his ears straining for sounds of a growl or a rush of paws up the stairs. He heard nothing except human voices. They were muffled, indistinct. For a heart-stopping moment, Brogan's imagination played with the idea that they were discussing a plan of action to deal with their home invader.

But then the voices sharpened as Jack and Pam came into the hallway.

'How long will you be gone?' Jack said.

'I'm only going down the road. Ten minutes or so. I'm sure you can last that long.'

'I'm starving. Going to the doctors always makes me hungry. It's something to do with the medical smells.'

'It's called hygiene, Jack. Something you should try to get more familiar with. And anyway, if you insist on having burgers tonight, you're not leaving me with any choice. Put the oven on while I'm gone. Oh, and I expect to see that Ralph is still in the house when I get back.'

'Ha ha! Stitch my sides back together.'

Brogan lowered the cover gently back into place. A broad smile was stretched across his face.

Happy now?

Ecstatic.

Good. Then let's have some fun.

He felt like dancing across the joists as he crossed to the Fairbrights' house. With his earlier worries now behind him, his anticipation of what might lay ahead was ramped up to maximum. What delights would Colette put on display for him tonight? Would she look directly at him again? Would she introduce a few little innovations that she'd spent all day dreaming up?

He almost slobbered more than Ralph at the prospect of it.

They were both home: he could hear their garbled voices filtering through the floors beneath him, but his inability to draw meaning from them was frustrating.

No matter, he thought. I can wait. I can sit here all night if need be. It'll be worth it. You'll make it worth the wait, won't you, Colette?

And wait he did. For hours. Neither of the pair seemed interested in coming into the bedroom. Occasionally, a wedge of brightness would intrude through the half-open door as the hall light was switched on, but it only ever signified a toilet visit. Brogan would hear the flush and the use of the washbasin, and then the light would be shut off once more. Minutes later, the conversation would start up again. It was clearly intense – something of great importance and gravity – but all it did for Brogan was to take his frustration to breaking point. He felt as though he were being deliberately shut out, like a child sent to bed while the adults discussed issues too grown-up for his ears.

'Get up here,' he said in a harsh whisper. 'Stop being a tease. I don't like to be teased.'

It was almost 11.30 before the couple came to bed. By that time, Brogan was aching all over with the effort of keeping still and silent in that cramped void. He was almost angry at being kept waiting.

But now she was here, only feet away, looking radiant. Admittedly, she seemed more serious than the previous night – a lot less playful – but perhaps that was tonight's role. Perhaps she was about to act the vamp or the dominatrix.

But what she did – what she *did!* – was take a T-shirt away with her to the bathroom. Brogan heard the shower running for a few minutes, and then she was back, dressed in the long T-shirt. No expanse of naked flesh. No sexy lingerie. And worst of all, not even a glance in Brogan's direction. No shrug of apology or a raised-eyebrow promise of future impishness. Her attention was only on her husband and her bed.

It was as if she was completely unaware of Brogan's existence.

'It's been a long day,' she said to Martyn.

A long day? She doesn't know what a long day is. She should try sitting on her own in complete darkness from morning to night.

'Yup,' said Martyn. 'Don't know about you, but I'm knackered.'

What a wuss! He has a woman like that lying next to him, and he can't even be bothered to take advantage of the situation?

What kind of man is he?

'Goodnight, Martyn. Love you.'

'Love you, too. See you in the morning.'

When they kissed, Brogan wanted to throw up. He wanted to heave a high-powered stream of vomit through this hole in the ceiling, directing it right into their stupid, love-twisted faces. This wasn't supposed to be about romance, about sugary sweetness. It was supposed to be about carnal desire and sins of the flesh. It was supposed to be about Colette showing Brogan what was his, what she had promised him.

This isn't right. Not right at all.

And then, as if in a final insulting gesture, the bedside lamps were turned out. Brogan had his sight taken away from him yet again.

He wanted to scream at them at that point, to yell obscenities through the ceiling, make the couple think they were under attack by supernatural forces. It occurred to him that he could quite easily kick his way through the thin plaster of the ceiling, then drop into their bedroom as they cowered beneath the duvet. He would pull the knife from his waistband, and he would bring his torch to his chin, shining it up at his menacing features, and he would approach them slowly, soaking up the sounds of their screams. And then he would raise the knife, bring it to an apex above the figures huddled beneath their pathetic shield of cotton and feathers . . .

He thought all this, but he didn't act. He didn't move from his prone position in the Fairbrights' attic, his eye still aimed at the couple, now snug and warm and unknowing in the refuge of their bed.

Stay calm.

Easy for you to say. This was meant to be a special night. They're not going along with it. The day has turned to shit. They were supposed to make things better.

I know, but don't let anger take control. You know how unsatisfactory it is when you do things in anger. It's much better when it's a game, when it's done for pleasure. Like the Carters, for example. Remember how much you enjoyed that? Remember the thrill of their steaming blood flowing through your fingers? And your parents. Remember the priceless looks on their faces? Their acceptance of your power over them? Compare that with what came before. Recall the fury and the dissatisfaction with everything in the world. See the difference? See how much better this could be?

Brogan nodded in the darkness.

A minor setback, that's all this is.

Yes.

Tomorrow will be better. There will be other opportunities. If Colette is going to be awkward, you can make things even more awkward.

Just watch me.

That's the spirit.

Brogan pushed the insulation material back into place, covering the hole. Only then did he switch his torch back on and start to creep back towards his decrepit hovel.

It was at that point, the roaring within his head having subsided, that he realised how hungry he was. Because of the fiasco at Jack and Pam's house, he'd eaten nothing since breakfast.

A midnight feast was called for.

He felt more confident about entering Elsie's house this time, even though the sound of her snoring suggested her sleep was more fitful tonight. He reasoned that, even if she awoke, she wouldn't hear anything happening on the floor below.

It was as he passed her bedroom door that the hall clock began to chime the stroke of midnight. It reminded him of the clock next door that had seemed to command Ralph to attack him, and a shiver passed through him.

He stood motionless during the countdown, wondering how anyone could possibly sleep through that racket. But when all that Elsie did was emit some pig-like grunting before resuming her more steady rumble, he recalled that she took out her hearing aid at night.

I think you'd have to start banging pans together to get through to her.

Fortunately, that's not on my list.

Either that or a shotgun blast.

Really? Do you have to bring that up now?

It's my job.

Then resign.

On these wages, don't tempt me.

Brogan went downstairs. Into the kitchen again. Back to the fridge.

Elsie hadn't stocked up yet. From Elsie's previous discussions with her carer, Brogan had gathered that her main dish of the day was delivered by Meals on Wheels at lunchtime. In the evenings, Elsie would make herself soup or a sandwich. Groceries were delivered once a week, and right now her provisions were severely depleted. It would be hard to take much without it being noticed.

Brogan's stomach growled.

I'm growling too. This is ridiculous. We're living in four houses and we can't even get one decent meal.

Brogan closed the refrigerator door, then crossed the kitchen and helped himself to another handful of dry cereal while he considered his situation.

Sod it, he thought. Needs must.

He opened a cupboard. Started pushing aside packets of flour and boxes of tea. At the very back of a shelf he found some tins. He held them up to the moonlight to read the labels. He found some curried beans, lentil soup and canned meatballs. He didn't fancy eating any of them cold, but worried that the smells generated by heating them up might find their way to Elsie's nostrils, which could still be a lot more functional than her ears. But then, beneath a box of gravy granules, he found a small, square tin. Sardines!

Brogan popped off the lid. He was not generally a lover of tinned fish, but right now he was salivating. He pinched a round of bread from the brown loaf, which had more slices than the white, then poured the contents of the tin onto it and folded it over, mashing down the fish.

He took a massive bite out of the bulky sandwich. Rolled his eyes heavenward with the ecstasy of it.

He decided he needed to slow down a little. Make it last. He took a seat at the table while he ate, and forced himself to chew each mouthful twenty times.

This is more like it.

See? It's not all doom and gloom. And tomorrow the situation with Colette will be improved.

Too right. We'll make damn sure of it.

Brogan took another bite. He looked out of the window. The nearly full moon seemed to beam a smile at him.

He started thinking about what he could eat next. A couple of biscuits, maybe. Some grapes. A chunk of cheese.

He didn't get much time to ponder, because that's when the light came on and he turned to see Elsie in the doorway.

Brogan leapt to his feet in shock. He hadn't heard a thing. And now he'd have to do something to fix his disastrous mistake.

Better get a move on, before she starts screaming blue murder.

He started towards the old woman, his hand reaching for the knife at his waist. But Elsie stood her ground. There was no fear or anger on her face; only puzzlement. And that made Brogan somehow less certain of his decision to kill her.

Stop pissing about. Get rid of the old bat. Do it!

'Alex?' said the woman.

Brogan stopped in his tracks. 'What?'

'Alex? Is it really you? Have you come back to me?'

Elsie reached up a gnarled, skeletal hand. Her rheumy eyes filled with tears. Brogan realised then that, in addition to being as deaf as a post, she was also myopic and not entirely in tune with reality.

'Yes,' he said. 'I'm here.'

She shuffled towards him, tilting her silver-fringed head in an attempt to get a better view. Brogan noticed that she was wearing her hearing aid.

She put her fingers to his face, and he allowed it. Allowed her bony claws to comb through his beard. He'd grown it to avoid looking like the photograph of him currently doing the rounds in the media. Strange that it should now act as a clue to mistaken identity.

Her behaviour opened a closet in his memory out of which stepped Nanny Brogan. He had been so young when she died that his image of her was fuzzy, but he recalled her touching his face and marvelling at the smoothness of his chubby cheeks, and he vaguely remembered a toothy smile and an undeniable glint of kindness in her eyes.

'I knew it,' Elsie said. 'I always knew you'd come back. They told me you were dead, but I said no. I know my son. He wouldn't leave me. You've been gone a long time now, Alex.'

Ha! She's loopy! The old bird's as nutty as a fruitcake!

'Yes,' he said to her. 'A long time. I'm not even sure how long it's been.'

'Almost thirty years to the day. And yet . . . and yet you haven't changed a bit. It's a miracle.'

Brogan glanced towards the hall. He ought to get out of here. But, crazy though it seemed, he felt compelled to know more. He wanted to experience the surreal nature of the situation.

'You'll have to help me,' he said. 'I don't remember too well. What happened to me?'

'A car crash. You were driving home after a party, and you were drunk, and you went the wrong way on the motorway, straight into oncoming traffic. Well, that's what they said. I knew it wasn't true. I didn't even ask to view the body. Why would I want to look at somebody else's corpse?'

She reached both hands out now, and cupped his chin. 'My son. My son. I've prayed for you every night, and now my prayers have been answered.'

She wrapped her arms around him, pressing her weightless head into his chest. Brogan stroked her thin hair, feeling the bumps and indentations of the skull bones beneath her papery skin. He wondered about the neural misfirings taking place within that head. What was it that prevented her from questioning how it was possible for her son, who would now probably be in his fifties or sixties if he'd lived, to be standing here in front of her, not having aged a day?

'You seem thinner,' she said. 'Have you been eating properly?'

Mothers always ask that. It must be in their genes or something.

My mother never did.

Yeah, well, your welfare was never top of her priorities, was it? Not after what happened to the baby.

'Actually,' he said, 'I'm pretty hungry.'

She grinned, displaying crooked, discoloured teeth. 'Then let me make you something. What would you like? I've got soup. Or beans. And I think there's some frozen fish—'

'Beans on toast would be perfect. Thank you.'

She patted him on the shoulder. 'You don't have to thank me. That's what mothers are for. They look after their children, till the day they die.'

She toddled towards one of the cupboards and opened it, then started pulling out tins and holding them up to the light, exactly as Brogan had done earlier.

Like mother, like son, eh?

'I haven't got my glasses,' said Elsie. 'Are these beans?'

He went over to join her. 'Yes, they're beans. Here, let me.' He took the can from her grasp. 'Do you have a tin opener?'

She raised a crooked index finger. 'Now *that* I can find.' She opened a drawer and put her hands on the opener without difficulty. She handed it to Brogan, and he set about preparing the first hot meal he'd had in days.

Elsie watched him light the gas under the pan of beans and load bread into the toaster. Then something seemed to occur to her.

'Oh, oh! We should tell Jeanette the good news. Lord, what was I thinking?'

'Jeanette?'

'Your wife, silly. She'll be over the moon to hear you're back. I'll phone her now. She won't mind my waking her up, seeing as it's so important.'

Elsie started walking out to the hall, and Brogan had to drop the spoon in the pan and intercept her.

'No. Please don't.'

Elsie's roving eyes tried to search his face. 'Why? What's wrong?'

'It's . . . Nobody must know I'm here. It's important you don't tell anybody.'

'Even Jeanette?'

'Especially Jeanette. You have to keep this to yourself.'

'Why? I don't understand.'

'I . . . I can't explain. I shouldn't even be here. If anybody else knew, I'd have to go away again. I'd have to leave you forever. You wouldn't want that, would you?'

'Oh, dear me, no. I wouldn't want that, Alex. That would be awful.'

'Yes. It would. I'd hate for us to be torn apart so soon. We've only just found each other again.'

She took his hand between hers. His meaty fist looked massive in her pale talons, and her flesh felt so cold, as though her blood found difficulty in forcing its way through her shrivelled blood vessels.

'I don't want you to go away. It's lonely without you.'

Listen to that. Trying to manipulate you. Acting all weak and pathetic. It makes me sick. You need to show her you can't be bought so cheaply.

This counsel threw Brogan into confusion, and he was relieved to be interrupted by the popping of the toaster.

'It's ready,' he said. 'I should eat now.'

'Yes, yes. Get some food down you, you poor boy.'

He buttered the toast, poured the whole pan of beans over it, then sat down to eat. Elsie collapsed her bones onto the chair next to him and watched, but he didn't mind. Halfway through, she offered him a glass of milk, which he accepted gratefully. And afterwards, she brought him a slice of cheesecake from the fridge.

He took his time over the food. He was in no hurry, and this house was far more comfortable than the dump next door. He left his chair only when it suited him.

'I have to go now,' he said.

He saw the upset on her face. 'No, no! That's not right, Alex. You said you were back for good.'

'Don't worry. It's only temporary. I'll come back again tomorrow night.'

'You promise?'

'I promise. Shall I wake you up?'

'Yes. Wake me. I'll make you some supper again.'

'I'd like that.'

'You need to eat more. Do you want to take anything with you? I don't have very much in at the moment.'

Brogan looked around the kitchen. 'Maybe some fruit? And some more of that cheesecake?'

Elsie didn't need asking twice. She leapt to her feet with surprising agility, then went to the bowl on the counter and gathered together several ripe pieces of fruit in the spidery cradle of her fingers. She brought them across to Brogan, who found homes for them in his baggy pockets. Then she cut off a massive wedge of the cheesecake and wrapped it in tinfoil.

'Thank you,' he said.

'Is there anything else you need?'

Brogan tried to think. 'Candles,' he said. 'Do you have any candles? And matches?'

Elsie smiled with satisfaction. 'You can always trust your old mum to provide.'

She opened a door beneath the sink, then came back with a pack of white candles and a box of Cook's matches.

When Brogan had managed to find a space in his pockets to take the items, Elsie grabbed his hand again.

'I just want you to know. I don't think I've got many days left, but this has been one of the best. I can die a happy woman.'

Something flipped over in Brogan's core. People didn't say things like this to him. Usually, they let him know they were extremely unhappy to die. In fact, they pleaded with him to let them live.

'I . . . I have to go,' he said, because he could find nothing else to say.

He left the room without looking back. Took the stairs two at a time so that she could not chase after him.

Behind him, he could hear her calling out: 'Alex! Alex!'

On the landing, he hopped onto the chest of drawers and then hauled himself up through the hatch.

And still he could hear the mournful cry of the woman for her long-lost son.

He slept in again, but he didn't care this time. Catching sight and sound of Colette and Martyn seemed less important this morning.

He had lit one of the candles that Elsie had given him, mounting it in a pool of its own wax. Sitting up on the lumpy mattress, his back against the wall, he watched the flame dance, and allowed himself to be hypnotised as the walls of the room seemed to shift to its erratic rhythm. He could see the primitive face of mould in the corner, grinning inanely at him.

Before you say it, that's definitely not me. I'm not exactly smiling at the moment.

Why's that?

Because you should have killed the old woman. She's seen you. She knows you're here.

And how would killing her have helped? The carer gets there about now. She'd have the cops swarming all over these houses in minutes.

It didn't have to look like murder. You could have suffocated her, put her back in bed. That would have bought us enough time to get out of here.

I don't want to get out of here.

Well, now there's no choice in the matter. Elsie knows you're here.

She won't talk.

And you're certain about that, are you? What are you going to do, use your manly charm on her?

She's mixed up. Confused. She doesn't know what's real and what's not. Besides, there are things I want to do first.

Like what?

Like the Fairbrights.

You still want them?

Why do you ask?

Because you've been doing your best to keep them out of your thoughts ever since you woke up.

I'm avoiding disappointment. Last night was the pits.

Is that why we didn't go over there before they got up?

Yeah.

Well, you'll just have to get over it. That house holds promise. Get to know them. Find their weaknesses and their fears. Turn this thing around. Just like you did with the Carters.

Brogan nodded. The Carters had been the best so far. He had managed to get right inside their heads. He had found their Room 101 and locked them up in there. It had made it so much more fulfilling than a straightforward slaying. It had depth. It had resonance.

The cops won't see that. They're philistines.

I know.

They'll come up with some half-baked theory, some psychobabble to explain it all away. All they're interested in is catching a killer. They'll never understand what we do. Can you imagine what the psychologists came up with when they were asked why we swapped your parents' heads?

Something nowhere near the truth.

Exactly. The truth being that it seemed funny at the time. I bet that doesn't feature in our offender profile.

Doesn't really matter what they think. We'll never explain it to them.

Nope. We'll be dead before that happens.

Brogan dragged himself off the mattress. Stretched until it felt like his tendons might snap. From the pocket of his discarded jacket he took out a banana, then ate it as he paced up and down, considering the possibilities that might lie ahead of him. When all that remained in his hand was limp peel, he felt renewed enough to out-grin the smiley face on the wall.

Minutes later, he was up in the attic, climbing through into Elsie's. He hadn't intended to pause there, but he could hear her in conversation with Kerry, her carer.

'Still in bed, Elsie?' Kerry was saying. 'You know it's well after nine o'clock, don't you?'

'I was tired,' Elsie said. 'I had a late night.'

Kerry laughed. 'A late night? You got a new boyfriend or something?'

'I'm not too old for a boyfriend. And anyway, it was better than that.'

'Better than a boyfriend? Come to think of it, most things in life are. Are you going to tell me, then?'

'Can't. It's a secret.'

Good girl.

'Oooh,' said Kerry, 'I like secrets. Go on. I promise I won't tell anyone.'

Brogan listened to the patronising tone in the carer's voice, and thought about how much that would change if only she knew the truth.

'Can't,' Elsie repeated. 'He said he wouldn't come back if I told.'

'I thought you said it wasn't a bloke.'

Elsie grew irritated then. 'It wasn't. Not any old bloke. Not a boyfriend bloke. This one's special.'

Kerry didn't reply for several seconds. Then: 'You've lost me, Elsie. I'm not very good at riddles. Was it someone on the radio?'

'No!' Elsie snapped. 'You don't understand. You'll never understand.'

'Well, I'm doing my best, Elsie, I really am. Give us a clue.'

And then Elsie blurted it out: 'It's Alex! Alex is back!'

Brogan felt a sudden adrenaline rush. He tensed, wondering whether he was going to have to take action to deal with this.

What did I say? I told you. I knew she'd blab.

'Alex,' said Kerry. 'You mean . . . your . . .'

'My son. Yes, that Alex. He came to see me last night. But I promised not to tell, and now you've made me tell. I broke my promise, and now he probably won't come back.'

The distress was clear in Elsie's voice, and it pushed back against Brogan's rising anger.

'Hush,' said Kerry. 'It's okay, Elsie. I understand now. I understand.'

But she doesn't, thought Brogan. She doesn't have a clue. She's putting it down to the ramblings of a deluded old woman who's at death's door.

He realised then that his secret was safe with Elsie. She could say what she liked. Who would believe her? Who would make the leap from Elsie's story of her beloved son's return to a wanted criminal in her attic?

Brogan stood up, content that he could shelve this one for now.

Feeling as though he could almost whistle, he made his way to the brick partition between this and the third house. He sprang onto it so effortlessly he could almost have completed it as a high jump.

And then he stopped moving, stopped breathing. He clung to the top of the wall like an animal that had just spotted a predator, his every sinew tensed to keep him motionless.

The hatch was open, and a human head was protruding through it.

He thought initially that he'd been seen, and that he and the other man, who was presumably Jack, were now engaged in some kind of gunslinger's stand-off, each waiting for the other to reach for their pistol.

If he makes a run for it, you'll have to go after him. He'll call the police or grab a weapon. You'll have to get to him first, and you'll have to kill him, and if his wife is at home, you'll have to kill her too.

All of this went through Brogan's head in a split-second. But then he saw that Jack wasn't looking directly at him: he was looking the other way, shining his torch over at the wall leading to the Fairbrights' place.

Brogan realised that his own torch was in his left hand, still dangling on Elsie's side of the wall. He flicked it off, praying that it had gone unnoticed by Jack.

And then he heard the voice that almost stopped his heart: 'What the hell do you think you're doing?'

It was Pam's voice, but she was calling up to her husband, not to Brogan.

Jack peered down through the hatch. 'I'm just looking. A man can look at his own attic, can't he?'

'Get down here. You'll do yourself a mischief. I thought you were supposed to have a bad back?'

'I *have* got a bad back. I can climb a few steps, though. I'm not a bloody invalid.'

'Just come down, Jack. I'm not taking you to that flipping hospital again. You can take yourself there if there's an accident.'

'Charming,' Jack muttered. But he climbed down nevertheless, pulling the hatch closed above him.

Brogan sucked in some much-needed oxygen.

That was close.

Far too close. That bloody dog.

You don't know it was the dog.

What else could it be? It's too much of a coincidence. Why else would a guy with a bad back go to all the effort of climbing a ladder to take a look around his attic?

Maybe it's you. You make far too much noise.

No, I don't. I couldn't be any quieter.

Whatever. We'll have to be a lot more careful from now on.

Brogan switched his torch on again, then lowered himself gently into Jack and Pam's attic. It sounded to him as though the conversation between the two had moved downstairs, but he was taking no chances. He moved across the joists with as much lightness as he could muster, flicking his torch frequently towards the hatch for signs of movement. It was a relief to climb over into the Fairbrights' house.

Having learnt his lesson to be hyper-cautious, he paused

and listened for a few minutes before opening the hatch door, listening again, then lowering the ladder. It was only after he had checked the rooms out thoroughly that he felt able to relax.

He helped himself to cereal, toast with jam and a mug of coffee. As before, he washed up and put everything back in its precise place. After he had refilled his plastic lemonade bottle with water, he put the toilet facilities to good use, but made do this time with a quick wash rather than a shower.

He wondered again what might happen if he made a mistake while here – something bigger and more noteworthy than a mere dark hair in the shower. It crossed his mind that the scenario was not unlike the story of Goldilocks and the Three Bears, but in reverse: the human householders wondering who might be eating their food, sitting on their chairs, lying on their bed, but with the ursine fierceness and terrifying ability to kill residing in the intruder rather than them.

It was time, he decided, for this bear to sniff out the honey.

He wasn't sure what he was looking for exactly, but there had to be something – something that would give him an insight into their psyches.

He began his quest with a more thorough search of the sideboard in the living room. He was more systematic than before, opening up each document in turn, even those that appeared mundane.

It was disappointing.

He unearthed a few interesting nuggets – Martyn once almost lost his driving licence for speeding; Colette underwent tests for a tumour that turned out to be a cyst – but there was nothing spectacular.

There's got to be more than this. Remember that dildo collection the Derwents had? Boy, we came up with some inventive uses for those.

Brogan had noticed a laptop on a low bookcase, but he wasn't prepared to turn it on. He didn't know enough about computers, either to search it properly or to be confident of doing so in a way that was undetectable.

Instead, he went back to the bedroom. He opened the drawers and doors of the triple wardrobe, but the only thing that called attention to itself in the tightly packed array of clothes was Colette's wedding dress.

He moved to the chest of drawers. Opened the first drawer. Colette's underwear, mostly – some of it fairly racy. Brogan pulled out a black lacy thong and held it up. He could imagine Colette in this.

I wonder what she'd think if she knew you'd been fingering her gusset?

He continued through the drawers. One of them contained Martyn's socks and underwear, but the remainder seemed to have been claimed by Colette. They housed tights, stockings, sweaters and scarves, but also female paraphernalia such as hair brushes, bangles and make-up.

And then Brogan reached the bottom drawer.

This was more like it. This seemed to be where Colette kept her personal stuff. Her birth certificate was here, as well as some education certificates. There were memorabilia from various stages in her life: sketches, notebooks of bad poetry, postcards from holidays, a collection of seashells, a miniature teddy bear.

Then came the box.

It was a small wooden chest with some silver latticework on it. It looked to Brogan like a jewellery box, but he had already seen Colette's jewellery box on a shelf by the mirror. He lifted out the box and went to open it, but found it was locked.

Why would she lock it if it just contained jewellery? The other box wasn't locked.

Brogan looked and felt inside the drawer for a key, but found nothing. Deciding he couldn't break the box open, he returned it to its position.

There was another box here, too: a white shoebox. Brogan took it out and lifted the lid. Saw that it contained a stack of photographs.

Most of those near the top of the pile were of Colette and Martyn. Some had been taken on holidays, others at parties or with friends. One of the pictures was a close-up of a plaque naming Martyn Fairbright as Salesman of the Year, dated two months ago. Several other snaps showed him celebrating with his wife and colleagues, the plaque on the table in front of him. In one of the images, Martyn had been caught with his eyes firmly fixed on the décolletage of a buxom brunette sitting next to him.

Who cares about Salesman of the Year? They should be giving out trophies for Boobs of the Century. That woman would win hands down. Or even tits up.

It looks like she'd get Martyn's vote.

Yeah, and have you seen Colette? If looks could kill, we wouldn't have to worry about dispatching Martyn.

I wonder why she kept it.

Farther down the pile were photographs from Colette's younger days. They showed her with her parents and her sister and her dog. She was always happy, always beautiful.

At the very bottom of the box, Brogan found an envelope stuffed with more photos. Many of them were couple shots again – Colette with her man.

The difference here was that the man was not Martyn.

He was tall and good-looking, but he was not as muscular as Martyn. Colette was glued to his side, her arm wrapped around his, her wide eyes gazing up adoringly. In one of the stills, Colette and her mysterious partner were in a restaurant, their clasped hands resting on the white tablecloth. Colette was wearing an engagement ring.

Brogan puzzled over this. He could tell that these were old photos, and not evidence of an ongoing alternate life: Colette's hairstyle was very different then, for example. But what had happened to this guy? Why was he no longer in her life?

Brogan looked down at the photographs. There were probably hundreds more of them stored in digital form, but again, he wasn't about to risk trying to access them on her computer. What he had here were just fragments of Colette's life. And yet, Brogan gained the feeling that he could use these fragments in some way – that putting them together would provide him with the razor-sharp implement he needed to slice away Colette's outer layers. But he wasn't sure how. Not yet. He needed to bide his time, to watch and to listen. It would come to him, he was certain.

He gathered the photos together, ensuring that the ones of Colette and her fiancé went back into the envelope, and that the others were kept in order. Then he returned the stack to the shoebox and placed the box back in the drawer.

Interesting, thought Brogan.

Very interesting.

He returned to the Fairbrights' house just after ten o'clock in the evening. He knew he was early; he felt a little like the guy who insists on getting into the cinema before everyone else, for fear of missing even a second of the movie trailers.

We should have popcorn.

Yeah, or one of those phallic-looking hot dogs.

Dim the lights and start up the music. We've got a show to watch.

The day had gone more quickly than he'd expected. Sitting in the derelict house, he had lit a candle and allowed his brain to play with the information it had absorbed earlier that morning. Some of it was sheer erotic fantasy, heavily featuring the underwear that Brogan had seen in Colette's drawer; but other thoughts had concerned the ex-fiancé in the photographs. Brogan had dreamed up a game in which he invited Colette to say what she preferred about that guy over her present husband. Martyn would be forced to listen to her answers, reducing him to a gibbering wreck. It would act as a nice diversion before Brogan slaughtered them both.

He wondered if he would do it tonight.

Colette was the first to enter the bedroom. She came in at about ten-thirty, alone. Brogan watched her walk barefoot across the carpet. She took off her watch and her jewellery, and placed them on her bedside cabinet. For a few moments she disappeared from Brogan's view, and when she entered his field of vision again the television was on. It was the local news.

'Police are continuing their search for Thomas Brogan, wanted in connection with a string of brutal murders in the Mayhill area. The most recent of Brogan's victims, Ann and Edward Carter, were found dead at their home on Monday night . . .'

From his hiding place, Brogan watched as Colette suddenly stopped what she was doing and became immersed in his story. He couldn't see from here, but he wondered if the broadcasters were displaying the usual image of him.

Was that it? Was Colette looking at his face right now? Was she wondering what went on behind those piercing eyes? Was she fascinated by his cold-blooded disregard for society's rules? Was she frightened, but also intrigued, perhaps even excited by the prospect of a murderer in such close proximity?

I'm closer than you think, Colette. I can see your widening eyes and the flutter of the quickening pulse in your neck. I can hear your breathing and the gentle popping sound as you part your lips. I can smell your perfume as it rises. I can almost touch you.

I'm here, Colette. The real thing, only feet above the flat televised image you find so enthralling. Just look up, or give me a sign. That's all you have to do.

She started to undress. Keeping her eyes fixed on the television, she idly began undoing the buttons on her shirt.

Was this the sign? Was she teasing him?

Brogan tried to slow his breathing, even though his heart was furiously attempting to supply oxygen to his highly aroused system. He wished he had a camera to film this, but he didn't even possess a mobile phone. He would have to rely on his memory to replay what he was seeing. But it would never be as good. Like Colette's photograph collection, there would always be layers that it failed to capture and to project back at him in all their glorious living detail.

And then, when she was down to her underwear, she left him. She picked up her nightshirt from the bed and strolled casually out into the hall.

Brogan wanted to let out a low groan. He ached for release. He craved the merciful climax of violent death.

Minutes later, he heard the steady hiss of the shower. His inability to watch her soaping herself seemed unmercifully depriving.

When she came back into the room, she was wearing her long nightshirt. The television had moved on to something boring, and Colette turned it off and climbed into bed. Rather than go to sleep, she propped herself up against her pillows, then reached for the book on her bedside cabinet.

She didn't complete the manoeuvre.

Something had caught Colette's eye. Brogan followed her line of sight.

The chest of drawers!

Oh, shit. What did you do?

I . . . nothing.

You made a mistake, didn't you? You left a clue.

I didn't. What can she possibly see from all the way over there?

Colette threw back the duvet and swung her legs out of bed. She paused for a moment, still peering ahead. Then she stood up and walked over to the chest of drawers.

Shit, shit, shit.

Colette bent down. Slipped her hand into the narrow gap between the wall and the side of the furniture. Pulled something out.

A photograph! You dropped one of the photographs!

Brogan wanted to groan for different reasons now. Colette would know something was wrong.

Don't look up now, he willed her. Don't connect what you've just seen on the television with the photograph. Don't build that mental bridge between the two.

But Colette simply continued to stare at the rectangle of paper in her hand. She stood there for a full minute, staring and thinking. And with the passing of every second, Brogan found himself edging inexorably towards the acceptance that this was the Fairbrights' final night.

A sound intruded. Martyn, singing the tune to an advertisement for cheese. He was coming up the stairs.

Brogan tensed. He fully expected Colette to show Martyn the photograph, and together they would try to work out the reason for its presence.

But she didn't. Instead, she hastily opened one of the top drawers and pushed the photo beneath her underwear. Martyn entered the room just as she was closing the drawer again.

'That MP's been at it again,' he said. 'They've found more evidence of bribes.'

'Really?' said Colette, doing her best to feign interest.

'Yeah. He won't go to jail for it, though. That lot never do.'

Colette slipped back into bed. 'I had the local news on for a bit. That killer's still on the loose.'

'I saw that. No way he'll have stayed around here. He'll be well away by now.'

'I hope so.'

Martyn didn't answer. As he began to undress, Colette picked up her book and opened it at what Brogan was sure was a random page. Right up until the moment Martyn pulled on some pyjama shorts, Brogan kept his eye on Colette. He could tell she was only pretending to read. She gazed unseeing at the book, not even bothering to turn the pages.

When Martyn went to the bathroom, Colette put the book down and leaned her head back. Her line of sight was now directly aligned with Brogan's.

What's going through her mind? Why didn't she mention the photograph to her husband?

I don't know. It's weird.

Martyn came back and slipped under the duvet, then picked up his own book. He nodded at the one in Colette's hands. 'Any good?'

'Just all right,' she said. 'My mind's on other things.'

'Oh? Like what?'

'Clothes, mainly. I've got too much old stuff. I can't remember the last time I went through those drawers.'

'Hmm,' said Martyn, flipping through the pages in his own book to find his place.

'I mean, I've got a load of things in that bottom drawer I could probably get rid of.'

A grunt from Martyn.

'Wouldn't you like some of the space I could make in that drawer?'

It took Martyn a while to realise that a response was required from him. 'What?'

'I said, wouldn't you like more space in the chest of drawers?'

'More space? Not really. Why?'

'I just thought ... I mean do you ever go through that bottom drawer?'

'The bottom drawer? Those are your things. Why would I go through them?'

'Well, there are some photos of us in there, for example. Don't you ever get an urge to look at them?'

'Why? Do you?'

'Sometimes. But what about you? Would you like to take a look at them?'

'What, now?'

'No, not now. But some time. You'll tell me if you ever want to see them, won't you?'

'Sure. But I'm okay for now, honestly. If I ever get a burning urge to see your old photos, I'll let you know.'

'Right.'

'Can I read now?'

'Yes. Go ahead.'

They both returned to their books. But again Colette did

not get lost in hers. Her gaze was roving all over the place. To Martyn, to the chest of drawers.

Brogan knew what she was thinking. The same questions would be circling in her mind: Did I drop that photo there? If I did, when did I do it? When was the last time I had that shoebox open? And why have I never noticed the photo on the floor before now? But if *I* didn't drop it, it must have been Martyn. He must have been going through the photos. Why? And why deny it?

It was while Brogan was pondering the machinations of Colette's brain that he had an idea of his own. A light bulb moment.

He suddenly knew exactly what sort of game he was going to play with these two.

Knocking on Elsie's door wasn't working. He had to walk right in, put a light on and shake her by the shoulder before he could rouse her.

Unafraid of the apparition of an uninvited man standing over her bed, she peered at him through fogged eyes. 'Alex? Is it you? Are you back again?'

'Of course it's me. I told you I'd come back again, didn't I?'

'What? What did you say?'

Brogan opened his mouth to repeat himself, then realised it was a waste of time. He saw the box containing her hearing aid on the table, and handed it to her.

She plugged in the earpiece, then touched a withered hand to his cheek. 'Oh, Alex. Thank you. Thank you for coming back. I wasn't sure . . .' She let her words trail away, afraid to complete her confession.

'It's okay. Look, I could really do with some supper, but if you prefer to sleep . . .'

'No! I wouldn't dream of it. Pass me my dressing gown.'

She pointed towards the back of the door. Brogan unhooked

the gown, then helped her into it. When she tied the belt around her impossibly thin waist, it seemed that she might cut herself in half.

'Come downstairs,' she said, beckoning. 'I'll find you something tasty.'

Ten minutes later, she was heating up a chicken korma ready meal. Brogan had the suspicion that eating a curry this late at night would play havoc with his digestion, but he didn't care. He didn't want to fall into too heavy a sleep anyway. He had things to do in the morning.

When he began tucking into the steaming mound of food, she said to him, 'I'm so happy you came back.'

'I promised, didn't I?'

'Yes, you did. But . . .'

This time he finished the thought for her. 'You were naughty, weren't you? That's why you were worried I might not return.'

'What? No. I wasn't naughty.'

He wagged his fork at her. 'Yes you were. You told someone about me. You told Kerry.'

Elsie clamped a hand to her mouth, as if to prevent it from letting further indiscretions come tumbling out. Her eyes watered with the sting of guilt. Brogan decided he wasn't going to assuage her pain too quickly: he needed the lesson to sink in.

Eventually, Elsie removed her hand. 'I'm sorry. She kept asking me. And I was so excited. I felt I had to tell someone. I'm really sorry. Please forgive me.'

Brogan swallowed down another mouthful. For cheap supermarket curry, it wasn't at all bad.

'You see how it works?' he asked her. 'I see everything. I hear everything. I know what goes on, even when I'm not here. I'm special, you see. That I'm here at all is a miracle. You have to treat me with respect and do exactly what I tell you, otherwise I won't be able to come here again. You understand that now, don't you?'

She nodded, fearful not of him but of the possibility of losing him through being too loose-lipped.

'I won't do it again. You mean too much to me, Alex.'

He found a smile for her. 'That's all right, then. We won't talk about it anymore.'

They chatted about the things the real Alex did when he was alive. But the escapades of a complete stranger did not interest Brogan. What really amused him was the way in which he was able to slip so believably into the persona of the son she must know to be dead.

Do you think she does know? Is she just fooling herself?

Maybe she knows at some level, deep down. Maybe the truth is so buried she doesn't know how to reach it. Or doesn't want to.

That's a lot of disbelief she's having to suspend. She can't face death, but she can accept that you can pass through walls, that you know everything she says and does, and that you haven't aged since she last saw you. All that is okay as long as it means you're her Alex. How do you like being a ghost?

I could get used to it.

Yeah, me too. A-haunting we will go.

Brogan rose earlier than usual. He hadn't slept well, and it wasn't entirely due to the curry. His mind had been too busy. Sleep could wait until after he had set things in motion.

To bring himself fully awake, he did a hundred press-ups and a hundred sit-ups. Then he climbed the ladder into the attic. He moved cautiously through the houses, anxious not to repeat his mistake of the previous day. At the Fairbrights' house, he lowered himself carefully into position and uncovered the spyhole.

Sitting up in bed, Martyn was flicking through something on his mobile phone. Next to him, Colette was in a foetal position, fast asleep.

Two minutes later, Martyn seemed to become aware of the world outside social media, and he nudged Colette with his elbow. She groaned, but refused to rouse herself.

'Hey, sleepyhead,' he said. 'You're going to be late.'

Colette sat up abruptly and blinked at her clock. 'Shit. Did the alarm go off?'

'Yes. You decided to ignore it.'

'Then why didn't you wake me?'

'I just did.'

Colette harrumphed and jumped out of bed, then ran out of the room. After using the toilet and taking the briefest of showers, she marched back into the room stark naked.

Brogan noticed how Martyn suddenly lost interest in his phone.

Colette said, 'Don't look at me like that. I've barely got time for breakfast, let alone any shenanigans with you. Anyway, why are you still in bed?'

'I've got a nine-thirty appointment just two minutes away. I'm going straight there before heading to the office.'

'All right for some,' she muttered. She grabbed some clothes and threw them on, then dashed out of the room again.

'Cup of tea would be nice,' Martyn shouted after her.

'Fat chance,' she answered.

When she had disappeared, Martyn dived back into his world of social media, a broad smile on his face.

Brogan had a smile on his own face, but for different reasons.

Nothing exciting happened in the next couple of hours. Colette returned to the bedroom, sorted out her make-up, and then said goodbye. Martyn eventually dragged himself out of bed and started getting himself ready for work. Brogan watched and waited patiently.

This isn't exactly prime-time viewing.

It's real life. The humdrum existence of people up and down the country. The stuff they do because they have to, not because they want to.

They can keep it. I like the fact that we broke out of the vicious circle. We liberated ourselves from a life of banality. And now we liberate others.

We do. They're not always grateful, though.

They should be. We give them the most intense experience of their lives. By comparison, the majority of deaths are swift or painless or downright boring. Take your parents for example.

Which ones?

Yeah, you did have more than the average number. I mean the most recent ones.

What about them?

Well, they could have gone out in a car crash or had cancer, or something else that everybody else dies from. How much more interesting could it get than to have slices carved from your limbs by your own son? If that's not a talking point over a Sunday roast, I don't know what is.

Martyn left the house. When the noise of his car engine had faded into the distance, Brogan waited another twenty minutes, just to be on the safe side.

And all the while, his smile grew.

It was with great satisfaction that he opened the hatch and lowered the ladder. Luck was on his side for a change. Through the bedroom window, the day seemed brighter than usual.

He almost experienced happiness.

The reason for his uncharacteristic optimism was what he had just seen from the attic. Or, rather, what he had not seen.

He had not seen Colette return the photograph to the shoebox.

She had been too rushed this morning, too preoccupied. It was possible that the photograph had completely vanished from her mind.

But it hadn't left Brogan's.

He went straight to the chest of drawers. Opened the top left drawer. Dug the photo out from beneath all that lacy naughtiness.

It was as he suspected: a picture of Colette's ex-fiancé.

Why did she act all weird like that? She stood there for ages, just staring at it. And there was no way she wanted Martyn to see it.

I don't know. Somehow, I doubt she'd have acted like that if it had been a photo of her and Martyn on the beach. She would have casually mentioned it, or just put it back in the shoebox.

Exactly. So why the secrecy?

Brogan gently flicked the corner of the photograph while he decided what to do. He looked around the room for inspiration. When he found it, he laughed out loud at the deliciousness of his mischief.

The day had passed quickly for Brogan. He had filched a few scraps from the Fairbrights in the morning, and then completed his search of their house by going through the boxes in their attic. He had found only Christmas decorations, books, camping gear, decorating equipment and other items that saw the light of day on rare occasions. At lunchtime he had wolfed down some sandwiches and a pack of biscuits that Elsie had given him. Although he was starving again now, the excitement of what was to come took his mind off it. Besides, Elsie would happily fix that problem soon enough.

Why are we here so early?

I don't want to miss anything.

It's the end of the working week. Who turns in this early on a Friday night?

Maybe they do. Maybe they've got some bedroom gymnastics in mind.

Oh, well in that case . . .

It worried him that the house was far too silent, and that he could see only darkness through his peephole. When it got to ten o'clock, he realised the place was empty, and that worried him even more.

Where the hell are they?

How should I know?

They might have gone away for the weekend.

That's a useful contribution. Could you be any more negative?

But when eleven o'clock came and went, Brogan became even more convinced that they were not coming home. His wonderful plan was disintegrating before it had even started.

He pushed himself up from his ungainly position across the joists, then performed some stretching exercises. He was in great physical shape, but lying prone on sharp-edged wooden rails for such long periods was crippling him.

Then, at just after eleven-thirty, he heard the welcome sounds. The car first, pulling up outside. Then doors slamming and a raised voice: Martyn calling after Colette, and her not responding.

Brogan flew back to his observation post. He heard the front door being closed, then saw the hall light come on. Seconds later, Colette came into the bedroom and turned on the lamps. She was dressed in an old sweater and jeans – hardly the stuff for a night out – and her face was thunderous. Seemingly uncertain as to why she had come upstairs, she plonked herself on the edge of the bed and stared at the wall.

Martyn's entrance was more circumspect. He stood in the doorway for a while, studying his wife's back as though it was a part of her he'd never seen before. He was swaying slightly, clearly the worse for drink.

'Did you have a nice time with Emily?' he asked.

'Not really. She's just lost her job and her dog's on its last legs. We weren't exactly whooping it up in the same way you were.'

He hovered for a while longer while he dealt with this demolition of his attempt to lighten the mood.

'Col?' he said eventually. 'Do you want to talk about it?'

'No,' she said.

'Well, I'd like to. Talk about it, I mean. Can we talk about it, please?'

Colette swivelled on the bed to face him.

'Martyn, it's late and I'm tired and you're drunk. This is not the best time.'

'I'm not drunk. I've had a couple of pints, is all.'

Colette shook her head in despair. 'You know that's not true. And, to be honest, I'd be quite happy if that was the only lie you'd told me tonight.'

The force with which Martyn pulled his head back in mock surprise almost caused him to topple backwards. 'What do you mean? What lies?'

'A quick Friday night session with the lads is what you told me.'

'It *was* quick. Well, relatively.'

Colette sighed loudly. 'Focus less on the word "quick" and more on the word "lads".'

'I *was* with the lads. You saw them when you picked me up. Terry and Liam.'

Colette's eyes widened in astonishment. 'Martyn, I don't know what magic spell you thought you'd cast to make the fourth member of your party invisible, but I think you need to ask for your money back.'

'Oh,' said Martyn. 'You mean Gabrielle.'

'Yes, I mean Gabrielle. I don't think there's a hormone therapy programme been invented that could ever make her pass for "one of the lads", so can we stop pretending now?'

Martyn put his hands up in surrender. 'I didn't know she was coming. God's honest truth. Liam never once mentioned bringing her.'

'Fine,' said Colette. 'Whatever. But that's not the worst of it, is it?'

'What do you mean?'

'Tomorrow. I'm talking about tomorrow. Did you really have to invite the whole lot of them over for dinner?'

Martyn struggled to find adequate words. 'It was a spur of the moment thing. We haven't had a get-together with them for ages.'

Colette lost it then, and jumped to her feet. 'Martyn, the terms "dinner party" and "spur of the moment" don't belong together. I was supposed to have a quiet day off tomorrow. Instead, I'll be cleaning the house from top to bottom, doing the shopping, and cooking for hours on end. So thank you for that.'

'No, no, it's not like that. It's meant to be casual. Something simple. Pizza, or something.'

'Pizza. Yeah, sure. Like that's going to happen. Your colleagues from work turn up dressed to the nines, and I throw slices of pizza in front of them. Why don't we do hot dogs, too? Maybe some doughnuts for dessert?'

Watching from above, Brogan shook his head. Give it up, Martyn, he thought. Follow your wife's advice and drop the subject.

But alcohol had put Martyn beyond such reasonable behaviour.

'I'll help,' he said.

'Damn right you will. First thing in the morning, you will be on your knees with a bottle of bleach and a pair of Marigolds. It's the least you can do for putting me through this.'

There, thought Brogan. A good stopping point. Move on now.

But again, Martyn refused to listen to Brogan's helpful telepathic advice.

He said, 'You make it sound like it's going to be hell.'

'Not hell, no. Let's call it more of an ordeal.'

Martyn swayed a little more. Then he posed a question that almost made Brogan want to groan audibly.

'Why do you dislike Gabrielle so much?'

Colette glanced at her watch. 'How much time have you got?'

'No, seriously. What's so wrong with her?'

'You really need me to answer that?'

'Yes. Tell me.'

'She flaunts herself, Martyn.'

'Flaunts?' asked Martyn, as though the word was not in his personal lexicon.

'Yes. Flaunts, flirts, flourishes and . . . something else beginning with "f". Every time we meet her, she's almost climbing into your pants. What's worse is she doesn't even acknowledge that I'm in the same room when she's doing it.'

Martyn sputtered a weak laugh. 'That's just her way. She's like that with everyone.'

Colette raised a corrective finger. 'No, she isn't. She's not like that with Terry, and she's certainly not like that with Liam, even though she knows he fancies her like crazy.'

'Well . . . they're both unattached.'

'And that's your defence of her, is it? Her philandering – which, by the way, is the word I was searching for, even though I now realise it doesn't begin with "f", and I'm also not sure whether it can be applied to a woman – is perfectly acceptable because she doesn't extend the same service to saddo bachelors?'

It took Martyn a while to parse the lengthy sentence. When he did, his own utterance was less accomplished.

'Terry and Liam aren't saddos.'

Colette shook her head again. 'I'm going to get ready for bed now, but let me just finish with a warning. Tomorrow evening, Gabrielle will turn up in a dress cut to her navel, her jugs hanging out like overripe melons, and with a ruby-red pout that could suck an egg from a hen's arse. She will—'

'Eggs don't come out of—'

'Don't interrupt! She will be wearing a scent that could stun a rhino, and she will try to sit so close to you that you won't know which body parts are yours and which are hers. But I'm telling you, Martyn, that if you so much as glance at any square inch of flesh below her neck, if your trousers betray any hint of arousal beyond the flaccidity of a jellyfish, I will come at you with a pair of scissors and I will turn this house into the talk of the town because of its novelty doorknocker. Do I make myself clear?'

Although the tirade contained another long sentence, this time Martyn appeared to get the gist more quickly.

'Message received and understood. Tomorrow night, you'll think I'm a priest.'

'In the current climate, that's not exactly reassuring. Anyway, that's all I'm saying on the matter.'

She started unbuttoning her shirt, and while Brogan kept his hugely dilated eye on her, he realised something. Gabrielle was the one in the photograph – the brunette whose cleavage was the object of Martyn's undivided attention at his Salesman of the Year presentation. That photograph was Colette's proof – something she could produce any time Martyn tried to defend himself against accusations of lechery.

And speaking of lechery . . .

Colette was down to her flimsy underwear now, and Brogan wasn't the only one appreciating the view.

'You look very sexy tonight,' said Martyn.

It was a clumsy attempt at winning her over, and drew from Colette the look of disdain it deserved. She wagged a finger at him.

'Uh-uh. Don't even think it. You're not coming anywhere near me while you've still got images of that woman floating around in your head.'

With that, Colette picked up her nightdress and left, clearly intent on completing her change of clothing in the bathroom.

Martyn stood there alone for a while, still rocking back and forth on his heels. He eventually made the decision to strip off, don a pair of pyjama shorts, and climb into bed. He was out barely seconds after his head hit the pillow.

When Colette returned, she stood looking down at the unconscious, snoring form.

She said, 'Well, so much for that idea, Casanova.' Then she walked around the bed and slipped under the duvet. She took another look at Martyn, frowned, and picked up her book.

The book! She's got the book!

I can see, can't I?

All right. I was just getting excited for both of us.

He watched as Colette opened the novel at the page containing her bookmark. He saw how her face registered a rainbow of emotions, from surprise to confusion to upset to anger.

Colette shifted her gaze from the book to the chest of drawers. Back to the book. Then to Martyn.

'You bastard,' she hissed at him. Then louder: 'You bastard!' She accompanied this with a shove to his chest.

Martyn came awake with an undignified snort. 'What? What's up?'

'You bastard,' she said again.

Martyn rubbed a hand across his face and blinked at her. 'What have I done? If this is about Gabrielle again, I swear—'

'No, it is not about fucking Gabrielle. It's about this!'

She snatched the item from the pages of the book. Held it up in front of Martyn's alcohol-fogged eyes.

'It's a photo,' he said. 'Of Jeremy.'

'Yes,' she said. 'And?'

Brogan had to put a hand over his mouth to stifle a snigger. This was wonderful stuff.

'And what?' said Martyn. 'I don't get it.'

'This isn't funny, Martyn. I don't know what the hell you're playing at, but—'

'Wait,' said Martyn. He pulled himself into a sitting position, looking suddenly a lot more sober, as though the intensity of his wife's emotion had burned off the alcohol in him. 'What are you talking about?'

'This! This photograph. Why did you put it in my book?'

'Your book? I'm sorry, Col, but you've totally lost me. This photo of Jeremy was inside your book?'

'Yes! And you're the only one who could have put it there!'

Martyn stared in bafflement. 'Why the hell would I put a photo of Jeremy in your book?'

'You tell me. I don't even know why you got it out of my drawer in the first place.'

Martyn was on his knees now, his voice rising steadily. 'I didn't get it out of your drawer.'

'Well, somebody did. I found it on the floor last night. You must have dropped it and not realised.'

'*I* must have dropped it? Why does it have to be me? And what do you mean, you found it on the floor?'

'I mean precisely what I say. It was over there, on the floor.'

'Where exactly?'

Colette tossed the duvet aside, spun out of bed and marched across to the chest of drawers. 'Here! In there!'

'In that gap? You found the photo in that gap?'

'Yes!'

'So then what did you do?'

The question seemed to defuse Colette's anger. Suddenly she was in the witness box, accounting for her own actions.

'I . . . I picked it up. And then I put it in this drawer.'

She didn't sound so certain of this, and like a quick-witted barrister, Martyn was swift to pounce on the weakness.

'So let me get this straight. Last night, you spotted a photograph that could have been accidentally dropped down that gap months ago. Then you—'

'It wasn't there months ago. It wasn't there before last night.'

'Are you sure?'

'Yes. I would have noticed it.'

Her testimony was faltering now. She was losing the jury.

'Not sure I would have,' said Martyn, further destroying her credibility. 'But anyway, you spotted it and you picked it up. Then what?'

'I just told you. I put it in this drawer.'

'Your knicker drawer?'

'Yes.'

'Why? Why didn't you just put it back in the shoebox?'

Brogan wanted to know the answer to this question too.

'I just didn't, okay? The point is, it was in my drawer last night, but in my book tonight, and it didn't just jump there by itself.'

'No, it didn't. But maybe . . .'

'Maybe what?'

'Maybe you forgot where you put it. Maybe you *did* put it inside your book. I mean, your knicker drawer would be a weird—'

'No, Martyn. I was putting it in the drawer when you came back from the bathroom, and I think you saw me doing it. That's why you're playing this cruel trick on me.'

Colette was getting all worked up now. On the edge of tears.

'Col, you're not making any sense.'

'I am. You saw me hiding the photo, and sometime today you looked to see what it was, and when you saw it was Jeremy, you decided to teach me a lesson. That's why you moved it to where I'd find it again.'

'That's not—'

'It is! And it's not funny, Martyn. If it had been a photo of anything else, I would have seen the funny side. But not this. You knew how much this would hurt me.'

She was sobbing openly now. Brogan remained transfixed by the spectacle as Martyn climbed across the bed and went to her.

'Hush now,' said Martyn as he took her in his arms. Brogan wasn't sure she would allow it, but she did. She rested her cheek against Martyn's broad shoulder, wetting it with tears that flowed more copiously now.

And then she said something so shocking that Brogan wasn't sure he had heard correctly.

'I killed him, Martyn. I killed him.'

What? What did she say? She killed him?

That's what it sounded like to me.

Someone needs to tell her that's our job.

'Hush,' Martyn repeated. 'Stop that now. You didn't kill Jeremy. He took his own life. You know that.'

'I drove him to it, though. I must have done.'

Martyn pulled away slightly and cupped Colette's face in his hands. 'Let's get a couple of things straight, okay? First of all, I would never play such a nasty trick on you. I know how much Jeremy meant to you, and I wouldn't do anything to tease you about it or bring up painful memories. You loved him, you were going to marry him, and I'm fine with that. I'm not jealous. Can I please ask you to believe me that I did not take that photo out of your shoebox, and that you must have slipped it into your book without thinking?'

Colette sniffed wetly a few times, but eventually nodded her agreement.

'Good girl. Secondly, you are not to blame for Jeremy's death. He was a depressive. The doctors explained it all, didn't they? They told you how even the happiest and most beautiful things in the world are sometimes not enough to help people who are severely depressed. It wasn't Jeremy's fault either. He just couldn't see the light at the end of his very dark tunnel.'

'I know all that,' said Colette. 'I've told it to myself a million times. But why couldn't he at least have come to me and explained how bad he was feeling? Why didn't he at least offer me a chance to help him? That's the thing I can never get my head around.'

Martyn rubbed Colette's arms. 'Who knows? We're fortunate that we've never been in that position. I guess the mind just closes down and refuses to deal rationally with things.'

'But why didn't I see the signs? I knew him better than anyone in the world. And it's not like I hadn't seen him for days. We were on holiday, for Christ's sake. I saw him almost constantly, and I still didn't spot what was coming. I didn't have the faintest inkling that the only walk he chose to go on alone was the one that would take him straight over a cliff. How can that possibly be?'

'I think it just shows that we never know people as well as we think we do. Everyone has secrets.'

Colette stared into her husband's eyes. 'Do *you*, Martyn? Do you have things you've been keeping from me?'

Martyn's face became more grave. 'Only one.'

'Care to tell me?' she said apprehensively.

'It's that for the past five minutes I've been bursting for a pee.'

Colette found a smile as she slapped Martyn on the arm. 'Get out of here, then.'

When he had waddled from the room like a kid about to lose control of his bladder, Colette stared after him for a while. Then she raised the photograph she was still clutching and studied it. She looked over to her book on the bedside table, then back to the chest of drawers. She walked across the room and pulled open her underwear drawer. After studying it for a few seconds, she used her free hand to rummage through it. Finally, she closed the drawer, opened the bottom one and returned the photograph to the shoebox. She was closing the drawer just as Martyn returned.

'Okay now?' he asked.

She nodded. 'Okay.'

'Then come here.'

She joined him in bed, and he put his arm around her shoulders as she lay her head on his chest. A couple of minutes later, Martyn was sound asleep again, but Colette's eyes were still very much wide open.

Brogan watched her carefully from above. Her recent years had been filled with death and drama and self-recrimination, and yet all had failed to scar her appearance. She was still so innocent-looking, so beautiful.

Just goes to show: don't judge a book by its cover. I mean, what do you see when you look in the mirror? Mr Average, right?

Well, I like to think a bit better than average.

You need to get a new mirror.

It was another ten minutes before Colette turned out the light. Brogan remained perfectly still until he was certain he could hear her soft snoring alongside Martyn's less gentle throat noises. Only then did he make his way back to Elsie's house, and allow her to prepare the fattened calf for her prodigal son. But the food was just something to quell the emptiness in his belly. Elsie rambled on nonsensically as usual, and Brogan interjected encouraging noises whenever they seemed called for, but it all fused into a drone that became a backdrop to his fierce mental activity.

He hadn't thought it possible, but Colette had suddenly become infinitely more fascinating. Both her past and her present had been opened to Brogan at a level of detail and candour of which nobody else was aware.

Not even Martyn.

That's right. Not even her own husband.

He didn't see how she glared at him when she came across the photograph in her book. He doesn't know that she checked her underwear drawer one final time, even though she'd already told him she accepted his version of events. He didn't see her a few minutes ago, unable to sleep while she entertained doubts about him. Whereas we . . .

We know everything.

Exactly. She shares with us. We're the only ones in the world who know what she's thinking.

That's a special bond.

It is. And you know what else I've been thinking?

What?

The spooky stuff with Elsie. If you can be a ghost for her, why can't you do the same for Colette?

Brogan blinked. In front of him, Elsie pressed on with her stories, but she may as well not have been there. He had a whole new perspective to consider.

The prank with the photograph had been purely that: a minor adjustment to perceived normality in order to test reactions. It had been intended as a starter dish – something to whet his appetite for the altogether more bloody main course.

But now a theme was developing. Jeremy was dead, and Colette felt responsible. That offered Brogan an opportunity to turn his practical joke into the start of something much less whimsical.

How would Colette react to attempts by her dearly deceased to make contact with her from beyond the grave?

Would she be terrified out of her wits?

Or would she seek rational solutions closer to home?

Brogan decided it would be worth finding out.

SATURDAY 8 JUNE, 10.15 AM

Anticipating that the rest of the weekend would be a washout, Brogan permitted himself another lie-in. With the dinner party imminent, the Fairbrights would probably be at home for most of today, and tomorrow they would no doubt just veg out with hangovers, leaving Brogan no opportunity to implement the next phase of his plan.

But he was undaunted. The thoughts still going through his head after last night's revelations were more than enough to see him through.

Saturday fairly rushed by. He spent the time doing exercises, sitting at the back door staring into the wilderness of the back yard, eating the sandwiches that he had asked Elsie to make for him, and making occasional forays into the attics.

Each trip to the Fairbrights' abode confirmed that at least one of them was at home. Sometimes he heard their voices; other times the sounds of a vacuum cleaner or running water or a radio. Once he caught sight of Martyn tidying the bedroom, only to be ousted by Colette because he was 'making a right pig's ear of it'.

It crossed Brogan's mind that he might drop in on Elsie, but he rejected the idea. Doing so during daylight hours just didn't seem the wraithlike thing to do. Besides, there was the danger that someone might turn up at her door while he was there. A panic-stricken sprint up the stairs followed by a noisy and clumsy ascent into the attic would definitely not be in keeping with his otherworldly façade.

Things warmed up after about six-thirty in the evening.

For one thing, Brogan was treated to copious eyefuls of Colette as she sorted out her hair and makeup and changed into her tiniest underwear and a clingy black dress. Clearly feeling the pressure, she was snappy with Martyn when he entered the room and spruced himself up in a fraction of the time and with minimal effort. Seemingly oblivious, he then compounded his error by asking her if she was nearly ready. The sheer force of her response was enough to propel him out of the room.

Half past seven was when the doorbell began ringing. Colette was still making last-minute adjustments to her makeup, but she clearly had one ear tuned in to what was going on downstairs as Martyn received their guests.

She pulled a face at herself in the mirror, and in a quiet, mocking voice she said, 'You look lovely tonight, Gabrielle. And my, what wonderful tits you've brought with you. Come over here and sit on my lap, Gabrielle.'

When she had purged that bit of antagonism from her system, Colette pushed the corners of her mouth up into a smile, then went downstairs.

Two minutes later she was back again, her smile having

wilted considerably. She stood in front of her mirror, unzipped her dress, removed her bra, then zipped herself in again. As a final touch, she tweaked her nipples through the fabric to bring them to attention.

'Two can play at that fucking game, missy,' she said before disappearing once more.

Brogan let loose a low snigger. That's my girl, he thought. I'd take you any time over that tart. Want me to slice her out of your life for ever? Just say the word.

He suspected he wouldn't see much of the couple for the next few hours, and so he slipped back to his lonely den to stare at the shapes in the flickering candles.

He returned at midnight, only to find that the party was still ongoing. The bedside lights had been left on, as if to taunt Brogan with a view of the room's emptiness. He could hear voices and raucous laughter from downstairs, and it was starting to irritate him.

What's bugging you?

I can imagine what's going on down there.

Which is what, exactly?

Picture it. Good-Time Gabrielle, with her dress cut down to her navel and up to her hip.

Okay, I can visualise that.

She's all over Martyn, nudging him with her boobs and touching his thigh while she lets out a constant stream of innuendo and downright filth.

Good, keep going.

Martyn is lapping it up. He can't keep his eyes off her. His face is burning with all the suggestiveness.

And? And?

There's Colette. On the other side of the table. She tries not to look. Tries not to show the others how upset she is. Some of Gabrielle's jokes are aimed directly at her, undermining her as a suitable lover for Martyn. She wants to run away and cry her eyes out.

Oh. Okay. Not so fruity now. So what do you want to do about it? Shall we go down there?

What?

Yeah, let's gatecrash the party. Why not?

Brogan considered this. Allowed the suggestion to trundle through his mind like a snowball, building in mass as it went. He could drop in on them, couldn't he? Instead of wine he would bring a knife. He would see mouths fall open in shock as he appeared in the doorway, and he would watch the revellers transform, mutating into quivering playthings as he introduced them to a party game of his own. While Gabrielle got the attention she craved, Martyn would see more of her than he ever thought possible. He would literally get an eyeful of what lay beneath all that superficiality.

And Colette? Well, she would be queen for the night, observing the subjugation of her tormentors in triumphant silence. That would be Brogan's gift to her before he took her for himself.

He lost track of how long his fantasy persisted, but when he drifted out of it he realised that the noise below was dimming. Doors were opening and closing. Cars – presumably taxis – arrived, idled and left.

And finally – *finally!* – Colette and Martyn came up to bed. Brogan's antennae bristled in anticipation of the drama that was surely about to unfold. The yelling, the tears, the recriminations. Perhaps even physical violence might not be out of the question. This would be fun.

Except that it wasn't.

The couple brought drunken smiles with them, and unfocused eyes that were only for each other. Colette in particular wore a dreamy, untroubled expression.

'So,' said Martyn.

'So,' said Colette.

'Wasn't so bad, was it?'

'Was all right.'

'It was better than all right. Go on, admit it. You enjoyed it. Even with Gabrielle here.'

'She still had her boobs out.'

'Did she? I didn't notice.'

She slapped him hard on the arm. 'You must be blind, then. They were bouncing all around the room.'

Martyn laughed loudly. 'You make it sound like we've been in a ball pit all night. Okay, so she was a little uncovered. That's just Gabrielle. I, for one, only had eyes for my darling wife.'

Colette began to make a show of putting her finger down her throat, but quickly changed her mind. 'Better not do that,' she said. 'Might cover you with vomit.'

Martyn grimaced. 'It's the innocent charm like that which really attracts me.'

Colette smiled and moved towards him. She tried to make her action sinewy and sensuous, but the alcohol got in the way and turned it into more of a tightrope walk. Martyn, however, seemed to read her intentions.

She said, 'I have to admit, you've been a very good boy tonight.'

'Hmm. Does that mean I get a reward?'

Her reply was to slip out of her dress. It was as if she had practised the motion a hundred times. One second she was clothed; the next she was standing there wearing only a thong, heels and a raised eyebrow.

Martyn needed no further encouragement. He was suddenly a blur of motion, on his wife like a spider on a fly. Above, Brogan waited for his moment. Waited for Colette to find her position and lock eyes with his. Waited for her to smile at him, to make promises to him, to offer herself to him.

But she was lost. Wrapped up in Martyn's web. Her movements became frenzied as his became ever hungrier. She lost sight of what lay beyond, forgot about the world and her place within it as Martyn grasped her, manipulated her, devoured her.

She's betraying you.

She's had too much to drink.

And? Since when has drunkenness been an excuse for infidelity?

You're right. It hasn't.

She hasn't looked your way once. Not a single glance. She's not even attempting to put on a show for you.

I was on her side about the Gabrielle thing. I was willing to help her.

And how does she repay you? By snubbing you, that's how. She's doing this for herself. For herself and for Martyn. Not you.

She might as well be telling me to go to hell.

That's right. That's exactly what she's doing. She's giving you the finger, just like Martyn's doing to her right now.

It's disrespectful. She's an ingrate.

She's worse than that. She's a bitch. She's tossing you aside like a used tissue. She hates you.

I think she does. I really think she hates me.

You know it. The question is, what are you going to do about it? How does this make you feel?

Like . . . like I need to kill.

That's it. That's my boy. So, are we going down there or what?

Not now. I'm saving her.

For a rainy day? What are you talking about? Look at her. Look at how quickly she's forgotten you.

I know, but . . .

No buts. You need to kill. I can see the hunger in you.

I know. And I'm going to.

How? How will you do that if you don't go down there?

I'll find another.

Really? Who?

Elsie.

SUNDAY 9 JUNE, 1.27 AM

The pulsating thirst for death in his head demanded to be satisfied, and Elsie would be easy prey. Her sacrifice would keep the demons at bay for a while, allowing him to think more rationally.

He dropped onto her landing like a cat, and felt his eyes were glowing in the night. He moved silently towards her bedroom. He pushed open the door, then took out his knife and torch. He hadn't worked out exactly what he was going to do to her yet, but it would be imaginative. He liked a bit of variety when it came to dispatching his victims.

He stood in the darkness for a while, listening for her breathing, perhaps a snore. But he heard nothing. He worried for a moment that she had already died in her sleep – a spiteful act to rob him of his chance to become whole again. He thumbed the switch on his torch.

She wasn't there.

The duvet had been tossed to one side, as though she had woken and climbed out of bed. So where was she?

Brogan went back out to the landing. He aimed his torch

towards the bathroom, but the door was open and there was nobody inside. Then, as he moved to the top of the stairs, he saw a faint light from below. He turned his torch off and headed towards the light, like a moth drawn to a flame.

The glow was squeezing through the gap in the half-closed kitchen door. Brogan put his torch away but kept his knife in his hand. He stepped towards the door and opened it.

Elsie sat at the table in her dressing gown. She had turned her chair around to face the door. Her eyes were closed and her lips slightly parted. She didn't move even a fraction as he entered.

'Elsie?' he said. He took a few steps closer. '*Elsie?*'

When she jolted awake, it was as though an electric shock had just restarted her heart, and Brogan jumped back, startled. Elsie blinked her rheumy eyes, then narrowed them as she struggled to focus on his face.

'Alex? I was beginning to think you weren't coming.'

'I'm here,' he said. He kept his tone cold. He wanted her to understand what was happening.

'I couldn't sleep. I kept thinking you would come, but you didn't, so I got up. You don't mind, do you?'

Brogan shook his head. 'It makes no difference. Upstairs or down here. It's all the same.'

'Are you hungry?'

Oh, yes. We're hungry, all right. Just not for food.

'I'm okay. There's something I need to do first.'

Her mouth twisted into a shrewd smile. 'Yes. I know.'

The remark threw him. He became suddenly uncertain. 'You know?'

'Of course. This is a special moment for you.'

'Yes. Yes, it is. But how did you know?'

She cackled. 'I might be old, but I'm not senile.' She pointed a gnarled finger. 'My brain is as sharp as that knife.'

Brogan looked down at the knife, then back at Elsie, her eyes now mischievously wide.

How can she be like this? How can she be so blasé about dying?

She's ancient. She has the wisdom of the old. They have a sixth sense for when their time is up.

A sixth sense?

Absolutely. Like when a knackered old lion walks off into the desert to die.

That's a thing?

It's definitely a thing. Google it.

Brogan stepped slowly towards her, bringing the knife up to her eye level, moving its deadly point closer and closer. Still she seemed unafraid. Amused, even.

She shouldn't be like this. She should be scared witless, begging for her life.

I told you. It's what she expects. She's resigned to her fate.

'It's all right,' she said. 'You can go ahead and start cutting now.'

He didn't understand. Her attitude was confusing him and deflating his sense of purpose.

'What?' he said.

And then she turned. He thought at first she was showing him the side of her neck, presenting the wrinkled, veiny flesh as a target. But then she gestured towards the table behind her.

'Happy Birthday, Alex!' she said.

He could see now that on the table stood a chocolate cake, a single candle at its centre.

'What?' he said again.

'It's after midnight, so it's officially your birthday. I know this is a strange time of the day for cake, but this is when you come, isn't it? You come only at night, so that's when we have to celebrate. Your present isn't quite ready yet, but if you can come back tonight before midnight—'

'You made a cake?'

'Yes. Of course. I always make a cake for you. I'm not as good at it as I used to be, but, well, it's all right, isn't it?'

Brogan moved around her, lowering his knife arm. He stared at the cake. It was covered in chocolate shavings and buttons. It looked delicious.

'It's for me?'

'Of course it's for you, silly. Would you like a slice?'

Brogan looked again at the knife, and then at Elsie.

Go ahead, take a slice out of the old woman. That's what you came here for, isn't it?

Yes, it's what I came here for.

Then do it. What are you waiting for? You still get the cake afterwards, so do it.

But Brogan remembered when he was last given chocolate cake. It had been when he was much younger. It was back in the happy time, when he was part of a proper family. He recalled smiling faces and singing and presents. The pain and the blood were still a long way off.

'I would,' he said. He started moving the knife towards the cake, but Elsie stopped him.

'Wait, wait! We have to light the candle. Can't have birthday cake without lighting the candle.'

She tottered over to her under-sink cupboard and brought out a box of matches. Returning to the table, her jittery fingers removed a match, struck it, then brought its flaring tip to the candle. When she blew out the match, its smoke drifted towards Brogan, and he inhaled it to add substance to his memories.

He raised his knife again, but then the singing began. It was only the brief repetitive lines of 'Happy Birthday', but Elsie's voice surprised him. Tremulous, yes, but with its own fragile beauty. A voice he could listen to for hours.

And something strange happened.

Tears found their way to his eyes.

The sensation shocked him. He couldn't remember the last time he had cried. It was evidence of feelings he thought he had long put behind him.

'Make a wish,' Elsie said.

'What?'

'Blow out the candle and make a wish. That's what you do on your birthday.'

He did as he was instructed. He didn't have to think long about his wish. It was already there at the forefront of his mind.

He wished for the unfamiliar feeling of contentment to remain there for ever.

Wishes don't come true. He'd always known that.

He sat on the edge of his mattress, a single candle providing his only light. He tried to transport himself mentally back to Elsie's kitchen, but the feelings were already distant and fuzzy. It was like trying to make out shapes through frosted glass. If someone told him now that he'd actually cried, he would call them a liar before killing them.

Some memories were much sharper. The cake, for one. Best cake he'd had in a long time. Being home-baked made all the difference. The Carters had only supermarket crap in their fridge. He'd eaten it, but it had made him feel bloated and full of chemicals.

He had talked to Elsie for at least an hour. Mostly about Alex, of course, but then why not? That's whom she believed he was. When he left, he almost thought of himself as her son.

He didn't like the fact that it was Sunday now. The Fairbrights would probably be home much of the day. No opportunity to drop into their house, pinch their food, use their shower. He'd have to make do with what he had here, which wasn't much. Fortunately, Elsie had once again insisted on giving him enough food and drink to get him through the day.

You shouldn't go back there again tonight.

Why not?

She makes you weak. She makes you unsure of yourself.

Do you think that's how other people feel? Because of their emotions, I mean.

All the time. It's why they don't survive. You're a survivor, but you need to stay strong.

I like Elsie.

You were supposed to kill her.

It would have been too messy. The police would have been called. I would've had to leave.

I already told you that you could have made it look like natural causes.

I could, but where's the fun in that? Besides . . .

Besides what?

I like her.

See what I mean? She's a bad influence. You need to focus.

Focus on what?

On the Fairbrights. What else?

Brogan nodded as he stared at the face of mould on his wall. The advice was sound. He needed to pull himself together.

But over the course of a long, empty day, with little else to occupy his mind, he found his thoughts returning to Elsie and the way in which she was utterly consumed by her desire for the son she had lost. Profound absences of his own slithered into his brain – of companionship, of friendship, of love

– darkening his mood and making him wish for this interminable day to be over and done with.

He knew it hadn't always been this way, but the days of an untroubled existence were so long ago. His early years were spent on a farm in Shropshire. He had no siblings, but his parents were always there for him. Life was happy, carefree. Idyllic, even. He sat on tractors and stone walls, he pushed through tall grass and waded through burbling streams, he talked to sheep and cows and horses. He had started school in the village and loved it. His teacher, Miss Lumley, was friendly and pretty. She had a smile that seemed wider than her face.

He was unprepared when the clouds rolled in.

He was five years old. Sitting halfway down the stairs in the big, echoing farmhouse. He was there not by chance, but because he had heard raised, anguished voices – unprecedented in his brief experience.

He didn't understand most of the conversation, but it was something about money, and about losing the farm. Thomas couldn't comprehend how it was possible for someone's home to be taken away from them, but that seemed to be what they were saying. Both his father and mother were crying. He wanted to go to them, to comfort them, but something prevented him – a vague sense that his sudden intrusion would cause them to crumple up their true feelings and hide them behind their backs.

Life seemed different from then on. His parents became more serious, more distracted. Even when they attempted to play with him, unseen forces tugged at their attention. They kept exchanging soulful glances, the meaning lost on their son. He often heard their voices in the night, and he shed tears into his pillow at the thought of their distress. When he asked them if everything was okay, they told him not to worry, it would be all right in the end.

It wasn't all right in the end.

He jolted awake at the sound of a thunderclap. At least he thought it was thunder. But when he went to the window, he saw that there was no rain, the moon was smiling down at him through an unblotched sky, and the trees slumbered peacefully, their arms open to the heavens.

He climbed out of bed and his feet slapped the short walk to his parents' bedroom. There were no raised voices that night, and so he felt it was safe to seek reassurance from them.

He pushed open their door. Halted. His eyes widened as he struggled to make sense of what he saw.

His mother and father were in bed. But that was the extent of the normality.

His mother had no face. It had been replaced by an open flower of glistening crimson. Next to her, his father had the twin barrels of his shotgun in his mouth. His legs were drawn up, and his toes were curled around a pen that had been inserted through the trigger guard. His eyes were closed and his breathing heavy, like he was trying to suck oxygen through the gun barrels.

'Daddy,' Thomas said.

His father opened his eyes, looked at his son with a sadness that was devastating in its finality. And then, with a flick of his toes, he depressed the trigger and scattered his brains up the wall behind him.

There followed a long period of nothingness. It stretched into days, weeks. A piece of Brogan's life had been obliterated from his timeline.

His next firm memory was of being with his new parents: his Aunt Janice and her husband Brian. They had no children of their own and took Thomas into their home with apparent glee, albeit fuelled by a sense of familial duty.

It wasn't like the farm. He was in a city now. There was dirt and noise and litter and aggression here. His new school was grey and unwelcoming, his teacher male and unapproachable. Thomas had to attend regular meetings to talk to psychiatric counsellors about his feelings. He hated it. He endured long periods of gloom and irascibility. Janice and Brian did their best with him, but their patience was bounded. They often left him to wallow in his misery.

And then lightning struck for a second time.

Janice became pregnant.

Suddenly it was all about the bump. Whether it would be a boy or a girl. What name they would give it. How they would decorate its room. What clothes they would buy for it.

Thomas was forgotten. At the tender age of seven he was sensitive to the changes in the atmosphere. He felt the coldness. He could walk into a room unnoticed, while Janice and Brian marvelled and cooed over the bump. Sometimes even the words he uttered went unheard. He was made to realise that he was secondary.

When the baby was born, there was little attempt at integration. Thomas was not encouraged to regard the new arrival as his little sister. Instead, he was constantly shoved aside

– sometimes physically. He was repeatedly warned not to handle her, or to do anything that might put her at risk – so much so that he was sometimes afraid to breathe on her. He absorbed the phrases like 'Isn't she a miracle?' and 'I always wanted a girl', and 'Finally we have a child of our own', and brick after brick was added to the walls going up in his head.

Strike three: the baby died.

Later, Brogan would wonder what cruel twist of fate drew him to the infant's side, and he would reason that it was an affinity with death. The same strange connection that took him to the scene of his father blowing his brains out.

On that fateful day, he was passing the bedroom and he sensed something was wrong. He walked over to the cot and he looked down and he saw it.

Death.

He knew this instantly. He could smell it. Taste it. The experience was curiously electrifying.

He didn't hear Janice come into the room behind him until it was too late. He watched in detached silence as she went into meltdown. The room was filled to bursting with her emotions. And among it all, the accusations, flung at him with venom: *What have you done? What in God's name have you done?*

He tried to protest his innocence, but his exclamations were ineffective against the barrage of allegation. He shrank away from the banshee of a woman clutching her dead baby, and his soul shrank inside him.

After that, the counsellors and therapists returned in force. They consoled both parents and elder sibling, but a rift had been opened that was beyond healing. They assured the family that it was nobody's fault – that such things just happen. Janice and Brian nodded their acceptance, but it was a lie. When the professionals moved on, the shroud of doubt and suspicion remained. What few ties of love that ever existed had been severed. Thomas became just an entity in the house. He was given meals and clothing and . . . well, hardly anything else. He was not taken on days out or on holidays. He was not allowed to have friends over, or to visit them. Conversation was kept minimal and functional. He spent most of his time alone in his room, out of sight and out of mind.

And nobody, least of all Thomas Brogan, realised what it was doing to him.

He woke up hungry but excited. This was going to be a great day.

He hadn't visited Elsie last night, and a part of him wondered whether she would be upset.

Stop caring about her. She's not important.

He hadn't visited the Fairbrights either. He didn't want to see them all lovey-dovey. He wanted to see how they coped when it all started going wrong.

He crunched on an apple while sitting cross-legged at the kitchen door, the wooden board pulled away to allow in some fresh air. He had become so used to living in darkness that the bright sunlight hurt his eyes.

Hot day ahead. It's going to get pretty toasty up in those attic spaces.

Yeah, I know.

Maybe you should go up there naked.

What?

Yeah. And then you should drop in on them. Just appear naked in their house. Imagine their surprise. You could put the willies up them!

That joke's still funny if you're about nine years old.

When Brogan had eaten, he put the board back in place, bolted the door and headed upstairs. At Elsie's place he paused for a while and listened to the conversation from below.

'Elsie, did Tammy bring food with her yesterday?'

'I don't like Tammy. If I must have someone, I'd prefer you.'

'Yes, well sometimes I need a day off like everybody else. And you haven't answered my question. Did she bring you some food?'

'She never brings me anything. You don't, either.'

'Not my job. So why is there cake in the fridge?'

'I made one.'

'And very nice it looks too. What I'm asking is why it's there. You've got diabetes. You're not supposed to be eating sugary stuff.'

'I only had a sliver.'

'There's more than a sliver gone, Elsie. There's barely half of it left. And there's a candle in it.'

'It was a special occasion.'

'What was?'

'Yesterday. It was a special day.'

'What kind of special day?'

'A birthday.'

'It wasn't your birthday. Your birthday is in September.'

'I didn't say it was *my* birthday, did I? It was someone else's.'

'Whose?'

'Alex's.'

Stupid old cow. I told you. She can't be trusted.

'Al— Oh, I see.'

'Do you?'

'Yes, I . . . Look, Elsie, you need to start being sensible.'

'Sensible? What are you talking about?'

'I'm talking about looking after yourself. You need to get out more. Meet some new people.'

'I don't want to meet new people,' she snapped. 'I like it here. With Alex.'

'Yes, all right. Don't get all hot and bothered. I'm just saying that having so much cake isn't good for you.'

'And I told you that I didn't eat it.'

'No. All right, Elsie. If you say so.'

There came an awkward silence best left unfilled by either party. And then Elsie said, 'I made him a present too.'

'A present? For Alex?'

'Yes. I was going to give it to him last night, but he didn't come.'

'No, well—'

Brogan got the feeling the carer was about to say 'well, he wouldn't, would he?' and that she then thought better of it.

'I hope he's all right,' Elsie said.

'I don't think you need to worry. Right then, what shall we have for breakfast?'

Brogan smiled at the carer's diversionary tactic. The woman clearly wasn't comfortable talking about the dead. Little did she know how close her charge had come to being in that state.

Brogan abandoned his listening post, but knew he would have to visit Elsie again soon. She had a present for him. He couldn't recall the last time someone had given him a present. Gifts were something he gave to himself now, usually involving great sacrifices of others.

He moved on. He wasted no time at Jack and Pam's house – their demon hound had convinced him to delete it from his list of local attractions – and continued on to the Fairbrights' attic.

It's different.

What do you mean, different?

Look at it. Things have been moved around. They've been up here.

Well, they're entitled, aren't they? It's their house.

I don't like it. This is our domain. They should stay down there where they belong.

Brogan tried to dismiss the fact as being unworthy of further contemplation, but it drove home to him how precarious his situation was – how, at any time, someone else could easily explore the route he had come to regard as his private footway.

Slightly unnerved, he spent a few minutes listening to satisfy himself that the property was empty before he made his way down the ladder.

In the bedroom, the smell of Colette washed away his anxiety. He closed his eyes while he inhaled her scents. He pictured her on the bed, asleep and unaware of his presence. His excitement grew.

He headed downstairs. In the kitchen cupboard he discovered a fresh loaf of bread. He took great care in unpeeling the dated sticker holding it closed, then he extracted a slice and resealed the tab. He toasted the bread lightly, then scraped a thin layer of peanut butter onto it. As he ate with his back to the sink, he scanned the kitchen, his mind toying with the possibilities this house might offer him when he finally confronted the Fairbrights in person.

His eyes alighted on a small music system on the counter opposite. He went across and switched it on. It started to play 'I'm a Believer' by The Monkees.

A great song.

Absolutely. A classic.

The opening bars pulled him in. He found himself nodding along, and then singing. The lyrics seemed so fitting to his situation. They could almost be about Colette. He became lost in the song, his voice growing louder.

And then he noticed the shadow.

It passed across the wall in front of him, and at first he thought he was imagining it. But then he heard the noises too.

He dropped to the floor.

Shit!

A fucking window cleaner!

Has he seen you?

I don't think so. I don't know.

Get out of there, man.

I can't move. He'll see me.

Well, at least turn off the fucking music.

I can't! I can't reach it without him seeing me.

Brogan stayed where he was, flat on the tiled floor. He listened to the heavy footsteps outside, the splashing of water onto the ground.

He'll do the upstairs first, right?

I think so. That would make sense.

Because if he starts on this window, he'll definitely see you.

I know. Stay cool.

You'll have to kill him.

What?

If he sees you, you'll have to kill him.

Shut up. It won't come to that.

Brogan lifted his head slightly – enough to see out the window. A dark shape passed in front of it, and Brogan pressed his cheek against the tiles again.

He heard a heavy slap against a window, then a steady waterfall hitting the yard just outside the door. The cleaner was definitely tackling the upper storey first.

Cut the music!

I'm doing it.

Brogan crawled towards the counter. He couldn't risk standing up, as the window cleaner was working from ground level using a telescopic brush attached to a pressure hose.

Brogan stretched up an arm. During the several seconds it took him to locate the off switch, he hoped that the cleaner wasn't staring at his floundering hand in amusement.

Commando-style, Brogan snaked his way out of the kitchen and into the hall. The only glass there was in the front door, and it was frosted. Breathing a sigh of relief, he sat up and pressed his back against a wall.

You got cocky.

What do you mean?

You were complacent. Careless. Stupid. How many more adjectives would you like?

All right. Don't go on about it. It's over.

Is it?

Brogan waited for some time, listening to the cleaner work his way around the house. When the light coming through the kitchen doorway was suddenly eclipsed, he found himself drawing in his legs and holding his breath. He didn't feel frightened; it was more that he was overcompensating for his earlier recklessness.

He listened to the soft slide of a soapy pad across the glass, and then a bright squeal as a squeegee dragged away the dirt-laden suds.

The cleaner moved on to the other windows. In a few minutes it was all over. Brogan heard the yard door being latched shut. He could relax again. He stood up.

See? Nothing to worry about.

But then, as if knowing it had just been challenged, the shadow returned. It loomed outside the front door. As it neared the frosted glass, it crystallised into colours and the more precisely defined shape of a heavy-set man.

The doorbell rang.

Brogan stayed perfectly still, staring at the distorted figure, waiting for it to give up and come back for the money another time.

You need to answer. Get him in here.

What are you talking about? He'll go away in a second. He doesn't know I'm here.

No? Then listen.

Brogan listened. The window cleaner was whistling softly. It was the melody of 'I'm a Believer'.

He heard you!

So?

What do you mean? He knows you're there. When he comes back for the money, he'll tell them. They'll know you were here.

He won't do that. He won't even remember.

He will. Open the door. Drag him in.

Don't be ridiculous. He has equipment. A van. What am I supposed to do with that?

But then it was too late. The cleaner moved away, his shadow thinning, his whistle fading.

You're an imbecile. You need to think about your actions.

Brogan couldn't help himself. He began laughing.

What the hell are you laughing about?

You. You're such a worrier. We're fine. We'll always be fine.

Yeah? Well, keep thinking that way. See where it gets you.

Brogan got to his feet and returned to the kitchen. He retrieved his half-eaten toast from the floor, then ate it because he didn't know what else to do with it. He cleaned the butter knife and put it away, then brushed up any crumbs he could see and flushed them down the sink. Lastly, he switched the toaster off at the wall – exactly as it had been when he arrived.

When he was done in the kitchen, he went back upstairs to the bedroom. There was something he needed to do.

MONDAY 10 JUNE, 5.58 PM

Brogan made sure to be back in position just before six. It was hot up here. Stifling. The sun had been beating down on the rooftops all day, turning the loft spaces into ovens.

But soon the Fairbrights would be home, and then the heat would be turned up even higher.

When he heard the first noises from downstairs, he let out a low laugh.

Come up here, Colette. Come and find your surprise.

She kept him waiting longer than he would have liked. He began to wonder if she was doing it on purpose, simply to frustrate him.

But then he heard her coming up the stairs. She entered the bedroom. She kicked off her shoes, then sat on the bed and rubbed her feet as though they might be sore.

She's got beautiful feet.

What are you, a foot fetishist now?

I'm just saying. They look delicate. Smooth. I'd like to massage them for her.

I'm starting to worry about you.

Colette stood up and began to undress. Brogan always enjoyed these moments. He suspected he'd enjoy it even more on this occasion.

She removed her skirt, her blouse. Brogan's excitement mounted. He knew what was coming next.

Colette moved towards the chest of drawers. She would probably want a T-shirt and jeans, perhaps leggings. She would want to get comfortable.

She slid open a drawer. Gasped. Brogan had to clamp a hand over his mouth to prevent an exclamation of his own.

He could see directly into the drawer from here. See the photographs of Colette's dead fiancé placed carefully on top of her clothes.

Tentatively, Colette picked up one of the photographs. She studied it carefully as she tried to work out what it meant. She opened another drawer, and another. Photographs in each and every one of them. She let out a cry and staggered back to her bed, the picture of Jeremy still clutched in her hand.

'No!' she said. 'No!'

I think she likes your little gift to her.

I do, too.

Colette began to weep. She stared at the photo, then back towards the drawers, then at the photo again.

'What's happening?' she said quietly. 'Why? Why would he do this?'

Do you think she's talking about Martyn or Jeremy?

Not sure yet. But I think we're about to find out.

Brogan had heard the car pulling up outside. The next few minutes would be unmissable.

At the sound of the key in the front door, Colette burst into life. She dashed across to the chest of drawers, moved a couple of photos aside, then yanked out the first clothes that came to hand. After putting the pictures back in position, she threw on the clothes.

Looks like there's gonna be a fight.

Yeah. Hard to be taken seriously when you're standing there in skimpy underwear.

Martyn shouted up the stairs: 'You there, love?'

Colette went to the bedroom door. 'Could you come up here a minute, please?'

She walked back into the room, folded her arms, waited.

Martyn appeared. 'What's up?'

Colette untucked a hand and waved it towards the chest of drawers. 'This! This is what's up.'

Martyn took a few steps forwards. 'I don't get it.'

'The photographs, Martyn!'

'Yes, I can see them. What I don't understand is why you've laid them out like that.'

'I was about to ask you the same thing.'

'What are you talking about? This is nothing to do with me. You must have done it.'

'I didn't, Martyn. Which means *you* did. What I want to know is what the bloody hell you're playing at. Why did you do this?'

Martyn stared at her for several seconds. He shook his head. 'You know what? I don't need this. I've just got in from work, I'm tired and I'm hungry. I don't want to play stupid games.'

He began to turn away, but Colette grabbed his arm and spun him around.

'Don't you leave. This is important. I want to know what you're trying to do to me.'

'Trying to do to you? What the hell does that mean?'

She stabbed a finger towards the drawers. 'Those pictures are all of Jeremy. The other day I found one in my book. Now I find them in my clothes drawers. They didn't get there by themselves. Somebody put them there.'

'Well, it wasn't me.'

'No? Then what are you suggesting? That somebody broke into our house without leaving a trace, laid out those photos of Jeremy, and then left again?'

'No, because that would be stupid. What I'm suggesting is that you put them there.'

Colette waved her hands wildly. 'Why? Why would I do that?'

'I don't know. Maybe you're still fixated on him.'

'Fixated? I'm not fixated. I hardly ever mention him.'

'Doesn't mean he's not on your mind. The mind can play funny tricks. Maybe you're not even aware that you keep getting his photos out.'

'What? Oh, don't even go there. I may be upset, but I'm not crazy. I would know if it was me who moved those photos.'

'If you say so.'

'What's that supposed to mean?'

'It means that there aren't many alternatives here. Who was the first one to leave the house this morning? Me, right? And who was the last one to come home tonight? Oh, that's right, it was me again. So when am I supposed to have had this amazing opportunity to piss around with your old boyfriend's pictures?'

This threw Colette. 'You ... you could have dropped in during the day.'

'Is that what you think? That I drove ten miles to get here in my lunch hour, took out the photos, then dashed back again? What possible motive could I have for doing that?'

Brogan could see the uncertainty creeping into her expression. 'I ... I don't know.'

'I mean why would I move those photos at any time? The guy is history. I don't want to think about him. I certainly don't want him interfering in our marriage. I don't even know why you keep those photos. How would you like it if I kept a shoebox full of pictures of my old girlfriends?'

'He wasn't just a boyfriend, Martyn. We were going to be married. I loved him, and those pictures are all that's left of him.'

'Well, it's becoming perfectly clear how much love you had for him.'

Colette looked stunned. 'What?'

'You can't let him go. Whether you're conscious of it or not, you're still in love with him. That's why you keep going back to his photos. I'm no psychologist, but maybe that's why your brain is wiping out your memories of it, because you feel guilty.'

Now it was Colette's turn to glare. 'I don't believe this. After all we've been through, after all the explaining I've tried to do about what happened to Jeremy and how it affected me, you're still accusing me of being unfaithful.'

'Not in the physical sense, no.' He tapped his temple. 'But up here, where it also counts, then maybe. I don't know how else to explain your behaviour.'

'You don't? Then piss off, Martyn, because I've had it up to here with this. I'm not crazy and I'm not unfaithful, but if you're going to keep throwing insults at me like that, you can just fuck right off.'

'Fine. I'll do that, then.'

'Fine.'

Martyn turned and stormed out of the room. Colette slammed the door behind him. Then she opened it and slammed it again, just to make sure he got the message.

Brogan watched as she sat down on the bed and put her hands over her face. She cried and sniffed for a minute, then abruptly uncovered her face and stood up again.

'I'm not crazy,' she said to the room.

She went to the chest of drawers and gathered the photographs together. She sat back on the bed and flicked through the images.

'What's going on, Jeremy?' she asked. 'What the hell is happening?'

She went back to the chest of drawers and returned the photographs to their box, then she moved to the door and stood there for a while, as if debating whether to go after Martyn.

Ten seconds later, she backed away, chewing on a fingernail.

'I don't know what you're playing at, Martyn,' she whispered, 'but it won't work.'

Brogan smiled. He thought otherwise. He thought it was all working perfectly.

The door opened, and Martyn stuck his head into the room as if expecting to be shot at. Colette was curled in the foetal position on the bed, and didn't turn to look at him. He went over to her, lowered himself gently onto the mattress.

'I've made dinner,' he told her.

She gave no reply.

'Col? I've made dinner. Come and eat with me.'

'I'm not hungry,' she said.

He was silent for a few seconds. Then: 'It's bolognese. You love bolognese. I've done garlic bread, too. The one with the cheese. Loads of carbs, I know, but I think we could do with some comfort food.'

'I can't eat it.'

'Why not?'

'I'm upset, Martyn.'

He waited, then tried again. 'You need to eat. Being upset uses a lot of calories.'

'That's not even funny.' She finally turned her head to look at him. From above, Brogan could see the sheen on her

137

tear-stained cheeks.

She said, 'This is serious. I don't know what's going on here.'

Martyn shrugged helplessly. 'All I know is that I didn't move those photographs.'

She stared into his eyes, as if searching for the glint of deceit. 'Well, neither did I.'

'Okay. I believe you.'

'Do you? Do you really?'

'Of course. If you really don't remember moving—'

'No, Martyn! It's not a question of remembering. There's nothing to remember. It didn't happen, okay?'

Martyn raised his hands in surrender. 'All right. I'm sorry. Bad choice of words. But then I don't know what the answer is. Only you and I have been in this house today. And even if somebody had somehow managed to break in without causing any damage, why the hell would their only act be to dig out some old photos? It doesn't make any sense.'

'So you still think it was me, right?'

She turned her face away from him again.

'No. I didn't say that. Look, can we forget about this, please? Let's have dinner. I'm starving.'

'Go and eat then. I'm not stopping you.'

He placed a hand on her shoulder, and she didn't shrug it away.

'Come on, Col. It's not important. It's just a few photos. It doesn't mean anything.'

'That's not what you said before. You said I was still in love with Jeremy.'

'I . . . I didn't mean it. I know that's not true. Let's just mark this down as one of those freaky things that sometimes happens in life. Things we can't explain. Like UFOs. Or the Bermuda Triangle.'

'Or ghosts?'

'What?'

She turned to him again. 'Is that where you're going with this? The supernatural? Jeremy back from the dead, haunting me because I didn't do enough to stop him killing himself?'

'No. That's not what—'

'Because that's just ridiculous, Martyn. I don't need you trying to scare me like that.'

'I wasn't trying to—'

'There's a perfectly rational explanation for this. I just don't know what it is. Okay?'

Martyn surrendered again. 'Okay. I was just trying to lighten the mood. The total opposite of scaring you. It's not a ghost. I don't even believe in ghosts. It's just . . . weird. Can we leave it at that?'

Once again, Colette showed him the back of her head.

'Col? Can we eat now? Let's go downstairs and talk about something else. We'll have a glass of wine and I'll tell you about the latest stupid things that customers have said to me today. All right? Is that a plan?'

Colette made him wait a while before answering. 'I'll come down in a few minutes. I need to wash my face.'

Martyn suddenly brightened. 'Okay. Great. I'll lay the table.' He leaned down, kissed her on the cheek, then rubbed her shoulder. He opened his mouth to say something else, then thought better of it. He stood and went to the door, then watched her for a few seconds before disappearing.

When he'd gone, Colette climbed off the bed. She stood staring at the chest of drawers for a full minute. When she lifted her gaze to the ceiling, Brogan instantly pulled his head away from the hole.

She's heard you! She knows you're here!

No. Wait.

He brought his eye back to the hole. Colette was still staring upwards, but not directly at him. Her eyes were fixed on another point entirely.

'Jeremy?' she whispered to the heavens. 'Was it you?'

Brogan felt a childish impulse to reply, to issue veiled threats in his best spectral voice.

Colette lowered her head. 'Don't be stupid,' she told herself before leaving the room.

Brogan smiled. The seeds were sown. All he had to do now was keep them nurtured.

Brogan got into position early. He had been back to his empty house for a couple of hours, mainly to stretch his muscles and ease his joints, but he didn't want to miss any of the action.

As it turned out, the action was minimal. The couple came to bed not long after ten-thirty, but it was not for any reasons of lust. Brogan listened to Martyn doing his best to remain buoyant, but Colette was in no mood for it. Her responses were courteous enough, but there was no real feeling in them. She showered and changed into her nightwear in the bathroom, and when she returned, she got straight into bed and turned out her light. When Martyn said goodnight, she grunted an unintelligible response. Brogan saw how Martyn shook his head in despair before turning out his own lamp.

Remember that?

What?

That atmosphere. The sense that nobody in the house wanted to communicate with you. The realisation that you may as well have been living there alone for all the attention you were getting.

I remember it. The silence hurt more than words.

Brogan gave the couple the time they needed to drift into unconsciousness, then took his own leave.

You know you got off lightly, don't you?

How do you mean?

That business about Colette saying that Martyn could have slipped away from work to come home.

What of it?

Think about it. If the window cleaner says anything to Colette about hearing the radio on or someone moving about inside, it will just confirm her suspicions about Martyn.

Yeah. I never thought of that.

Still doesn't excuse your stupidity, though.

Brogan opened the hatch into Elsie's house and dropped down. When he reached the door outside her room, he could hear her gentle snoring. He decided not to disturb her, and headed downstairs in search of food.

He found a steak pie in the fridge and slid it into the microwave. He'd have preferred it done in the oven, because microwaves make the pastry go all limp, but he didn't want to hang around that long.

While the pie cooked, he found a tin of beans in one of the cupboards. He emptied the contents into a bowl and placed it next to the microwave, awaiting its turn to be nuked. He opened a fresh loaf of bread, pulled out two slices, and began to butter them.

The smell of food made him realise how hungry he was. A full stomach now would keep him awake for the next few hours, but his body clock was all messed up anyway. It actually made more sense to sleep during the day, when there was nothing better to do.

It was as he was carrying his food to the table that Elsie materialised in the doorway. He almost dropped the plate in surprise.

'Shit!' he said.

'You shouldn't use such language, Alex. You never used to talk like that.'

'I'm sorry. You're quite right.' He hefted the plate in his hand. 'I hope you don't mind. I was starving.'

'You should have woken me up. I'd have done it for you. I'd have made a proper meal.'

'I didn't want to disturb you. You sounded fast asleep.'

'I can sleep anytime. I'd prefer to see you.'

He nodded, then tilted his head towards the table. 'You mind?'

'Go ahead,' she said. 'Eat. I wouldn't want you to fade away.'

He sat down, began to stuff the food into his mouth.

'I'll make you a nice big mug of tea,' she said. 'Help wash it down.'

'Thank you.'

While the kettle boiled, he could sense her staring at him.

'Did you come last night?' she asked.

'Er . . . no. I couldn't make it last night.'

'Why not?'

'It's . . . it's not always easy. I have to come a long way.'

She nodded, as if comprehending some profound truth. 'I stayed up. I wanted to give you your present.'

The present! He'd forgotten about that.

'I'm really sorry. I wanted to come, but I couldn't. I hope it didn't upset you.'

'I was disappointed, but it doesn't matter. You're here now. Eat up and then I'll fetch it.'

He wolfed down the food and swallowed the steaming tea in massive gulps. Elsie sat observing him in awe.

'Heavens,' she said. 'I think somebody still has room for dessert. How about sponge and custard?'

'That would be fantastic,' he said. 'But . . .'

'Yes?' she said, a twinkle finding its way through the mist in her corneas.

'You said something about . . .'

'A present? I did, didn't I?' She stood up. 'Give me a minute.'

He watched her shuffle out of the room. She seemed incredibly frail tonight. A wisp of a person that would not withstand the slightest breeze.

What are you doing?

She's got a present for me.

And since when did we start accepting presents? When did we decide it was a good idea to become indebted to people? Especially people we might have to kill?

I won't be indebted. It's for my birthday. I don't have to give something back.

It's not your fucking birthday! It's all in her head. She's mental!

We all have our own reality.

Don't we just? All I'm saying is, don't get too cosy with her, okay? You know what happens when you like things too much. They get taken away from you.

Elsie returned, one hand behind her back and a twist of

anticipation on her lips. She came right up to him at the table, and for a second he thought that the excitement was getting too great for her and that she might fall onto him.

'It isn't much,' she said. 'My fingers aren't as nimble as they used to be. It took me all day.'

She brought out her hand, opened up her spidery fingers. On her crumpled palm sat a small knitted toy. A black and white cat. Its eyes were a little askew and its whiskers over-long, but it was unmistakably a cat.

See? She brings you crap. I could do better myself, and I can't even knit.

Brogan stared at the pathetic object and wondered why anger wasn't already surging through him, why he wasn't seeing Elsie as a deluded ancient trout who deserved only to be put out of her misery.

'You had one like this when you were little,' she said. 'Do you remember?'

And then it hit him.

Mitzy.

The toy looked uncannily like Mitzy.

He reached out a hand, but felt almost fearful to touch it. It had been a long time since he'd last experienced fear, and the emotion felt alien in his soul.

'Do you like it?' Elsie asked.

'It's . . . How did you know?'

He must have been about nine or ten at the time. Most of his days were spent alone, even when he was surrounded by people. It was like he was invisible.

But not to Mitzy.

He had been standing in the mouth of the open garden shed when she wandered into his life. The heavy clouds had begun to release their load in a fine drizzle, as if to trick those below into complacency before opening the bomb bay doors.

Young Brogan loved to watch the rain crashing down mere centimetres in front of his face. The world looked so different when viewed through that constantly shimmering curtain. It seemed more distant, somehow. Less painful.

The cat appeared to have sensed that a drenching was imminent. It was heading towards the back fence of the garden, presumably to hop over in search of shelter. When it saw Brogan hovering in the shed doorway, it halted. Stared at him with piercing green eyes. Sniffed the air for traces of his scent.

'Hello, puss,' Brogan said. 'What's your name?'

He expected the cat to run away, but it didn't. It stood its ground as it appraised this unexpected stranger on its route.

Intending to stay a while, Brogan had come to the shed with his lunch. A ham sandwich.

'Are you hungry?' he asked.

He sank slowly into a squat, then lifted the top from his sandwich and peeled away the slice of ham. Tossing the bread aside, he held the meat out towards the cat. It stared at the offering, then up into Brogan's eyes, then back to the food. It sniffed again, searching for the scent. Clearly enticed, the cat took a step forward, then another. It stretched out its neck, but would come no closer.

Brogan ripped away some of the meat and tossed it out onto the wet grass. The cat gobbled it up.

'Wow, you're hungry, aren't you?'

He continued throwing pieces of ham, each time bringing the animal a little closer. Eventually, he was able to reach out a hand and stroke the cat's fur as it ate. In response, the feline arched its back and straightened its tail. When all the food was gone, though, the cat decided it was time to leave. It hastened away from the shed and jumped lithely over the rear fence, just as the heavens opened and the rain began to slant down.

Throughout the long summer holidays, when both his adoptive parents were at work and he was left to wander the house alone, he spent many hours in that shed, just watching and waiting. Sometimes the cat would come, sometimes it wouldn't. But each time it showed up, it grew a little bolder, a little friendlier. Even when he had no food, it would come to him. He would sit cross-legged on the floor and it would climb onto his legs, purring as he stroked it. As soon as he determined that the cat was female, he gave her a name: Mitzy, after a cat he'd once seen in a television programme.

Mitzy was his only real friend for a long time.

He never told Janice and Brian about her, because he knew they would find a way of ending the relationship. They would make up an excuse, of course, but he knew the real reason. Anything that would cause him misery was justifiable in their book.

But all friendships come to an end.

He was in the house when he heard the wailing from outside. He dashed to his bedroom window just in time to see Mitzy being chased by a large ginger cat. Mitzy ran out onto the street, and the driver didn't even seem to notice as his car ran her over. Brogan could hear the bang from his window. He watched as Mitzy somersaulted crazily in the air and landed in the gutter, all nine lives snatched from her in one fell swoop.

He ran outside crying, but there was nothing he could do. His only friend was now just a lifeless furry bundle.

Looks nothing like her.

Shut up.

I mean black and white, yes, but that's about it.

I said shut up!

'Are you all right, dear?' Elsie said.

'I . . . I'm . . .' He took the knitted toy from her. Stared into its wonky eyes. Then he stood up abruptly. 'I have to go now.'

'Alex, no. Stay a little longer. Please.'

But he was already on his way out. He heard Elsie's fading pleas for him to return, to have some dessert. He ran up the staircase, made short work of climbing up into the attic.

Seconds later he was back in his empty house.

He lit a candle and placed the toy Mitzy in front of it. He watched its magnified shadow on the wall, and imagined life in the shifting image.

It was a full minute before he realised tears were staining his cheeks.

See? I told you not to get too friendly with her. She hurt you.

No. It wasn't her. She was just being nice.

She's a witch. She reached into your mind and pulled out painful memories. Something that was dear to you and that was taken away, just like all the good things. She found Mitzy. She'll find others.

No. It wasn't like that.

Then why are you crying?

148

He had no answer. He couldn't explain. His thoughts were too confused. There was pain there, yes, but also a memory of exquisite happiness. The two didn't go together, and yet they seemed to mesh perfectly. As if one couldn't exist without the other. Pain and pleasure. Grief and joy. Yin and yang.

Mitzy was the light. Her death was the darkness. And from that completeness came his own growing.

He had befriended another cat after Mitzy. The ginger one that had chased her. He had laughed as he listened to the cries of its owners when they found it mutilated at the bottom of their garden.

That had been Brogan's beginning and end.

TUESDAY 11 JUNE, 6.37 AM

It felt to Brogan as though he were on a boundary between life and death. From the rooms below came nothing but a graveyard silence. Just feet above his head, though, he could hear the scratching and chirruping of the birds on the roof tiles. A plane flew over. A car started up and drove away. Brogan waited for the activity of the world outside to extend its tentacles into this house and shake it alive.

Sleep had become a fair-weather friend lately. Brogan used to be able to sleep soundly almost anywhere, in the harshest of conditions. But things were different now.

You're losing it.

What's that supposed to mean?

The old bat got to you. Made you cry like a girl. And now you've lost your edge.

I haven't lost my edge at all.

Yes you have. You're like Samson. Elsie has cut your hair and now you've lost your powers. You're starting to make mistakes. Like you did with that window cleaner. It's going to get worse unless you pull yourself together.

A radio came on. The seven o'clock news. Seconds later, a dim finger of light poked its way through the peephole in the ceiling. Brogan moved his eye to the hole.

Colette was staring right back at him.

Brogan's heart suddenly leapt into overdrive. Did she know he was there?

There was no fear on her face, no anxiety. Brogan realised that she had been lying there for a long time, staring into space. Perhaps she'd been as deprived of sleep as he had.

Next to her, on his stomach, Martyn groaned. The noise caused Colette to turn and look at him, as if she had only just realised he was there. She didn't reach out to him or even smile. Almost as if she preferred he didn't wake up and intrude into her thoughts.

When he yawned and turned towards her, she tossed the duvet aside and bounded out of bed, leaving his arm floundering for her warmth.

Brogan smiled. He had worried that the interlude of the night hours might have banished Colette's fears. It looked as though he needn't have been concerned.

He watched as Colette left the room, but noticed how she couldn't stop herself glancing towards the chest of drawers as she passed it. Brogan wondered how many times the contents of those drawers had occupied her mind during the night. He wondered how many explanations she might have considered – how they might have oscillated between the supernatural and the downright malicious, and how she might have even begun to question her own sanity.

Brogan listened to the hissing of the shower. Below, Martyn

didn't budge from his nest in the bed. Minutes later, Colette was back in the room, a large bath towel wrapped around her. She seemed in an unusual hurry this morning.

Her back to the bed, she dressed speedily, and Brogan was able to get only fleeting glimpses of her nakedness. When she slammed a drawer in her haste, Martyn jolted from his reverie and raised his head from the pillow. Opening one eye, he said, 'Put the kettle on.'

'I've got to go,' she answered.

'What, now? What about breakfast?'

'No time. I'll grab something from Starbucks.'

Martyn raised himself into a sitting position. 'Surely you've got time for a cuppa with me before you go?'

'Martyn, I've got to do that presentation tomorrow. I need to be ready for it. Okay?'

'You've done lots of presentations. What's so special about this one?'

'I'm behind. I'm not prepared and it's stressing me out. See you later.'

'Well . . . okay, I suppose.'

He was clearly unhappy about it. He could tell, as could Brogan, that Colette was making excuses. She just wanted to get out of there. Away from Martyn and away from that house.

Martyn said, 'I'll see you tonight. Love you.'

Colette didn't respond in kind. She simply blew him a passionless kiss before racing for the door like a sprinter off the starting block.

Brogan studied Martyn's face as he listened to his wife flying down the stairs and then out through the front door.

His expression ranged from bemusement to disbelief and then sheer annoyance.

'Fucking hell,' he said, before flinging the duvet aside.

After he had showered, every one of Martyn's movements betrayed his irritation. He banged around the room like a petulant child, muttering and growling to himself. When he eventually left the house after breakfast, the screech of tyres as he drove off showed he hadn't calmed down.

Brogan found himself laughing as he came down into the house, the events with Elsie painted over for the moment. In the kitchen he followed his usual pattern of stealing items of food that would go unmissed: a small amount of cereal, a piece of toast, an apple. The apple was probably the most risky, but Brogan figured that, even if the Fairbrights noticed, each of them would assume the other had taken it.

He wandered around the house for a while, just looking and thinking. Dreaming up new plans. He wasn't quite sure what his next move should be, but he knew it would come to him when it was ready.

You stink again.

Thanks.

No. You do. You've spent too much time in those roasting-hot attics. You need another shower.

It wasn't such a bad idea. He'd done it before.

He went upstairs to the bathroom. It had been left in a bit of a state after the quickfire showers by Martyn and Colette: towels and nightwear on the floor, a cabinet left open, an empty bottle of shampoo in the sink. Brogan made sure not to touch any of it.

He undressed, turned on the shower, stepped in. Even once he was clean, he remained under the stream of hot water, turning on the spot and allowing it to massage his muscles.

That's enough. Don't push your luck. Get out now.

He turned off the shower and wiped the water from his eyes. The whole bathroom had filled with steam.

Great. If anyone comes back in the next few minutes, we're busted.

You're the one who told me to shower in the first place. Anyway, nobody will come back. They don't do that. The only one here is the ghost of Jeremy.

He laughed again, but stopped suddenly.

The idea had found him, as he knew it would. Everything he needed was here.

Brogan made sure to get there well before either of them was due home. He didn't want to miss any of what was to come.

He hoped his rumbling stomach wouldn't reverberate through the ceiling. In his haste to leave Elsie last night he hadn't loaded up with snacks, and now he was famished. Another trip to see Elsie was definitely on the cards.

Are you two becoming an item?

Shut up. That's sick.

Right. Because everything else you do is completely normal.

Colette was the first to get home, just before six. When she came into the bedroom, she looked hot and flustered. The first thing she did was to draw the curtains and begin to strip off.

Here we go.

Looks like. I was hoping it would be later, when Martyn was in the house.

Beggars can't be choosers. Just enjoy the ride.

Colette left the room. A few minutes later, Brogan heard the shower going on.

Won't be long now.

What if she doesn't see it?

She'll see it. Have patience.

He waited, and the longer he waited, the more he became convinced this wasn't going to work. He had reasoned that Colette was always first into the shower in the evening. But if she didn't see what he'd left, and Martyn did when it was his turn, it would ruin everything.

The shriek told him he needn't have worried.

Colette came running back into the bedroom. She was wearing a shower cap and had a large white towel wrapped tightly around her body. Her hand was pressed to her mouth, and she was staring in apparent horror towards the bathroom. She shook her head, took a step forward, then a step back. She didn't seem to know what to do, where to go.

A few seconds later, she turned to look at the chest of drawers, as if her answers might be found there. She started to yank open the drawers. When she reached the bottom drawer, she removed the lid from the shoebox and began to push the photographs around, as if to check they had not escaped and were now wandering mysteriously around her house.

She closed the drawer and straightened, then turned again towards the bathroom. Brogan could see the tears on her cheeks.

It had been the work of a couple of minutes for Brogan. A cotton pad dipped in shower gel, which he had then used to write on the bathroom mirror, ready to be revealed by the steam.

The message was: WHY DID I HAVE TO DIE?

The question in Brogan's mind was which explanation would she choose for its appearance? The natural or the supernatural?

'Bastard,' she muttered. Then, louder: 'BASTARD!'

I guess that answers that one.

She started crying again. 'Why would you do this?' A couple of minutes later, her anger resurfaced. 'No,' she said. 'You're not doing this to me. I won't let you.'

She began to pace the carpet, chewing her nails, deep in thought. Making a sudden decision, she dressed quickly. As she left the room, she muttered a final, 'Fuck you.'

Brogan heard her in the bathroom again and guessed that she was wiping away the message. When she returned, she sat on the bed and resumed chewing her nails. She looked unsure, as if still full of doubt that her husband might do such a thing to her.

She stood abruptly, then headed towards the other end of the room, beyond Brogan's field of vision. He listened carefully, and thought he heard the creak of a door, but he wasn't certain.

When she moved back into shot, she was at the chest of drawers again. She stooped and opened the bottom drawer, then took something out. Brogan held his breath. This time it wasn't the shoebox but the small wooden jewellery box she was holding.

She placed the box on top of the chest of drawers. In her right hand she was holding a tiny key. She used it to unlock the box, but as she raised the lid she shifted position, so that her head was blocking Brogan's view of the contents. He could tell that she was lifting things out and studying them, but he had no idea what they were.

Another few minutes passed. Finally, Colette closed the

lid and locked the box again, then returned it to its place in the bottom drawer. Once more she disappeared from view. Brogan heard the creak again, then a click. He tried to lock those sounds in his memory, but his attention was immediately diverted by a noise elsewhere in the house.

Martyn was home.

Colette had obviously heard it too. She seemed to go into a minor panic. She straightened her T-shirt and started taking deep breaths, as if she were an actor preparing to go on stage.

Perhaps that's exactly what she's doing.

'You up there, Col?' Martyn called.

Colette cleared her throat. 'Yes.' Then she added, 'Just took a nice hot shower.'

She waited for the reaction, but all she got from Martyn was, 'Okay.' She shook her head, her lips tightly pursed, then left the room.

She's calling his bluff.

Yeah.

She's decided he's trying to mess with her mind, and so she's stringing him along. It's a battle of wills now.

Yeah.

I think this is terrific. One of our best games yet. Even better than when we made the Carters hide broken glass on their persons while they were naked. Don't you agree?

Sure.

You don't sound very excited about it.

I am. It's really cool.

But?

The box. I need to know what's in that box.

The dynamic between the pair had changed. It was obvious to Brogan, and he was certain it must be obvious to Martyn too.

They had finally come to bed. While Colette began tidying things away and getting clothes out for the morning, Martyn studied her, a look of puzzlement on his face.

'You worried about tomorrow?' he asked.

'Not especially,' she answered. 'Like you said, I've done lots of presentations before.'

'You were stressed about it this morning.'

'Was I? Well, that was this morning. It'll be fine.'

'Okay. Good. So you're all set, then.'

'All set.'

Brogan guessed that their conversation had probably gone like this all evening.

Colette began to strip, facing her husband while she peeled off her clothes. It was crystal clear to Brogan that she was injecting a hint of sensuality into her actions, but she maintained an expression on her face that told a different story. She was acting as though she could be thinking about something as mundane as whether to have one egg or two for breakfast in the morning.

When she slipped her nightie over her head and climbed into bed, Martyn was immediately drawn towards her. She stopped him with a cold look.

'Have you had a shower yet?' she asked.

'What? No.'

'Don't you think you should? I had mine earlier. A nice hot one. Really steamed up the place.'

She watched his face. He simply looked puzzled.

'Er, okay. I'll do that.'

He climbed off the bed and walked out to the bathroom. While he was gone, Colette sat staring straight ahead, as though planning her next move in this psychological game.

The shower lasted only a couple of minutes. As soon as the noise stopped, Colette took it as her cue to rearrange her pillows, turn out her lamp, and settle down onto her side. Martyn's lamp was still on, and Brogan could still just about tell that Colette's eyes were open. As soon as Martyn returned, she closed them.

Martyn stood looking at her for a few seconds, then got into bed himself. He studied the back of his wife's head for a minute, then leaned towards her.

'Col?' he whispered. 'Col?'

But Colette kept her eyes firmly shut. Didn't move a muscle.

Martyn wasn't giving up so easily. He cuddled up behind her, slid a hand across her arm to fondle her breast.

Colette groaned, but not in pleasure. 'I'm tired, Martyn. Busy day tomorrow.'

Martyn rolled away again, his frustration evident. As Colette had done, he sat staring at nothing. Then, abruptly, he turned off his bedside light.

Show's over. Let's go.

Not yet. Martyn's too wired to sleep. We need to wait for him to drift off.

I'm sick of waiting. All we ever do is wait.

Anyone ever tell you that patience is a virtue?

I have patience in spades. Remember Jamie Wragg? I couldn't have been any more patient.

Wragg was a bully who had felt the compulsion to stamp his authority within the first few days of secondary school. Like most bullies, Wragg had an unerring knack of selecting the meekest, most friendless of kids as his victims. Naturally, his attention alighted on Thomas Brogan. At that age, Brogan was scrawny and ate all the wrong food. The many hours of intense fitness training would come much later, as would the hunger for tearing any opponent to shreds.

The initial fight was hardly worthy of the name. It involved Brogan suddenly being surrounded by a mass of pupils who had obviously heard the jungle drums, while Wragg insulted, shoved and finally punched Brogan. Brogan was left on the floor with a bloodied nose and a depletion of self-esteem that had already been close to negligible. What had hurt him most, though, was not the physical assault but the fact that nobody had come to his aid, nobody had stood up for him.

Subsequent confrontations intensified the psychological torment. Wragg tied Brogan up in the gym. He made him climb into the school rubbish bins. He commanded Brogan to go down a set of steps to fetch a football while, above, Wragg and his mates gathered round and spat at him. He ran home that day, dripping with saliva and phlegm, and when his adoptive parents saw the state of him they said nothing.

Patience.

Young Brogan bided his time. One day, he saw Wragg heading home alone, and followed him. He kept his distance and managed to remain unseen. He was surprised to discover that, despite Wragg's propensity for violence and torture, he was capable of immense affection. In particular, his love was reserved for a pair of guinea pigs that he kept in his back garden.

Patience.

Brogan returned to that house day after day. He spent hours at the back fence, his eye glued to a knot-hole in one of the panels while he watched Wragg with his precious animals.

It was on a fine spring evening that Wragg was called in by his mother, leaving the guinea pigs to roam. Brogan seized the opportunity and scaled the fence. It was the first time he had ever trespassed on somebody else's property, and the thrill was electric.

At lunchtime the next day, Brogan sat alone as usual, sucking orange juice through a straw. He watched as Jamie Wragg entered the school dinner hall, his lunchbox tucked under his arm.

Wragg seemed in a particularly unpleasant mood. He ignored the unoccupied chairs and instead dragged away a kid who was only halfway through his pasta, then took his place. He shoved the lad's plate to the far side of the table, then wiped up a splash of sauce from in front of him and flicked it onto the white shirt of another boy opposite.

Patience.

Wragg unsnapped the catches on his lunchbox. Brogan sucked more heavily on his straw.

Wragg stared into his lunchbox. He looked puzzled at first, then began to reach in.

He jumped back in his chair so hard that he sent the trays of food flying from the grasp of two pupils behind him. At the sound of his uncontrollable screaming, everybody else in the vast hall became deathly silent. A teacher dived onto Wragg and tried to restrain him. Other students craned over the lunchbox to see what had affected Wragg so intensely. Some pulled faces of disgust; others looked ready to regurgitate their own lunches.

And then the eyes began to turn on Brogan. First the pupils at his own table, then those at other tables. Whispers skipped across the hall. Even the teachers and canteen staff stared in his direction.

They left him alone after that. The bullies, but also almost everyone else. His isolation was virtually complete.

*

It was almost half past midnight when he finally got a meal with Elsie. Fish pie with green beans, to be followed by the sponge and custard he didn't get the previous night.

'Is everything all right, Alex?' she asked him.

Brogan swallowed down a burning mouthful of food.

'Yeah. Why?'

'I thought you acted a little strangely last night. You just ran off.'

'I had to go. Things to do.'

'What kind of things?'

'Just things.'

'I don't really know what you do all day.'

He shrugged. 'I have people to see.'

Nice.

Thank you. I thought so.

'You have friends, then?'

'Kind of.'

'Oh. That's good. Although . . .'

'What?'

'I just think it would be lovely if you could spend a bit more time here, with your old mother.'

'You see a lot more of me now than you have for years.'

'Yes. Yes, I know. I'm sorry, am I being selfish?'

Brogan put down his knife and fork. He reached out a hand and placed it across Elsie's cold bony fingers.

'Not selfish at all. I'll keep coming back here. Every night, if that's okay with you.'

She stared at him with wet eyes. Nodded. 'That would be wonderful. Everything is better now you're with me again. The house seems less empty.'

Brogan smiled. It wasn't often he smiled at anything that wasn't at somebody else's expense.

'I'm not very well, you know,' she said.

'Yes. I know.'

'I think . . . I think that if you ever went away again, I'd have nothing left to live for.'

Brogan patted her hand. 'Now, now. Don't talk like that.'

You should put the old dear out of her misery. Look at her. She's at death's door as it is.

'Tell you what,' said Brogan. 'Why not start getting that sponge ready? I'm nearly done with the main course.'

'Of course, son. Anything for you.'

Secrets.

Brogan liked secrets.

Other people's secrets, that is. The kind of thing a woman would keep even from her husband, or a man from his wife. Tales of infidelity, of past shame, of current loathing. Brogan always delighted in the reveal – the shock on the partner's face on being confronted by a truth they were never meant to hear.

There were such secrets in this house. They were contained in that small wooden jewellery box.

Brogan slid open the bottom drawer once more and lifted out the box. He stared at it for a full minute. Then, almost as an afterthought, he attempted to lift the lid. It didn't budge.

He looked across the room in the direction that Colette had walked when fetching the key. Against the far wall was the large triple wardrobe, with drawers along its bottom. One of the doors was slightly ajar. He pushed it closed, and was sure that the click it made was exactly like the one he had heard the previous evening. He pulled it open again, swung the door wide.

No creak.

Yesterday he had definitely heard a creak prior to the click.

He moved on to the adjoining door. Same result. A satisfying click, but no preceding squeal.

So, one more door to try. He pulled it wide in one swift motion. The shrill complaint was like fingernails on a blackboard. This was the door that Colette had opened.

Brogan took a longer look at the array of clothes on their hangers. Tucked away on the very left, as though hiding its glamour and expense from its more workaday peers, was Colette's wedding dress, sheathed in protective plastic. Brogan wondered if she'd ever worn it since her big day. Wondered, too, whether it differed significantly from the one in which she had imagined getting hitched to Jeremy.

Brogan flicked through the rest of the clothes. They were mostly dresses and a few jackets. Despite the paucity of pockets in women's garments, he didn't relish the prospect of rummaging through them.

He turned his attention to the items stuffed into the space below the hanging clothes. Shoes, mainly, but also a collection of bags of varying sizes. One of them, a clutch bag, was protruding slightly. Brogan pulled it out for inspection. Its outer material was iridescent and scaled like snakeskin. He opened it up and began searching through its multitude of internal compartments.

Bingo!

Yup. This is the key.

Doesn't look much. I hope the thing it's safeguarding is more impressive.

Brogan tossed the bag onto the bed, then moved back to the wooden box. He inserted the key and turned it. The lock mechanism's answer was smooth and decisive. Brogan raised the lid.

The contents were minimal. A ring and a few scraps of paper. Brogan recognised the ring as being the one on Colette's engagement finger in the photographs with Jeremy.

Brogan unfolded the first piece of paper. It was immaculately handwritten in blue ink. He speed-read it to grasp the gist, but the gist decided it would be more fun to leap up and strike him with the force of a sledgehammer.

Fuck me! It's the guy's suicide note!

Brogan read it again, more carefully this time.

My dearest Colette,

This is so difficult for me to write, but it has to be done. It would be unfair of me to leave without some parting words.

I can't carry on like this. It's too painful. Every day I see the look of optimism on your face, and it tears me up inside.

I wish I could talk to you face to face about this, and I feel so cowardly for not doing so. You would try to talk me out of it. You might even succeed. But it would be for only a short while. The pain would return, and sooner or later I would have to end it.

I'm sorry it has come to this. You deserve so much better. You deserve a future. But it has to be a future without me in it. I hope you understand.

J. xx

Brogan turned his attention to the other bits of paper. They were all cuttings from newspapers. One of them showed a close-up photograph of Jeremy alongside a headline that announced the 'Tragic Death of Holidaymaker on Welsh Coast'.

Dyfed-Powys Police have released the identity of a body recovered on Tuesday from the rocks below the coastal path just outside St David's in Pembrokeshire, South Wales.

Jeremy Dawsbrook, 27, a schoolteacher from Nottingham, had been staying at a nearby holiday cottage with his fiancée, Colette Lamb. He left the cottage early in the morning, saying he was going for a walk, but never returned. Ms Lamb reported him missing when she found a note left on the mantelpiece. Police and coastal rescue services launched a search, and an RNLI lifeboat spotted the body of Mr Dawsbrook within hours of the alert.

Access to the cliff edge is unrestricted at many points along the Pembrokeshire coastal path, and police have said that foul play is not suspected.

Brogan looked through the other newspaper reports, written at later dates. Some of them described the effects on Jeremy's school colleagues and pupils. Another contained the passage:

> Evidence discussed at the coroner's inquest included a note found at the cottage where Mr Dawsbrook had been holidaying with Ms Lamb, and post-mortem toxicology reports that indicated a significant quantity of anti-depressants in the deceased's bloodstream. Pembrokeshire coroner Geraint Owens recorded a verdict of death due to suicide.

Brogan looked again at the newspaper photograph of Jeremy, and wondered if it was one of the last ever taken of him, perhaps by Colette herself. Now that he knew the full story, he thought he could perceive in Jeremy's eyes a hint of the darkness that had weighed so heavily upon him. Brogan could easily imagine this man to have lost his appetite for life. He had seen that look in other eyes – where, having glimpsed a world absent of pain, they resigned themselves to making it their final destination.

Why'd she keep all this shit?

Why not? These and the photos are all she has left of him.

Maybe. But this is pretty morbid stuff, don't you think? God knows what Martyn thinks of it.

That's probably why she keeps it locked away. Maybe he doesn't even know what she keeps in this box.

You think? Because if that's the case . . .

Yeah. Exactly what I was thinking.

He had been looking forward to this all day.

He wanted to experience the tension all over again. The cold shoulders, the shallow conversation. It would be such a delight.

That's what Brogan had anticipated.

It's not what he got.

Six o'clock came and went. Then seven. Then eight. Nobody came home.

Anger began to crawl around inside Brogan. He could feel its heat as it moved around his body.

Where are they?

How the hell should I know?

They're pissing me off. They are so going to regret this.

Brogan had to keep leaving his sentry post so that he could move around in the small loft space, relieving the pain that was building up in his muscles and joints. The last thing he wanted was to get cramp while trying to observe the happenings below.

But it was beginning to look as though tonight might be a washout.

Shit. Maybe we should get down there.

And do what, exactly? They have to come home at some point.

And then Brogan heard the noises.

A car pulling up outside. Sounding like Martyn's car.

The front door opening. Voices. Laughter.

Laughter? They're laughing? Why are they laughing?

Brogan's stomach sank.

Surely not. They can't have patched things up.

But the distant voices continued, and although Brogan couldn't hear what was being said, he could tell it was proper conversation, full of warmth and emotion and happiness and all those detestable things.

And, worst of all, the laughing. Each explosion of humour carried up the stairs and punched Brogan in the gut.

I knew you should have gone down there. You need to put a stop to this. They're ruining everything. They're laughing at you.

It went quiet.

Brogan put his ear to the hole. Nothing.

He waited. Tried to imagine what could possibly—

And then it started up again. It was getting louder, because—

They're coming up the stairs!

Giggling now. Naughty, throaty, heat-filled giggling.

Brogan watched. He saw.

He saw the door being thrown open. The couple staggering into the room, clearly the worse for alcohol, even though Martyn had just driven home. They were clutching at each other, kissing, panting, circling as they danced clumsily towards the bed. They reached for buttons, for zips, for clasps, and the clothes came off. The mattress pinged in surprise as it was thumped by the weight of the two naked bodies landing on it.

Brogan's eye grew wider and wider. He watched the contortions, the jiggling flesh, the stimulation, the arousal, the raw lust. He listened to the slurping and the slapping and the wetness and the cries and the gasping and the swearing and the yearning calls for more, God, more. He remained transfixed as rhythms speeded up and slowed down, as passions increased, as new positions were sought and found and adapted. And then he tensed for the final moments, as the heat from below grew to boiling point, only for everything suddenly to burst apart in a frenzy of spasmodic, breathless writhing.

And as Martyn rolled away and onto his back, his chest rising and falling as though it feared never to be able to inhale oxygen again, Brogan was able to get a much better look at the object of the man's ardour.

She glowed. Her cheeks, her body, her eyes – they all shone up at Brogan.

He spoke her name soundlessly.

'Gabrielle.'

Brogan's smile was as wide as it had ever been. This was delicious. A turn of events worthy of celebratory fireworks.

Gabrielle.

She was a stunner, all right. Splayed out directly below Brogan, she possessed a topology of undulating curves that commanded his eyes to rove back and forth across them. Whatever fault lines lurked beneath them in her personality were worth the journey.

Gabrielle, though!

That was the point. She was not Colette. She was the very antithesis of Colette. She represented Colette's worst fears and anxieties about her relationship with her husband. Well, other than what she thought he was doing to drive her insane over Jeremy.

And, Martyn, you sly dog! What has got into you? Why are you even taking this risk?

'This is so bad.'

Gabrielle turned to Martyn as she said this, her fingers plucking at his chest hair.

'Really? I quite enjoyed it.'

She flicked his left nipple, making him wince. 'I mean it's wicked. We shouldn't have . . . I mean, don't you think . . . ?'

'It's fine. Colette will never know. She's giving a presentation up in Edinburgh.'

'Okay, but even so . . .'

Martyn leaned in and stroked her breast with the backs of his fingers. 'Wasn't it worth it?'

'For me, yes. I like the excitement. For you, though? Why couldn't we have gone to a hotel like we usually do?'

'Because I have an empty house tonight. I've got a comfy bed, wine, food . . .'

'You mean it's cheaper.'

'That's not what I said. If you had your own place, instead of living with your sister—'

'She wouldn't say anything. What happens in our flat stays in our flat.'

'I'm not taking any chances. Louise knows me, don't forget. All it would take is for her to say the wrong thing to the wrong person—'

'She wouldn't do that. Anyway, I don't think that's the real reason.'

'What do you mean?'

'For bringing me here. You did it because it turns you on to have me in your wife's bed.'

'Rubbish.'

She poked him in the ribs with a gaudy false fingernail. 'Go on, admit it.'

'No.'

'I'm right, aren't I? The only reason I'm here is because you like the idea of rubbing Colette's nose in it. That's a metaphor, by the way, so no dirty comments, please.'

'Who, me?' He paused. 'All right, I confess. Maybe it does give me a thrill. But I've got to get my kicks where I can at the moment.'

'Oh? Colette putting you on rations, then?'

'More of a starvation diet, really.'

'Really?' Gabrielle sounded too pleased with the revelation.

'Well, it's not like it's been going on for ages, but she's suddenly gone all cold on me.'

'Why? What brought that on?'

'Dunno. She's been acting really weird. Keeps going on about her ex.'

'What, the guy who topped himself?'

'Yeah. And whatever you do, don't mention him to Colette when you next see her.'

'Right, because I'm likely to do that, aren't I? I'm going to say, "Hey, Colette. Why don't you tell me about that boyfriend of yours who committed suicide?"'

'You know what I mean.'

'So . . . why is she talking about him? Doesn't seem very diplomatic.'

Martyn pushed his hair away from his forehead. 'It's not just the fact that she mentions him. She's been getting his photographs out and putting them in her drawers.'

Gabrielle laughed, then put a hand over her mouth. 'I'm sorry. You mean her clothes drawers, right?'

Martyn gave her a disapproving look. 'Yes, I mean her

clothes drawers. But the really freaky thing is that she forgets she does it, and then she blames me for it.'

'What? Is she losing the plot?'

'I have no idea. I think she needs to see a doctor, but if I suggest anything like that it'll be like a red rag to a bull.'

'Sounds like you need to start taking precautions.'

'What kind of precautions?'

'Oh, like strapping her into bed at night in case she goes sleepwalking and comes at you with a rolling pin.'

'Very funny. She's not batshit crazy. She's just . . .'

'Off her head?'

Another stern look from Martyn. 'Anyway, I don't want to talk about Colette. That's not why I brought you here.'

'We've already discussed why you brought me here. But right now I think I should be going.'

She started to roll out of bed, but Martyn put his hand on her hip.

'Already? I thought we could—'

'I think we've taken enough of a risk tonight. You have the nosiest neighbours in the world. I saw the curtains twitching across the road when we pulled up.'

'It's called community spirit. We look out for each other.'

'And talk about each other, too, no doubt. I don't want to become the subject of this week's gossip, Martyn. Call me a taxi while I get some clothes on.'

She climbed off the bed and pulled on her underwear while Martyn got on the phone. When he hung up, she said, 'Oh, and when I'm gone, wash these sheets.'

'What?'

'She'll know, Martyn.'

'She won't know. How will she know?'

'Trust me, she'll know. Women are good at things like that.'

Martyn frowned, but Brogan could see the worry on his face.

The taxi came within five minutes. Martyn threw on jogging pants and a sweater and saw Gabrielle to the door. When the taxi departed, he came back upstairs and stared at the bed. Making a sudden decision, he started pulling off the sheets and pillowcases.

Brogan continued to watch. This had been quite a spectacle. Not at all what he had been expecting.

Despite Martyn's precautions, Colette would get to learn about this little escapade. And it would come straight out of Martyn's mouth.

Brogan would make sure of it.

WEDNESDAY 12 JUNE, 11.57 PM

A promise is a promise. And besides, he was hungry.

Elsie prepared him a full English: bacon, sausages, eggs, beans and toast. She didn't have any black pudding, but he didn't want it anyway. The idea of eating something made with blood repulsed him.

'Why do you only come here at night?' Elsie asked.

Brogan swallowed a mouthful of bacon dripping with egg yolk. He liked his eggs runny. 'It's hard to explain,' he said.

'Could you try?'

'My life is complicated. There are rules I have to follow. Night is the safest time for me.'

She nodded, but something was clearly niggling at her.

'I've been thinking,' she said. 'About you. About your accident.'

Uh-oh! She's on to you, man.

'What do you mean?'

'I . . . I don't know. I get so confused. You are *here*, aren't you, Alex? I mean, I'm not imagining it?'

He shook his head. 'No. You're not imagining it. I'm real.'

He rested his hand on the back of hers. 'See? Feel that? It's real, isn't it?'

'It seems real, but . . .'

'But what?'

'I don't see how you can be. They said you were dead.'

'Who did?'

'After the accident. The police. And I remember . . . I remember going to your funeral. I'm sure I did. And when I mention you to Kerry, she says the same thing. She—'

'Yes, you told her about me again, didn't you?'

He saw the look of horror on Elsie's face. 'I-I'm sorry, Alex. I forget things. I'm just so confused. Kerry keeps telling me you can't possibly come back. Is she wrong, Alex? How could everyone have got it so wrong?'

See? Her brain's not as addled as she makes out. She's cottoned on. She knows you're a fake.

And your answer to that is?

Kill the old biddy.

Yeah, I had a feeling it might be.

Brogan took a sip of his tea while his mind struggled to formulate a suitable response.

'I don't have all the answers,' he said. 'I only know that the universe is a strange place. Things happen that we can never understand. One person's reality is different from the next person's. What matters is what you believe, and not what anybody else tells you to believe.'

Get you, the armchair philosopher.

I have my moments.

'I know what I believe,' Elsie said.

Better get that knife ready. She's about to blow you out of the water.

'What do you believe?'

'I believe that you are a gift.'

'A gift?'

'Yes. I've thought a lot about this lately. I'm old, you see, and not very well. My time is limited.'

'It's limited for all of us.'

'Yes. And that's my point. We're all the same, really. We're born, we live, and then we die. The only difference is the length of that bit in the middle.'

'I'm not sure I understand.'

'I'm not sure I do either, but . . .' She paused, marshalling her thoughts again. 'It's what we do with that bit in the middle. That's what counts.'

Brogan began to think about his own bit in the middle.

Don't do that, man. It's not healthy. She's messing with your head again.

'And if we do a good job of it,' she continued. 'I mean, if we live a good life, then I think we're rewarded.'

'You mean in Heaven?'

'Yes. But sometimes also before that. Do you believe in Heaven, Alex?'

'I . . . That's a tricky one.'

'Not for me. But I'm not talking about angels and harps and people all dressed in white. That's just silly. A heaven like that would be completely boring and pointless. No, Heaven to me is a place where your greatest wishes come true. And sometimes, if we're really lucky, we get given a glimpse of that just before we die. It's like a trailer for a film.'

'That's what you think this is right now? A trailer?'

Jesus, she's really lost it.

'Yes, yes. And I think you know it, too. Only you're not allowed to say. That's what you meant before about sticking to the rules. I can't have you for every hour of every day, because this is just a teaser for the main event. In my heaven, you will always be with me, but if I got it now, there would be no point in dying.'

'Yes, but you're not dying. You could have years ahead of you yet.'

'No. Don't you see? Your return is what's telling me that my time is up. I'm about to come and see you properly, and we can do all the things we missed out on together.'

Well, she's got it right about being about to clock out. Not so sure we'll see her on the same floor of the afterlife, though.

Brogan returned to his meal and chewed furiously, refusing to look at Elsie.

'Alex,' she said. 'Is something wrong? Have I said something to upset you?'

'You shouldn't think that way,' he said angrily. 'You can't give up on life like that. It's not right.'

'Why? Why isn't it right?'

'Because life is precious. Life can only be surrendered as a last resort. You have to hang on to it for as long as you can, otherwise what's the point?'

'I have clung on as long as I can, Alex. And I know you're just testing me now.'

He slammed down his cutlery with a clatter. 'No. You're not

listening to me. This isn't a test. I don't do tests. If I wanted you to die, you'd know about it. I can do that, you know. I could make you want to die. But I haven't. I've spared you. Maybe I made a mistake. Maybe I should have sent you to the afterlife as soon as we met. But I didn't. I've let you live, and you need to be grateful. You need to start making the most of whatever days you have left.'

He picked up the dinner knife again. Pointed it at her face.

'You see this? I could stick it in your heart right now. I could rip open your throat with it. For most people, I wouldn't think twice. For you, though, I've made an exception, and that's what you don't seem to realise. My gift to you isn't death. It's life.'

Elsie's mouth opened and closed slowly. 'I'm confused,' she said. 'I thought I understood, and now I'm not sure.'

Brogan pushed the beans around his plate. 'Don't worry about it. Forget what I just said. It's not important.'

'But it is. Understanding this is the most important thing I've ever had to do. But I'm old and I'm tired.'

'You should go to bed. Get some rest.'

'Yes. I think that's best. Will you be all right on your own?'

'I'll be fine. I'll clean up afterwards.'

'But . . . you will come back tomorrow night, won't you?'

'I'll be here.'

'You promise?'

'I promise.'

When she had left the kitchen, Brogan thought hard about his words to her. He almost found it impossible to believe he'd uttered them.

Life is precious? Since when did that become your catchphrase?

I meant it. I don't want her giving up. Not because of me.

And you think you just convinced her not to, do you?

Of course. She was ready to lie down in a coffin just to spend more time with me. Now maybe she'll think twice.

You're an idiot.

What makes you say that?

Because now the old crow is totally confused, but whichever side of the fence she comes down on, she's going to shuffle off her mortal coil.

What the hell are you talking about?

Think about it, brainiac. If she still believes that Heaven is where she can spend all her time mothering her precious Alex, then it's lights-out time, right? On the other hand, if the only thing keeping her clock ticking is the promise of spending time with you, then she's still doomed.

How so?

Because, genius, you're not going to be around forever. As soon as you've finished with the Fairbrights, we're out of here. I still don't know what it is about Elsie that has made her get to you, but what you need to face is that, like it or not, you've already signed the old bat's death warrant.

He heard the raised voices as soon as he climbed into the attic. Elsie arguing with Kerry, her carer.

'What's been going on, Elsie?'

'What are you talking about?'

'All the food! Your cupboards are full of it.'

'What's wrong with that?'

'You can't possibly need that much food. How did it get there?'

'I had it delivered, of course, like I always do. The volunteer service. I phone them up, give them a list, and they deliver. You know that.'

'What I know is that they usually come once a week, and even when they've been, half your cupboards are bare. It looks like you're about to have a party down there. A lot of that stuff you don't even like!'

'Well, I'm changing my ways. I've decided I need fattening up. I'm wasting away here.'

'Whose fault is that? You don't even eat the meals that Reg brings you every day.'

'That stuff is horrible. And it's never hot enough. I only like the puddings.'

'And what about the sandwiches I make for you? Do you eat them?'

'Sometimes.'

'Well, you didn't eat the one I gave you last night, because I've just found it in your bin. And I'll tell you what else I found.'

'What? What did you find?'

'Eggshells and an empty tin of beans. And open packs of bacon and sausages in your fridge. How could you possibly have worked your way through that lot after I left you yesterday?'

'I got hungry. You don't give me the right things.'

'Those aren't the right things, Elsie. They're full of fat and salt. They won't do you any good at all.'

Elsie's voice suddenly rose in volume. 'Stop going on! I'll eat what I want. I'll die soon anyway, so what's the difference?'

There was a long pause, and then Kerry said, 'Elsie, is there something you need to tell me?'

'Like what?'

'Has someone else been in your house?'

Brogan stiffened. He heard how Elsie hesitated.

'Chance would be a fine thing,' she said. 'Nobody ever comes to see me.'

'Elsie. Don't play the martyr. Are you certain you haven't had a late-night visitor?'

Elsie laughed. 'What, like a man, you mean? A secret admirer, sneaking into my bed?'

'Well, if you're going to be like that, I'm going to go downstairs and prepare your breakfast. Assuming you still have room for it, that is.'

Brogan heard footsteps, and then Elsie muttering something to herself.

That was close.

No it wasn't. That carer doesn't suspect a thing.

She'll start smelling a rat soon if you're not more careful.

What did I do?

It's what you didn't do. You shouldn't have left all that rubbish in the bin. You should have taken it with you.

Yeah, that's going to look great in future, isn't it? Sorry, Elsie, I know you believe I'm the ghost of your long-lost son, but do you mind if I take your rubbish with me?

You should still do it. And then there's all that food in the cupboards.

How is that my fault? I didn't put it there.

No, but Elsie's buying it for you. You need to tell her to stop.

No fear. That's the only way I can get proper food at the moment.

It's your funeral. She's already told the carer her son has come back to her, and now it's clear she's cooking for someone. It won't take much for that carer to put two and two together.

She won't. She thinks Elsie has lost her marbles. She probably thinks Elsie cooks it for an imaginary visitor and then flushes it down the toilet.

Maybe. Just be careful, that's all.

Brogan shook his head, then continued to move through the houses. At Pam and Jack's he could hear voices from just below the ceiling, but he didn't stop to listen. They didn't interest him.

He just had to slow his pace to make sure he didn't make a noise.

At the Fairbrights' house he went through his customary routine of listening and spying from above before opening the hatch and lowering the ladder. When he reached the landing, he pushed the ladder back into place and closed the hatch, just in case Jack should decide to start exploring the roof space again. After that, he took the unusual precaution of going to the spare bedroom at the front of the house, then risking a brief glimpse of the street outside. Both cars had gone. He was safe, alone in the house.

Good boy.

Shut up.

It's worth the peace of mind. Now you can do what you like. How about a drink?

If you mean water, then yes.

Brogan wasn't particularly hungry this morning, but the carer had been right about the saltiness of the food. It had left him feeling severely dehydrated, with a rasping tongue and a niggling headache.

As he headed downstairs in search of fresh water, his mind was still focused on Elsie. He wasn't sure he had handled the situation at all well. His relationship with her felt precarious, as though it could all go tits-up at any moment. He didn't like that degree of uncertainty. Perhaps he needed to have yet another chat with her. Lay it on thick this time, to let her know how crucial it was for her not to give away news of his existence.

He was nodding to himself at this thought as he entered the kitchen.

Finding a stranger there was like being handed a live electric cable.

The man had just stepped down from the sink. Behind him, the kitchen window was wide open.

Brogan reached around his waist and pulled the knife from his belt.

'Who the fuck are you?' Brogan demanded.

The man was wearing a tracksuit, and had a shapeless knapsack slung over one shoulder. His head was shaven, but his chin bore several days' worth of stubble. His eyes were narrow and sly-looking, and there was a notch in one ear where it looked as though a ring had been ripped through the lobe.

He held up a palm. 'Steady, pal. This isn't what it looks like.'

'And what does it look like?'

'Like . . . like I've just broken in.'

'So you admit it?'

'That's . . . that's not what I said.'

'What, then? You were just passing, and thought you needed to wash your shoes in the sink?'

'Look. This is just a mistake, okay? I made a mistake. I'll go now. I'll get out of here.'

Kill him.

What?

He's seen you. He'll tell someone.

'Why should I let you go?'

'What?'

'I should call the police. You broke in. You're trying to steal my stuff.'

'*Your* stuff? You don't live here. I've been watching this place for ages. I've never seen you here. Who are you, anyway?'

Uh-oh!

'I'm the guy who caught a burglar, dickhead. That's all you need to know.'

And then something clicked in the man's head. His squinty eyes widened as he pointed a finger at Brogan.

'I've seen you before.'

Shit.

'Don't think so, fella.'

'I have. On the telly.'

Brogan took a couple of steps towards the intruder. 'No. You've got that wrong.'

The man suddenly seemed to place Brogan, and to realise the extent of the danger he was in.

'Look,' he said, 'this is nothing to do with me. I won't say anything. I'm getting out of here now. Okay?'

He didn't wait for an answer. Instead, he put his hands on the counter behind him and pushed his buttocks onto it.

You can't let him leave. He'll talk. For the right reward, he'll rat you out in a heartbeat.

The man gestured towards the open window. 'I'm going,

okay? Take it easy.'

You can't let him go. Stop him!

The intruder began to pull his legs up and swing them towards the sink, ready to stand in it and leap out of the window.

And then Brogan made his move, hurtling towards the man, teeth and knife bared.

But the burglar was no slouch either. He was already pumped with adrenaline, his wits as sharp as Brogan's knife, and as Brogan came at him he grabbed a heavy copper-bottomed saucepan from the draining board and brought it round in a wide arc. Brogan felt it slam into his skull with a force that seemed capable of splitting it in two, and he reeled across the room. He lost his footing and realised his face was about to embed itself in the oven door, and he put his hands out to protect himself, and the knife went flying away and he thought, *Shit, shit, this isn't good.* And then he knew he had to keep moving, because in all likelihood his enemy was going to make damn certain Brogan didn't try to stop him again, and so Brogan rolled on the floor and, sure enough, there was the burglar again, coming at him with that shiny steel pan, and Brogan whipped his leg round and caught the man on the side of his knee with his foot, and there was a cracking noise and the man screamed and dropped to the floor and Brogan lashed out with his foot again, slamming it into the man's chest and knocking him backwards. And as it penetrated the man's mind that he might lose this battle, he tried to scramble away, but now Brogan was up again, on his feet again, closing in on the scuttling insect that had dared to strike him . . .

Kill him! Kill the fucker!

Brogan dropped heavily onto the man's back, spearing one of his kidneys with his knee. There was another cry, and then Brogan sat astride the man and reached under his chin with both hands and started to pull . . .

Kill him!

Brogan lifted the man's head up from the floor, bent it right back, and the man tried to arch his body as much as he could, but there are limits to what the human frame can endure, and Brogan focused all of his strength and determination on his task, and . . .

KILL HIM!

The sound reverberated around the kitchen. A sickening combination of crunching and snapping. A noise that most people are fortunate enough never to hear. Brogan felt the sound waves shoot up his arms, and then the sudden give in the body beneath him, now broken. He sensed its life escaping, draining away like water down a plughole, and the thing he was holding became an empty contraption of inanimate tissue, as if infinitely less complex than it was just seconds ago.

It was over.

Brogan dragged himself off the corpse and stood panting at the sink.

You did it! Ha ha! What a piece of shit he was. He deserved everything he got.

Yeah. There's just one problem.

And what's that, o victorious one?

What do we do with the body?

Brogan stared out of the still-open window, breathing in the warm summer air that seemed to beckon to him. He touched the side of his head and winced. There was no blood, but he could already feel a bump forming. His headache was now a thousand times worse.

I think I have to leave.

What? No, we can't leave. What we've got here is too good.

In case you haven't noticed, there's a dead body on the floor. I think the Fairbrights might suspect something is wrong when they come home and find that.

Still doesn't mean we have to leave. It just means we bring the game to an end sooner than expected. Let them come home. Let them find the body. We can turn it into quite a little spectacle. Really freak them out. They see your display, they scream a lot, and then you step out of the shadows and take control.

Brogan felt his head again. Christ, it hurt. Made it difficult to think properly. But yeah, why not? Why leave now, when there was still fun to be had with the Fairbrights? Wouldn't it be great to see how Colette reacted when she came home to find a corpse sitting at her breakfast table? Or maybe lying in her bed? Wouldn't that be incredible?

A pity about the other stuff, though. The ghostly goings-on. Shame to bring those to such a premature end. It seemed like such a great plan.

Wait.

What?

Maybe all is not lost.

What are you talking about? Of course it's lost. Our dead friend here has seen to that.

Not necessarily.

No?

No. We can move him.

Move him? Move him where? Hide him in the broom cupboard? Stick him in the wheelie bin?

We take him out of the house.

Don't be stupid. How am I supposed to do that without being spotted? You heard what Gabrielle said about the neighbours. And where would I take him?

You go out the same way you always go. Up!

Brogan's eyes automatically rolled upwards. Of course! He could take the burglar up through the ceiling with him. Drag him back to the abandoned house.

It won't be easy.

I never said it would be. I think you could do it, though. Don't you?

Maybe.

Brogan looked down at the man again. They were of a similar height, but the burglar was much skinnier.

All right, let's do it.

Brogan went upstairs and lowered the ladder, then returned to the kitchen. He closed and locked the kitchen window, then used a cup on the draining board to take a much-needed drink of water.

He picked up a chair and moved it next to the body. Then he flipped the man over, grabbed him by his hoodie and pulled him into a sitting position. The man's head lolled as though it was about to fall off. Brogan slipped his hands under the man's armpits, then hefted him onto the chair.

He's heavier than he looks.

You've got a long way to go yet.

Thanks for the encouragement.

Go ahead. Fireman's lift. Use your legs, not your back.

Brogan bent forward, pulled the man across his shoulders, then straightened up with a grunt.

That's it. Now go.

Brogan carried the corpse out to the hallway, then began to ascend the stairs. Carrying a dead weight on level ground was one thing, but this was tough. He began at a good pace, but each step seemed much higher than the previous one, and Brogan's calf muscles began to burn.

He made it to the landing, but had to lean back against the wall. He looked at the loft ladder.

I'll never make it up there.

Don't put him down now. You'll never pick him up again. You've got to keep going.

Brogan's head was pounding again. Each beat of his rapid pulse threatened to burst his brain like an overripe fruit.

Go!

Brogan went. Adjusting the weight on his shoulders, he launched himself from the wall with a subdued roar and headed straight for the ladder.

Negotiating his way up the narrow, steep steps was difficult and painful. It felt like pushing a massive boulder up a mountain. The ladder creaked and groaned, and it occurred to Brogan that it probably wasn't designed to take the weight of two fully grown men. He worried that it would collapse beneath him, or rip from its moorings above.

Things became more difficult as he neared the top. The hatch wasn't huge: it was barely big enough for a broad man to get through. But a man with a body slung across his shoulders was another matter. Brogan had to manoeuvre the corpse's head through the hatch first, then its upper half. With one final gargantuan effort, Brogan pushed up, sliding the body along the attic floor as its legs went through.

Brogan followed it into the attic, then sat down and leaned against the low partition wall.

'Jesus Christ!' he muttered. 'That was hard.'

Stop whining. I knew you'd make it. Now what you have to do—

—Whoah! Stop there. I'm not moving a muscle for the next few minutes.

If you say so. Wimp.

Brogan closed his eyes while he tried to reclaim some calm. His whole body ached. His head felt ready to explode. He wanted a bath. A long, hot bath, soothing music and some ibuprofen.

When he had finished dreaming, he stood up again. He pulled his torch from his pocket and shone it over the wall. The distance from here to the next wall seemed like the Grand Canyon.

How the hell am I supposed to get him across there?

With stealth and patience. There's no rush. We've got all day.

There are no floorboards next door. I won't be able to put him down halfway – not without risking making a hole in their ceiling.

Then don't put him down. Do it all in one go. Have a proper rest first. Get something to eat. We'll do it in an hour or so.

Brogan took another minute while he assessed the route across the adjoining attic. Just how strong were those joists? Yes, they had coped with his weight, but what about almost double that focused on a single point? He really didn't want to go through the ceiling. Then there were the two partition walls to manhandle the body over.

He sighed. He didn't have much choice in the matter – not if he wanted to continue playing with the Fairbrights.

He switched off his torch. Stared into the blackness a moment longer.

And then came the noises.

Voices first. Loud male voices. Coming from the direction of Jack and Pam's house. The clatter of a stepladder. More voices – gruff, unfamiliar ones. And then a crack of light, quickly growing and spreading and spilling into the nooks and crannies.

The hatch was being lifted.

Brogan dropped down behind the wall. He saw a beam of light splash over the top of the wall, scanning left to right.

Cops! It's the cops.

A voice again, and now the words were clear: 'Get that other ladder, will ya, Kev? And some lights.'

Brogan glanced down at the body next to him.

Cover him up! Quick!

Brogan grabbed the edge of a roll of carpet and unfurled it over the corpse, then found a couple of cardboard boxes and placed them on top. He could hear ladders being shifted around.

'We'll get started then,' said the voice. 'Any chance of a brew, Mr Harris?'

Get out now!

Brogan practically slid down the Fairbrights' ladder. As he used the pole to push the steps back up and close the hatch, someone was already climbing into the attic next door.

'Toss those lights up, Kev!'

Brogan swung the hatch closed as swiftly and as silently as he could, but it still made a thump.

Shit! They must have heard that. They'll come over the wall any second now. We need to get out of this house before they catch us.

Wait.

No. We have to go!

I said wait!

Brogan ran to the front bedroom and peered out of the window. A white van, thick with dust, was parked in front of the neighbouring house.

Why are we still here?

Because they're not cops. Why would cops come through the attic? They're workmen.

All right, so they're workmen. They still probably heard you closing the hatch.

So?

So they might tell Jack and Pam. They'll know that nobody is supposed to be in here at this time of day.

Why would they bother to tell them that?

I don't bloody know. It might come up in conversation. They might say, 'Doesn't your neighbour go out to work, then?' or something like that.

They might, but they probably won't. Stop worrying. We're not even sure they heard me.

They could find the body.

Stop panicking. They're doing some work next door. Why would they climb over the wall?

I don't know. To nick stuff. We don't know who these blokes are. I think we should go.

Well, I disagree. I'm not running out of here on the minuscule chance that these workmen, who are probably perfectly reputable, will climb the wall and start unrolling carpets in the hope that they'll find a Ming vase. Forget it.

Your funeral.

Relax. We're safe. Let them do their job and leave, and then we can pick up where we left off.

But Brogan couldn't relax. His route back to the abandoned house now cut off, he felt trapped.

You may as well make the most of it. Get something to eat.

I'm not hungry.

Then take a shower.

They might hear.

Well at least make yourself useful. You need to sort that kitchen out.

Brogan had to drag himself away from his position below the hatch. As he reached the top of the stairs, he was startled by the sound of a drill whirring into life above him. He pictured the workmen up there, the attic fully lit up, and wondered if he'd covered the body properly. All it would take was a foot to be showing, or a hand.

And then an even more alarming thought hit him.

What if he's not dead?

What?

He might not be dead. He might come round.

What do you mean? You made sure, didn't you?

Not properly. I mean, he looked dead, but I didn't check his pulse or anything.

You're being ridiculous. You heard how his neck snapped.

Doesn't mean a thing. I've done worse than that to people without killing them.

Calm down. He's dead. We both felt the life leave him, remember? We've experienced that enough times to know the difference. One of the things that was so exquisite about the Carters was knowing precisely when they were at their limit, and then keeping them there.

Brogan nodded. It was true. What he carried upstairs had no life whatsoever left in it. He would have sensed it.

But he couldn't shake off the thought that the corpse wasn't done with him yet.

In the kitchen, Brogan picked up the burglar's backpack from the floor and took a look inside it. It was empty, obviously intended for carrying away valuables.

Brogan crouched down, feeling the strain in his back from carrying the dead weight up all those stairs. He found the saucepan under the table and returned it to the draining board. He shifted the chair back into position, then went to the sink and washed away any traces of shoe prints left by the intruder.

That it?

No. Your knife.

Brogan reached behind him to his belt. Of course. He'd lost his knife during the fight.

He crouched down again, but could see no sign of it on the floor.

Where the hell is it?

I don't know, but you'd better find it before the Fairbrights do.

It's not here.

It can't have just disappeared. You had it in your hand when that dickhead walloped you.

That's right. He hit me and I fell towards the oven.

Brogan flattened himself to the floor and peered beneath the appliance. All he could see were cobwebs and dust.

Jeez, don't these people ever clean? Use your torch.

Brogan pulled out his torch and flicked it on.

I see it! Right at the back.

Good. Then get it out.

How?

I don't know. Use your initiative.

In a cupboard beneath the stairs he found a feather duster with a red plastic handle. He took it back into the kitchen and got down on the floor again, then placed his torch next to his head while he poked around beneath the oven.

Crap. I can't get hold of it. It just keeps moving farther back.

Forget it. You'll have to leave it there.

I'm not giving up that easily. What I need is . . .

He trudged back upstairs. On the landing he stood for a minute listening to the hammering above, music blaring from a radio. Brogan shook his head, then entered the master bedroom. In the wardrobe he found a wire hanger stuffed behind the shoes.

As he retraced his steps, Brogan began unwinding the hanger. By the time he reached the kitchen, he had fashioned it into a long, thin hook.

Now that's what you call a knife-retrieval implement.

Great. You should take out a patent. Every serial killer should have one.

It took Brogan only seconds to get his knife back. As he sat against the oven, he blew the dust off the weapon and wiped the blade on his shirt. Having it back in his possession made him somehow feel complete again.

Happy now?

I'll be happier when those workmen have finished.

Well, until then you should take it easy. Get something to eat.

I told you, I'm not—

Eat! You'll need your strength to move that body later.

Minutes later he was sitting at the table, trying to force down some toast while staring into space. He could still hear the noises from upstairs.

What do you think they're doing?

I have no idea. Maybe I should go up there and ask them.

No need to be sarcastic.

It was a stupid question. I hate it when things go wrong like this. Today is a shitty day.

It'll work out. Doesn't it always work out?

In a word: no.

Tell you what. Why don't we make the most of the situation? We're here anyway, so let's move some more of Colette's stuff.

I can't even think about that right now.

Suit yourself. But you could be waiting here for a long time.

Listen.

What?

It's gone quiet. Do you think they've finished?

Brogan went to the bottom of the stairs and stared up. He could hear nothing.

He took the steps two at a time, then stood on the landing beneath the hatch. Still nothing.

I think they've gone.

Brogan opened the door to the spare bedroom and went to the window. The white van was still there. He checked his watch and sighed.

Lunch break.

Not necessarily. They might've—

Trust me.

He went back onto the landing and looked up at the hatch again.

Maybe now's a good time to check.

Check on what?

The burglar. I could make sure he's dead, and that he's

covered up properly.

I don't think that's a good—

I could easily go in and out of there before they come back.

Seriously, this is a bad idea. We don't know how long they've been—

I'm going in.

Shit!

Brogan manoeuvred the pole into position on the hatch cover, took a deep breath, then began to push.

Easy does it.

A dim light appeared through the crack, but Brogan could hear nothing. He moved his hand down the pole, ready to push the hatch open wider.

A more intense light suddenly flared above, dancing around the edges of the hatch. Brogan immediately lowered the cover.

'What are you doing, Kev?' said the familiar voice.

'I thought I heard something,' his younger comrade answered.

'Where? Next door?'

'Yeah.'

The older man laughed. 'It's only the rats. Back to work before one of them jumps up at you.'

The radio came on again, accompanied by less tuneful singing from the tradesman.

Damn, that was close. I told you it was a bad idea.

Brogan breathed again. His nerves were starting to wear thin.

What now?

Now maybe you'll start listening to me. We wait. They can't stay there all day.

Brogan leaned the pole against the wall again, then went downstairs. Hunger was finally beginning to gnaw at him, so he stole another slice of bread and smothered it with peanut butter. He ate that and followed it up with two plain biscuits and a mug of tea.

He spent the next hour and a half looking through the Fairbrights' possessions in the back bedroom and kitchen. It didn't add anything to his existing knowledge, but it killed some time.

Sitting on Colette's bed, he checked his watch again. It was past four o'clock.

I don't like this.

Don't like what?

This! What if they plan to stay until the job is done? They could be here for hours yet.

Relax. I've never met a tradesman who stayed after five o'clock. Except for that electrician we killed, remember?

I remember.

We really put his lights out, didn't we?

That's very funny.

Seriously, they'll be gone soon. In fact, it sounds a lot quieter up there now. Check the van. See if they're packing up yet.

Brogan went back onto the landing. He could still hear music from above, but it sounded more muted now. Another appearance at the front window seemed an unnecessary risk, but he did it anyway. The van was in the same position. The only difference now was that there was a car parked in front of it.

The car door opened and a woman climbed out.

It was Colette.

Move!

Brogan raced back onto the landing. He paused beneath the hatch, looking up at it. He could still hear the music, along with some conversation and laughter.

We can't go up there. Shit!

Then where?

We'll have to hide.

This isn't such a big house. Where do you suggest?

The spare bedroom. No, wait! Fuck!

What?

The burglar's knapsack! It's still downstairs!

Brogan flew down the stairs, taking them two at a time. He tripped at the bottom, nearly losing his balance, but just managed to regain his footing. In the hallway he could see the figure of Colette approaching through the frosted glass of the front door, and he ran into the kitchen. The backpack was on the table where he'd left it, and he grabbed it just as he heard Colette inserting her key into the lock. He ran back out to the hall, noticed that the front door was swinging open, and he thought, *Too late, too late*, but then the door stopped only partially open as Colette removed her key, and he bounded back up the stairs. He sprinted into the front bedroom once more, stood there for a fraction of a second wondering where he could possibly hide, then decided his only option was under the spare bed. He threw himself to the floor, shuffled into the tight space, the pack clutched alongside him, and he tried to make himself be as quiet as he could, but his breathing seemed so harsh, so loud, that it felt like it must be possible to hear him all the way downstairs.

'Martyn?' Colette called. 'Are you home?'

She heard you. She knows we're here.

'Martyn? Is that you?'

She knows!

Footsteps on the staircase.

She's coming up. Get ready.

Brogan reached for his knife and pulled it out. He tried to steady his breathing. He would kill her without hesitation if he had to, but he didn't want it to be like this, not as his last resort. This wasn't how he wanted it to end.

'Martyn?'

Footsteps again. Into the main bedroom, then the bathroom, and then . . .

This is it. She's on the way.

Brogan tightened his grip on the knife. Brought it up close to his chest.

The door was pushed open, but Colette didn't enter.

She knows you're in here. She's frightened. She's going to run or start screaming. Get her now, while you still can!

209

But then Brogan heard a muttering from Colette.

'What the hell is that noise?' she said to herself.

And Brogan knew that it wasn't him she was talking about, but the builders above. She could hear the radio and the chatter.

She came into the room and went straight to the window. Brogan watched her beautiful, slender feet in their high heels as they glided across the room, and he knew she was putting two and two together. She was looking at the van on the street outside, listening to the sounds from above, and her brain was connecting them in a nice, neat, logical package.

It was all good.

When she finally left the room, Brogan dared to let out a long, steady sigh of relief.

Now what?

We wait. What else is there?

There's also not waiting. You go down there now and you surprise her. Surprise Martyn too when he gets home and sees what you've done.

But that'll be an end to it.

Yeah, so? All good things come to an end.

I'm not ready to leave. We haven't finished the game. Besides, I like it here.

You like being stuck under a bed?

Actually, yes. You saw how close she got to me. I could have reached out and touched her leg.

Each to his own. Personally, I think lying about in dust for hours is overrated.

It was true about the dust. It was tickling his throat, and he had to keep rubbing his nose to prevent himself sneezing.

He listened out for Colette moving around the house. He heard the clinking of crockery, the clatter of cutlery. He heard more music – the smooth crooning of Michael Bublé from below clashing horribly with the wild outpourings of AC/DC from above.

Bublé gave up the fight after half an hour. Brogan tensed as he realised that Colette was back on the landing. He readied his knife once more.

But Colette didn't enter the bedroom. The sudden hiss of water told Brogan she had come up for a shower. He counted to a hundred, then wriggled out from under the bed, leaving the backpack there.

Where are you going?

I want to see.

See what?

Well, I'm not going to do a tour of the house, am I? I want to see Colette.

Are you crazy?

Probably.

He went to the door. Opened it a fraction. Colette was definitely in the shower: he could hear the slap of soap suds hitting the floor.

He moved along the landing. The workmen could still be heard above him, but even if they had gone, he couldn't risk the noise involved in climbing up there now.

He stood outside the bathroom. She hadn't fully closed the door, but it wasn't ajar enough for him to see much.

Step away now. It's not worth it.

I disagree. I think it's definitely worth it.

He brought his fingers to the door. Applied the slightest pressure. Just enough to open it by about an inch. Warm, damp air seeped through the gap. It carried to him the fragrance of Colette's soap, her shampoo.

He pushed the door again. Another inch. The room was filled with steam, the shower screen over the bath also steamed up, but he could see her, he could just make out her pink naked form as she stood beneath the hot water, and he could hear the slap of her soapy palms on her skin, her gasps as she ducked her head in and out of the water, and then she turned again so that she was facing him full on, and he could imagine her looking straight at him, wondering what he was doing there, what he planned to do to her as she continued to massage her yielding flesh . . .

We should go now.

What?

We should go.

In a minute.

He stood transfixed, watching and anticipating and dreaming of the near future. And then he pulled the door gently closed again and returned to his hiding place beneath the spare bed.

Brogan was starving. He'd had so little to eat today, and his stomach was rumbling angrily. If Colette came in here now, she'd be sure to hear it.

She wasn't helping matters. She was cooking curry downstairs. He could wolf down a curry right now. A huge plate of tikka masala with some naan bread and mango chutney and a cold beer.

He wondered if Elsie had any more curries in her fridge. He'd ask her later.

Later? Was that even going to be possible?

The men upstairs had finally stopped work. Brogan assumed they had packed up and gone home for their dinner. Curry, probably.

But when would he get an opportunity to climb up there? There was no way he could do so with Colette or Martyn in the house, and they very rarely went for an evening out in the middle of the week.

So when was he going to eat? Or, for that matter, drink?

We could die here. Without food or drink, we could die.

We're not going to die.

We could. One day, if it ever crosses Colette's mind to clean under her damn beds, she'll look under this one and find you shrivelled and dead. I know you want to freak her out, but that's taking it to extremes.

We're not going to die.

Couldn't we at least go back to the empty house?

What, you mean just stroll past Colette and say, 'See you later, babe'?

No. I mean at night. We wait until they're asleep and then—

How? How the hell will I be able to get up into the loft without waking them up?

We could go out the front door.

No. No, we couldn't. First of all, they lock the front door at night, so we'd have to find the key and unlock it, then put the key back and pull the front door shut as we leave, all without making the slightest noise. Secondly, there's no way back into the empty house once we're outside. The bolts are on the back door, remember? And all my tools are inside the house.

So that's it, then? We're staying?

That's it.

We're going to die here.

Colette had put her music on again. By pressing his ear into the carpeted floor, Brogan could almost make out the words.

Then another noise diverted his attention. The front door.

Martyn was home.

Brogan listened to the pair greet each other. Again, the voices were inaudible, but Brogan gained the impression that Colette was still acting like an ice queen. And why wouldn't she? She thought her husband was trying to drive her out of her mind. Why would a night away make her suddenly trust him again? If anything, the separation might have given her a more objective view of the situation.

Wait till she hears about Gabrielle.

Yeah. Won't that be a hoot?

Absolutely. On which note...

What?

Why wait? Why not do it tonight?

We've already gone over this. We haven't finished playing with them.

That's just it. Maybe we have *finished. We didn't foresee these circumstances. I really don't want to be stuck under this bed until morning, with nothing to eat or drink.*

Who said we would?

What?

Who said anything about staying under the bed?

Ah. Now you're talking.

Colette and Martyn had said little to each other all evening. The couple had eaten, washed the dishes and then relied on the television to fill the silence. It was as if they were strangers thrown together in a bed and breakfast. Actually, it was worse than that, because strangers would at least make an effort to get to know each other.

Brogan heard Colette come upstairs first. When Martyn followed a couple of minutes later, it sounded as though there was an awkward collision in the bedroom doorway.

'Where are you off to?' Martyn said.

'My suitcase. I left it downstairs.'

'I'll get it.'

'It's okay. I can manage.' Her tone was dismissive, as though she were forcefully rejecting the advances of a porter at a foreign airport.

'Colette. I'll get it. Okay?' Martyn's own voice was that of the alienated husband doing his best to regain his wife's affections.

'All right. Thank you.' The gratitude sounded like it had to be scooped out of her.

Martyn could be heard trudging downstairs, and then back up again. As he neared the bedroom, he said, 'Flipping heck. You only went for one night. It feels like you've got enough stuff in here for a fortnight.'

Colette muttered something that Brogan couldn't hear. There followed some toing and froing as the couple used the bathroom, and then Martyn said, 'I'll stick this in the spare bedroom so we don't walk into it at night.'

Brogan wriggled himself backwards as far as he could and pulled out his knife again. He watched as the door opened and Martyn's bare feet entered the room. Martyn plonked the suitcase down, but didn't leave immediately. He just stood there and sighed heavily.

He's annoyed. Frustrated.

Yeah. He was hoping she'd come back in a better mood, and she hasn't. He's in for a dog's life now.

At least we have an answer to something.

What's that?

The reason why things had been moved around in the loft the other day. They must have got the suitcase down for Colette's trip.

Finally, Martyn turned and left, fully closing the door with a click that seemed to echo around the room. Brogan detected a few words more from the adjoining bedroom, and then only silence.

And now all he could do was wait.

He waited until two-thirty in the morning, calculating that the pair would be sound asleep by that time. At least one of them was, judging by the heavy snoring.

Brogan shuffled out from under the bed. He stood and

stretched, and started to move towards the door, then paused. He crouched and untied his shoelaces, then removed his shoes and slipped them under the bed.

He turned the door handle slowly and carefully to avoid any clicks or rattles, then eased the door open and stepped onto the landing. His progress along the narrow passage was glacial, but he had only taken this route when the house was empty and he hadn't needed to make a mental note of any creaking floorboards.

It was as he drew level with the Fairbrights' bedroom that the snoring abruptly stopped. Brogan halted. He heard a murmur and the smacking of lips, and then the snoring started up again. Brogan pressed on, his confidence increasing as he descended the stairs.

He went straight to the kitchen.

Why did we come down here?

Because I'm thirsty and I'm hungry.

Seriously? You're going to put together a three course meal now? I thought we were going to have some fun.

I can't think on an empty stomach.

Well, good luck with that one.

Brogan took out his torch and shone it around the kitchen. He realised his choices were severely limited. One clink of glass or cutlery and it could all be over.

He went to the sink and took a pint glass from the draining board. He turned the tap until it was releasing barely a dribble, then waited patiently while it filled the glass. He downed it in one, then replaced the glass.

The glass touched against a wooden spoon.

The wooden spoon knocked against a metal spoon.

The metal spoon slipped from the draining board and dropped towards the floor.

Brogan caught it just before it hit the tiles.

Nice catch.

Thanks. I have good reflexes.

If you weren't so clumsy in the first place, you wouldn't need them.

Brogan moved to the fridge and opened it. Lots of stuff there, but looking at it just made him hungrier because he couldn't do anything with most of it, either because it was unopened or because it needed cooking. Same went for the contents of the cupboards. He couldn't use the microwave or the oven or the toaster. He couldn't use noisy implements like a tin opener, or anything that needed washing up afterwards. He didn't even think he could be quiet enough raiding a box of cereal.

Banana it is, then.

What?

Look. In the fruit bowl. A bunch of bananas.

They'll notice.

No, they won't. Who keeps track of how many bananas they have?

Some people probably do.

I don't think so. I don't think anybody in the world goes to bed knowing how many bananas they have.

Brogan took a banana. He remained standing while he peeled it, because he didn't want to risk moving the furniture. He ate slowly, relishing its taste and trying to imagine it expanding to fill his stomach, instead of becoming lost in its vast space.

Don't forget the peel.

I'm not eating the peel.

I mean don't leave it here, stupid. You'll have to take it with you.

Brogan stuffed the banana peel into his pocket.

Can we go now? I'm getting bored.

Yes. No.

Which is it?

I need to pee.

You need to— Jesus. You can't use the toilet! If you flush, they'll hear you, and if you don't flush, they'll see it in the morning. We're trying to make Colette believe she's being haunted, and ghosts don't pee!

So what do you suggest?

The sink. You'll have to pee in the sink.

That's gross. They wash their dishes in the sink.

I don't care if they lick round it. That's what you'll have to do.

Brogan peed in the sink. When he was done, he filled the pint glass again and used it to rinse the basin.

Right. Are you done? Can we go now?

We can go.

Are you sure you don't want to take a dump in the recycling bin first?

I said we can go.

Brogan left the kitchen. He was still hungry, but he could survive until morning.

His thoughts turned to the Fairbrights again, and he smiled.

He moved to the staircase. One step. Two steps. Three steps.

He halted when he saw Martyn at the top of the stairs.

It was dark, but not pitch black. Brogan could just about make out the shape of Martyn in his boxer shorts, scratching his head and farting.

Martyn was facing the other way, heading towards the bathroom. Brogan froze. Moved not a muscle or a sinew. Put a lid on his lungs as if to hold the air in them for ever. He felt his pupils dilating – stretching to their limit to admit as much of the scant light as they could. He saw Martyn go into the bathroom, leaving the door wide open. Heard the lifting of the lid and then a heavy stream of piss.

Brogan unwound his steps until he reached the bottom of the staircase, then retreated to the kitchen. He heard the flush of the toilet, the rush of water through the plumbing.

What if he comes down here?

He won't.

But what if he does?

Footsteps on the landing. For a moment, Brogan actually believed that Martyn was on his way downstairs. He squeezed himself into the space behind the kitchen door.

But Martyn didn't come down. Brogan allowed himself to breathe again. He waited in the kitchen for a full fifteen minutes before trying again.

On the staircase, he could hear that the snoring had resumed with an even greater intensity. It was only when he reached the landing that he realised there were two distinct tunes to the snoring, reassuring him that both were lost in their dreams.

He moved closer to their bedroom door, which was open just a crack, and paused there for a minute.

Are we going in? I think we should go in.

Brogan pushed the door open a couple of feet, then slipped inside.

It was much darker than it was on the landing, and he had to wait for a minute or two while his eyes struggled to adjust. It was as he was doing this that he felt a sudden stab of pain in his skull, and for a few seconds he thought he was going to pass out.

You okay?

I'm fine.

You really got a whack with that pan, didn't you?

I'm okay.

Good, because look . . .

He could see them now, dimly lit by the glow of the alarm clock. Martyn was on his side, his face turned away from Brogan. Colette was on her back, only half-covered by the duvet. Her snoring had become more of a gentle purr now, and her eyelids fluttered as though caught in the soft breeze she was creating. Her full lips were slightly parted, inviting the tender pressure of a kiss. The one leg that Brogan could see was bent slightly at the knee, and her nightie had ridden up over her hip.

Brogan stood in wonder, marvelling at the curves, the shadows, the prominences and indentations, the visible and the invisible. She excited him beyond measure, and not just because of what he could see, but also because of what he could envision.

He shifted nearer to the bed.

Careful.

He began with her foot. He put his hand out, brought it to within a millimetre of her flawless skin. So close he could feel the heat rising from it.

He moved his hand, brought it up the incline of her shin, letting it hover for a while at her knee before taking it on the descent across the expanse of her naked thigh. He sailed his palm over the roundness of her hip, stopping when it brushed against the material of her nightie.

He turned to her head, then. He reached out and touched her hair. It felt so incredibly soft, like down. He feathered his fingers over her forehead, then the bump of her nose, then her lips. He paused there for a while, savouring the heat of her breath, then continued on to her throat, her shoulder, the mound of her breast.

The movement was too rapid for him to react.

Colette took a sudden intake of breath as she arched her back and stretched out her arm. Her breast pressed into his palm before he had a chance to withdraw it. She groaned, and for an instant he thought she would wake up. But she simply turned onto her side and lay unmoving again.

We should go.

What's that?

Come on. I think we've taken enough risks for one night, don't you?

Yes. Okay, yes.

He left the room in a daze. Later, when he was back in the spare room, he found it difficult to remember how he had got there. He knew he must have taken his time to retrace his steps, but the journey was already barely a shadow in his memory.

What he *did* remember – oh so vividly – was what came before that. The way Colette had opened her eyes and smiled at him. The way she had deliberately pushed her breast into his cupped hand and groaned at the pleasure of his touch. The way she had mouthed the words, 'Come to me.'

He refused to listen to the suggestions of his fractured brain that it was a fiction, a corruption of the reality.

He wanted it to be the indelible, undeniable truth. And so it was.

He slept in the middle of the carpeted floor, making sure to squeeze back under the bed before the Fairbrights got up.

He heard the alarm go off, then listened to the trips to the bathroom, the washing, the dressing. Oh, and the occasional and brief exchange of words.

He listened to the clatter of bowls and mugs, a brief episode of happy radio music presented by an even happier DJ. He heard the front door being opened and shut, the starting and revving of engines and their fading into the distance.

And then, finally, he was alone. He was free.

But for how long?

Brogan wriggled out from under the bed and went to the front window. There was no van next door. He checked his watch. If they were coming again today then he probably didn't have long.

He went out to the landing. Grabbing the pole, he pushed open the hatch and unfolded the ladder, then stared up into the black void above him.

It'd be funny if he's gone.

Who?

The burglar. Imagine if he's not there anymore.

That's not funny. Why would you think that's funny?

It would be like the start of a murder mystery. I think it would make a great story, don't you?

No, I don't. Anyway, why would he be gone?

Any number of reasons. The workmen took him. Or maybe—

Why would the workmen take him?

Who knows? Maybe they have a thing for dead people. Maybe they're cannibals. Maybe they plan to blackmail the Fairbrights. Use your imagination.

I don't want to use my imagination. I just want to find out what they were doing up there.

So then my other theory is that he wasn't dead. He woke up and he escaped with the help of the workmen. Or he could be hiding up there, waiting to smack you with a pan again.

Will you shut up for a minute?

He started up the ladder. Pushed his shoulders through the hatch. He could see nothing. Hear nothing except for the tapping of birds on the roof tiles. And yet those sounds were different, somehow.

'Hello,' he said. The word sounded muffled. The air seemed to circulate less freely.

Try not to crap yourself if somebody answers.

I'm testing the sound. It's not the same.

If you'll forgive the pun, I'd like to suggest that using the torch would be more illuminating.

Brogan pulled the torch from his pocket and turned it on.

The suitcases, the crates, the bags – they were all in exactly the same places as before. The body was still covered in carpet and cardboard boxes.

But it was clear what the workmen had been doing. They had extended the brick wall. Built it right up to the roofline.

Brogan was now permanently cut off from the other houses.

Brogan stood in front of the new partition. He reached out and ran his fingers across it, almost in the hope that it would dissolve at his touch. But the bricks were cold and unrelenting. They made Brogan feel feeble and without control.

So that's it, then.

That's what?

The decision has been made for us. Today is our last one here. And the last day on earth for Colette and Martyn.

Does it have to be?

Of course it does. We can't go back the way we came. Our only way out now is through one of the doors of this house.

But why today? Why can't we stay up in the attic?

What are you talking about? We have no food, remember. We can't get to Elsie.

Oh, shit. Elsie!

Yes, Elsie. Our provider. We have to face up to reality now. This charade is over.

Brogan cast his mind back a few hours to that precious moment with Colette. Standing over her bed. Touching her.

Remembering the recent tender touch of another young woman.

No.

No? What do you mean, no?

We don't have to end it yet.

Really? And how the hell is that going to be possible?

We can come up here. Even if the workmen turn up again next door, they can't see us. We can hide again.

And food? What do we do about that?

I'll think of something.

Of course you will. What are you going to do? Eat the burglar?

Don't be ridiculous.

Then what? We can't live off a slice of bread and a handful of cereal a day.

Stop whining. I'll handle it, okay?

Fine, then. I'll leave it in your capable hands. And what about our friend here?

The burglar?

Yes, the burglar. If we're moving back up here, where is he going?

Nowhere. He stays here.

With us?

Yes.

You do know what happens to bodies after death, don't you? I mean, you haven't forgotten about that aspect of our activities?

Brogan closed down the conversation. He moved closer to the mound against the wall. He pulled away the boxes, and then the carpet.

He was not shocked by what he saw. To him it had always

been a marvel that flies were able to locate a corpse so quickly, and from such great distances. He had on many occasions been impressed at their ability to find a route through seemingly impenetrable barriers to get to their prey.

The flies were here now. They buzzed gently around the cadaver, flashing green in the torchlight. They landed and they ate and they laid their eggs, and they cared not a jot that this was once a human life. Tiny maggots were already crawling out of the man's nose and his mouth and his eyes and his ears.

Almost twenty-four hours had elapsed since this man had died. A full day in a warm, enclosed chamber. Brogan was fully aware that decomposition would be rapid in this environment, and that things were going to become substantially more unpleasant.

For Brogan, it was the moments leading up to death that were of interest. What fascinated him was how people reacted to pain, both mental and physical, and how they faced up to their final moments. There were endless variations on that theme to entertain him. What happened after life was extinguished didn't entice him in the slightest.

He was going to have to do something to make his time up here a little more bearable.

He climbed down the ladder and went to the kitchen. He scavenged a roll of bin bags, some parcel tape and scissors, then carried his haul back up to the attic.

He switched his torch on again, then wedged it into one of the rafters above his head. Its light didn't exactly fill the space, but it was enough for him to see what he was doing.

He ripped a bag from the roll and pulled it over the burglar's head and shoulders, then another for his feet and legs. He wrapped a couple more around the centre of the body, then used the parcel tape to hold them all together and seal any gaps. Feeling the need to play safe, he added another bag to each end of the corpse.

What are you going to do now? Put a stamp on it and take it to the post office?

Brogan grabbed the body and dragged it to the far end of the boarded half of the attic, pushing it as far under the eaves as he could.

Are you going to sleep up here with that thing?

That's the plan.

Well, I hope you've got a strong stomach. On which note . . .

What?

What's for breakfast?

The workmen had returned and started up again next door. More hammering and drilling and sawing. Brogan was glad to return to the relative peace of the kitchen.

Who knows? We may get another burglar today. We could start building a collection.

Brogan opened the fridge and studied the contents. He wondered if he could get away with stealing an egg, some cheese and some mushrooms. Maybe an omelette?

You know what would be great? A real show-stopper?

What?

Put the burglar's head in the fridge. Can you imagine that? Colette finding a human head in there next to her low-fat yoghurt and cottage cheese? That would be awesome.

Yeah. Remind me when the time comes. It might be nice to involve our burglar friend in the fun and games.

We could get them to play spin the bottle. Whoever it points to has to French-kiss the dead guy. Or maybe give him a blow job.

Brogan laughed out loud while he investigated the freezer.

'Yes!' he said out loud.

What?

He held up a Tupperware dish.

Leftovers. The curry from last night. Put this with a little rice . . .

Won't they notice?

I doubt it. They're not going to want curry again for at least a week, so why would they even go looking for it?

Fine. Go for it. Curry for breakfast is a weird choice, but right now anything looks delicious.

Brogan boiled a pan of water on the hob and dropped half a cup of rice into it. While that cooked, he microwaved the curry. When he was finally seated at the table, he was almost afraid to disturb the utter perfection of the steaming meal in front of him. But then the spicy aroma snaked into his stomach and twisted it into submission, and within seconds he was throwing the food down his gullet.

When he was done, he sat back and burped.

Damn, that was a good curry.

He washed up, put everything away, sat down again for a few minutes. He was aware of the pungent odour of curry in the room, but he reasoned that it would fade by the end of the working day, and the Fairbrights would just assume it had lingered since the previous night.

What now?

Now? Now I do what I said I'd do.

Brogan went upstairs to the bedroom. He found Colette's key and used it to open the jewellery box in the chest of drawers. He stared at its contents.

That's a nice ring. Expensive-looking.

Yeah. But I think she keeps it more for its sentimental value. It must be her closest connection to Jeremy.

So are you thinking what I'm thinking?

I'd be amazed if I wasn't.

Martyn had been the last to leave this morning, and the first one to come home. Brogan liked that. It left open the possibility that Colette could blame her husband for what she was about to discover.

Colette came up to shower and change before her evening meal. Brogan heard the shower start up.

He waited.

The shower was a brief one. Colette came thundering back into the bedroom. She was wearing a bathrobe and carrying a towel. She balled up the towel and threw it across the room.

'Bastard!' she said.

She jumped on the bed. Kneeling there, she pummelled Martyn's pillow with her fists for what seemed like a full minute.

When her energy was spent, she moved to the edge of the bed and sat there with her face in her hands.

It was obvious she had read the message on the mirror:

WHY DON'T YOU WEAR MY RING?

She thinks Martyn is trying to screw up her mind again. She's getting her anger out so she won't give him the satisfaction.

Brogan had figured it would go this way.

But he had also reasoned that this wouldn't be the end of it.

You think it's going to click with her?

Wait for it . . . Wait for it . . .

Colette suddenly lowered her hands. She sniffed back her tears.

Now. There it is.

Colette walked over to the chest of drawers. She took out the jewellery box.

That's it, Colette. I know what you're thinking. You're wondering how Martyn could know about the ring.

The fact that she kept the ring hidden away under lock and key had suggested to Brogan that she had probably never mentioned its existence to Martyn. Brogan had taken a gamble on that, and now it was paying off.

Colette pulled on the lid, confirming that it was locked. She went across to the wardrobe to retrieve the key, then came back into Brogan's field of view. She inserted the key and unlocked the box.

'Where is it?' she said.

She pulled out the bits of paper, tipped the box upside down.

'WHERE IS IT?'

Martyn appeared in the doorway then. His timing couldn't have been better.

'Where's what, Col?' he asked.

She turned her face towards him. 'Where is it?'

'What? What are you talking about?'

'You know damn well what I'm talking about. What have you done with it?'

'Col, I really don't know what—'

'Yes, you do. Don't lie to me. You've gone too far this time, Martyn. Where the hell is my ring?'

'What ring?'

'My fucking engagement ring! Where is it?'

Martyn sighed as if the answer was absurdly easy. 'It's still on your finger. You haven't taken it off. You never take it off.'

Colette's voice became a shriek. 'Don't talk to me like I'm an idiot! I'm not crazy, all right? I've had enough of your games. Give it back to me.'

'Honestly, love, I don't know what you want me to—'

'The ring! The engagement ring that Jeremy gave to me. You've taken it.'

Martyn stiffened. His expression of sympathy changed to one of annoyance.

'Jeremy's engagement ring? You've still got that?'

'I did have until you stole it from me.'

Martyn shook his head. 'Well, that's just fucking great, isn't it? Are you seriously telling me you've been keeping Jeremy's ring? What other goodies of his have you got in that box?'

Colette held up the scraps of paper. 'Newspaper cuttings and his suicide note. But I don't have to tell you that, do I, now that you've snooped around? How did you find the key, anyway? Have you been spying on me? Going through all my stuff? Is that what you were doing while I was in Edinburgh?'

Martyn threw his hands up in despair. 'Until now, I didn't

even know there *was* a fucking key. I'm not interested in your private things, Col. What I *would* like to know, however, is why you've kept this from me. Why couldn't you have told me you had all these mementos?'

'Precisely because I knew how you'd react. I knew you'd accuse me of loving Jeremy more than I love you, just like you did the other day. Anyway, we're getting off the point. I want my ring back, Martyn. Right now!'

'I haven't got it. Why would I take it?'

'Why would you do any of the things you've been doing? Why did you move the photos?'

'Oh, Christ, not that again. I thought we'd sorted that out.'

Colette pointed towards the bathroom. 'And the creepy messages you've been leaving me. What about those?'

'What messages?'

'On the mirror in the bathroom. Pretending they're from Jeremy.'

'What?' Martyn's voice was shrill. He turned and stormed out of the room. Seconds later, he was back.

'I can't see any messages.'

'That's because I rubbed it out.'

'Why? Why didn't you just show me this mysterious message and ask me about it?'

'Because I didn't want it there, and because I knew you'd deny it. You'd just say I'd written it.'

Martyn's face revealed that it was exactly what he would have said.

'Colette. I didn't move your photographs, I didn't write any messages on the mirror, and I haven't taken your precious ring.'

Colette opened the jewellery box and showed Martyn the empty interior. 'Well, it's gone. That means somebody took it.'

It was obvious from Martyn's body language that he was bursting to offer another explanation.

Colette could read it, too. 'No. Don't even go there. I would remember. If I'd moved it, I would remember.'

'Col . . . I didn't even know this stuff existed. How could I if you've never told me about it? And even if I did, I wouldn't know where to look for the key. Isn't it possible . . .?'

'No. It isn't.'

'All right, but can we at least *look* for your damn ring before you throw any more accusations at me? Don't I at least get a chance of putting up a defence case?'

She shook her head. 'It was in the box, Martyn. I know it was.'

'Indulge me, okay? When did you last see it?'

'Tuesday.'

'Tuesday?'

'What's wrong with that?'

'Nothing. It's just . . . I thought you were going to say it was a year ago or something. Do you look at it most days?'

'No, I don't. Why would you think that?'

'Well . . . you looked at it on Tuesday. You tried to look at it again today . . .'

'It's . . . Does it matter? It's lost. That's what matters.'

'And you definitely put it back in the box on Tuesday?'

'Yes. Definitely. Not a shadow of a doubt. How much certainty do you want from me?'

'Okay, okay. I'm trying to be helpful here. Where was the box?'

'In the drawer.' She said this with impatience, as if to imply to Martyn that he already knew that because he had taken it out and opened it.

'So let's look in the drawer.'

'It's not there.'

'How do you know? Have you looked?'

She harrumphed. Martyn went to the drawer and started taking things out. She made no move to help him.

'See?' she said when the drawer was empty. 'Not there.'

'Okay. Then let's try the other drawers.' He pulled out one of the top drawers and handed it to her.

'This is pointless. We could spend the whole night searching and still not find it.'

'Or we could find it in the next five minutes. Can we just give it a go, please?'

Colette went to the bed and tipped the contents of the drawer onto it. She moved the items around half-heartedly, then began stuffing them back into the drawer.

'Not here,' she announced in an I-told-you-so tone.

'Okay. No problem. We've only just started.' He handed her another drawer, which she treated in a similarly desultory manner while Martyn rummaged through her other clothes.

'Right,' he said. 'What about this box of photos?'

She sighed. 'Give it here.'

She turned the box over and pushed the photos around like she was mixing up a deck of cards.

'This is ridiculous,' she said. 'I don't even know why I'm going along with this.'

'Because you want your damn ring back, don't you? And I

want you to find it so that you stop blaming me for pinching it.' He scanned the room. 'Where can we look next?'

'Martyn, we're making a mess of my things. Everything's getting creased.'

'Yeah, but what's a few creases compared with the memories of your wonderful ex-fiancé, eh?' The scorn in his voice was unmistakeable.

'Martyn, I—'

'What about your other jewellery?'

'What about it?'

'Is that all in the big jewellery box on the shelf?'

'Most of it, yes.'

'Well, have you looked in there?'

'It's not in there. I wouldn't put it in there.'

'Not even by mistake? Maybe you weren't thinking straight.'

'My thinking is as straight as a ruler, thank you. The ring I got from Jeremy is kept in the chest of drawers. Always.'

'Fine. Have it your way. If you're not even going to make an attempt to look for it, then I'm giving up.'

'Oh, for God's sake, Martyn. Now you're acting like a child.'

'Me? *I'm* acting like a child? What about you?'

'Don't try to turn it around. I'm the injured party here. I'm the victim.'

'Victim!' he sneered. 'Is that how you see yourself? You've misplaced something and suddenly that turns you into a victim?'

'I haven't misplaced it, and it's not just about the ring.'

Martyn waved her away. 'Fine. Whatever.'

Colette let out a roar of anger, then stomped to the shelf. 'You insist on making me go through the motions, then all right. Here!'

She picked up a square box in black leather, then carried it back to the bed. She opened it up and turned it upside down.

'There! There's all my jewellery. My necklaces, my bracelets, my earrings, my . . .'

'What?'

Brogan watched as she reached down and picked something out from the glistening pile.

'What?' Martyn repeated.

'The ring. It's . . . it's the ring.' She turned and faced her husband, holding it up for him to see.

Martyn said nothing. He just stood there, shaking his head slightly.

'How?' she said. 'How did it get in there?'

'I don't think that's such a mystery, do you? Apology accepted, by the way.'

She stared at the shiny circle of gold as though it had magic powers. 'I don't understand.'

Martyn started for the door, anger still written on his face.

'You put it there, didn't you?' she said.

This stopped Martyn in his tracks. 'Excuse me?'

'You knew it was in there all along. That's why you suggested that I should look in there. You set up a pretend search, and then casually suggested my other jewellery box.'

Martyn lost control. 'For fuck's sake, Colette! What the fuck is this – Antagonise Your Husband Day? I am seriously on the verge of walking right out of this house now and never coming back. Is that what you want? Is that what you're trying to get me to do?'

'No. Martyn, I—' She burst into tears.

Watching her, Martyn softened. His shoulders slumped.

'Colette. Don't cry. Let's talk about this.'

She forced words out between the sobs. 'I don't know ... what's ... going on. What's happening ... to me?'

Martyn went to her, took hold of her shoulders, lowered her to the bed. She was shivering. Martyn sat down next to her and put his arm around her.

'Come on now,' he said. 'It's not the end of the world.'

'Promise me,' she answered.

'What? That it's not the end of the world?'

'No. That you didn't move the ring.'

'I swear to God. I didn't move it. Why would I? I didn't even know you had it. And if I had known, and I'd wanted to take it away from you, why would I just put it in your other jewellery box? That wouldn't make any sense.'

'And you didn't leave the messages in the bathroom?'

'Col, this is the first I've heard about them. What did they say?'

'The first one said ...'

'Go on. What?'

'It said, "Why did I have to die?"'

'Jesus.'

'And just now there was another one. It said, "Why don't you wear my ring?"'

Martyn stared at her for a while. 'That's ... that's pretty freaky.'

'Can you understand now why it's made me so upset? The messages. Things being moved around. And it's all about Jeremy. I'm getting a really bad feeling about this. If you didn't do any of it—'

'I didn't. Honest to God.'

'Then there has to be another reason. You don't think . . .'

'What?'

'I mean, do you think it's possible . . . Could Jeremy be trying to contact me?'

'Col, no. Don't start that again. Things like that don't happen in real life. There are no such things as ghosts.'

'How do you know? It would explain so much.'

'It wouldn't. It's not an explanation at all.'

'Perhaps Jeremy blames me. I should have read the signs. I should have seen it coming, and done something to stop it. I should have saved him. That's why he's contacting me now.'

'No. Stop it, Col. You're not being haunted. You're jumping to wild conclusions because you refuse to see what's right in front of your face.'

She looked into his eyes. 'You're going to bring it back to that again, aren't you? You're going to tell me I'm going mad.'

'No, not mad. You're stressed. Maybe you feel guilty about Jeremy, even though you shouldn't. It's making you forgetful. Perhaps you're sleepwalking, and that's when you move stuff around. Or maybe you're imagining things.'

'What things?'

'The messages in the bathroom, for example.'

'They were there, Martyn. I saw them with my own eyes.'

'Are you sure? Isn't it just possible that your mind told you they were there?'

She started crying again. 'I don't know what to think anymore. Why is it happening? And why now?'

'I don't know. But I do think we need to get you checked out.'

'You think I need to see a shrink?'

'I've no idea. Let's start with your GP first, see what he recommends. Like I said, maybe you're just overtired or stressed. Or maybe it's hormonal. The doc might want to do blood tests. Who knows – just talking it over with him might help to get rid of the symptoms. Either way, we'll get to the bottom of this.'

Colette nodded slowly.

'Good girl. Look, let's get the weekend out of the way first. We'll call the clinic on Monday and make an appointment. Deal?'

'Deal.'

He pulled her to him and kissed the side of her head. 'Don't worry. We'll get you fixed up. Now get dressed and come down for something to eat. Okay?'

She nodded again, and Martyn left the room.

When he had gone, Colette stood and walked to the mirror. Brogan watched as she stared deeply into the eyes of her reflection.

He knew what she was looking for, because he had tried to find it many times in the depths of his own pupils.

She was searching for the madness.

FRIDAY 14 JUNE, 10.17 PM

They came to bed earlier than usual, both of them clearly upset and drained. Martyn hovered around his wife as though she were a delicate flower, the slightest of breezes capable of dislodging her petals. He kept asking her if she was all right, and whether he could do anything for her.

He's pissing her off.

Are you surprised? He won't leave her alone.

He thinks he's won her over. He doesn't want to risk losing her again.

As the couple undressed, Brogan could see how Martyn's eyes constantly shifted towards his wife, then away again before he was caught.

He wants her.

Not tonight, Josephine.

You think?

He won't want to be thought of as taking advantage of her vulnerability right now. Plus, I don't think he's entirely sure what she thinks about him. He's got to be certain that she trusts him before he makes a move.

Pity. I could do with the entertainment.

The lights were switched off within minutes of the couple getting into bed. No reading, no further discussions. Brogan lay still until he was sure they were both asleep, then he covered up his spyhole. He switched on his torch, then eased himself across to the boarded section of the floor and rested his back against the brick wall.

Now what?

What kind of question is that? Now nothing. We sit here. We kill time.

That's boring. I don't want to kill time. I want to kill people.

And we will. Have patience.

Patience is not one of my virtues. I'm a doer. I like to be hands-on. Colette is in desperate need of some hands-on experience.

She'll get it. Think about something else.

Like what? Hunger? Okay, then, I'm hungry.

You're always hungry.

And it's about to get much worse. Have you looked at the pathetic provisions you brought up here?

Earlier in the day, Brogan had found another empty bottle in the recycling bin and had filled it with tap water. He had also taken a packet of crisps out of an open multi-pack, and wrapped two digestive biscuits and some cheese in tinfoil to keep them fresh. At the time, it had seemed substantial. Now, as he cast his torchlight over the meagre picnic, it looked barely enough to feed one of the mice that undoubtedly lived up here.

We'll manage.

We shouldn't have to manage. We should be taking control,

not hiding away like frightened animals. We should have these people at our beck and call, just like we did with all the others. Remember the Derwents? Remember how we got them to take bites out of each other? That's what we should have.

And we will! Just not yet.

Brogan thought about the authority he'd exerted over his victims. He had spent most of his early life subject to the whims of others; being able to wield such power was both liberating and electrifying.

He looked up at the wall behind him – the original crumbling red bricks surmounted by new dull grey rectangles. He was in a prison cell now. Solitary confinement with the measliest of rations. He wished there was still a way out, back across the houses, back to—

Elsie!

What about her?

How will I see her again?

Well, you won't, will you?

But you heard what she said. She needs me. She doesn't want to live without me, without her Alex.

Tough titties. To be fair, it was never going to be the longest of relationships, was it? It was always a question of whether she'd pop her clogs before we left.

She'll be missing me. It'll break her heart.

The only thing I'm missing about her is her food.

You have no soul.

Right. Because the welfare of our soul has always been at the top of our agenda, hasn't it? Get over it. You'll never see Elsie again, dead or alive, so put her out of your mind.

But Brogan couldn't. He never imagined his time with the old woman would be curtailed so abruptly. He would never have killed her. She was too special for that. Probably the only person to whom he had ever attached a label of immunity.

He tried analysing why that was, but it hurt his head. Too many confusing images and emotions and memories, all vying with each other to supply him with an answer.

But he would miss Elsie. And the last wish he made before he turned off his torch was that she would somehow come to terms with his abandonment of her.

SATURDAY 15 JUNE, 1.53 AM

Lots of things were bothering him about being stuck up here.

For one thing, he was tired. He wanted to curl into a foetal position on the floor and allow himself to drift off. But it was too risky. He might snore or roll around. The smallest of shifts in his position could be enough to alert the Fairbrights to his presence.

And so he remained sitting upright against the wall, even though his head insisted on lolling about on his shoulders.

Another thing was the stiffness in his joints and muscles. He hardly dared move, and when he did move it had to be done with painstaking slowness and care. What he really wanted to do was some star jumps, some press-ups, some running on the spot. His backside felt like it had permanently flattened out and lost all sensation.

Worst of all, though, were the sounds.

He hadn't noticed them before because he had always been too busy focusing on other things. He could cope with the creaks and the clicks. He told himself it was just the roof sighing as it released its warmth to the night air.

But the other noises were more troubling. They were not mechanical; they could not be readily explained by expansion or contraction of building materials or copper pipes. These sounds could only be the tiny but insistent emissions of living creatures.

There was scuttling, certainly. And also an occasional sudden scrabbling. Brogan was sure that live things kept dropping onto him from above, landing in his hair or slipping down the back of his neck.

But there was another noise, too. And it was coming from the direction of the dead body.

Brogan flicked on his torch and turned it towards the black plastic bundle at the end of the attic space.

What are you doing?

Checking.

Fine. You've checked. He hasn't gone anywhere.

He's making a noise.

A noise? What kind of noise?

I don't know. Just a noise.

No he isn't. He's dead. He's not likely to whistle, hum or click his fingers any time soon.

Brogan started to crawl towards the wrapped corpse. As he moved, one of his knees cracked, and the noise seemed to fill the air.

Quiet. You'll wake the neighbours.

Brogan continued to edge forwards. When he was only a couple of feet away from his target, he stopped and played the torch over it.

It was moving.

It wasn't as if the dead guy was struggling to get out of his wrapping or anything. The movement was much more subtle. Brogan leaned forward and stared at the tiny wriggling maggots that had somehow managed to escape from the bin liners. He wondered how many more were still inside, their combined weight causing the plastic to shift and contort as they crawled, making the noises he had heard. Shiny green flies circled the package, as though monitoring their progeny. As Brogan watched, a large beetle skittered across the body, closely followed by another. They seemed to be in a race to get the best place at the dining table.

Brogan grimaced, shuddered. He was also now more acutely aware of the smell.

He's a little overripe.

Just a tad.

I think he probably took a dump, too. I mean, not just now. When you killed him.

Brogan wrinkled his nose. He knew what happened immediately after death. How the body's sphincter muscles relaxed, often causing the deceased to soil themselves.

Death is never pretty.

It'll get worse before it gets better.

I know that.

And you still want to stick it out up here?

I do.

You still plan to eat that food you brought up?

Yes.

Well, you could have at least gone for the plain crisps. Those cheese and onion ones smell worse than this guy.

SATURDAY 15 JUNE, 9.26 AM

He thought they were never getting up. A part of him wanted to bang on their ceiling just to rouse them. He wanted them out of that room so he could move around a little more freely.

He watched as Colette stirred into life first. She groaned and wiped the sleep from her eyes, then spent several minutes simply staring at the still form of her husband. She looked thoughtful, as if trying to divine his truth. Was he as innocent as he claimed, or was he manipulating her?

She climbed out of bed eventually, took her dressing gown from a hook on the back of the door, then disappeared. Brogan listened to the sounds from the bathroom, then from the kitchen. After a few minutes, smells far more pleasant than the ones Brogan had suffered all night began to drift his way: toast and fresh coffee. He pushed his nose into the spyhole, eager to draw the aromas into his system.

Another twenty minutes went by before Martyn woke. He climbed off the bed and went to the door, scratching his crotch as he walked. He, too, grabbed a dressing gown before leaving the room.

Brogan waited until he was sure Martyn was downstairs before he emitted a drawn-out but quiet moan.

Jesus, that was a tough night.

You wanted it. I had other ideas.

Brogan switched on his torch and stood up. He stretched, reaching his arms up to touch the roof tiles. He bent over to touch his toes, and heard the vertebrae of his spine clicking. He moved around the cramped space, bringing his knees as high as he could. When he felt he had limbered up enough, he got down on the floorboards and performed some press-ups and stomach crunches, while trying to keep the noises of his exertions to a minimum.

When he had finished, he sat back against the wall and wiped the perspiration from his brow. He unscrewed the top from the bottle of water and took a long swig. The heat was already building up here, and it was only early in the day. Later it would become like an oven.

We should eat that cheese before it melts.

Brogan wished he were down in that kitchen, quaffing gallons of coffee and munching on toast and marmalade and cereal and bacon and eggs and sausages and . . .

But all he had was a packet of crisps, a couple of stale biscuits and a slice of warm, curling cheese.

Mmmm, doesn't that look yummy?

Brogan's plan had been to eke it out over the day. Instead, he devoured the whole lot in a couple of minutes, and was still famished afterwards.

Now what do we do?

Why don't you come up with a bright idea for a change? Something to take our minds off food.

Okay, then, I will. I spy with my little eye . . .

Brogan had fallen asleep. No longer preoccupied by the worry of alerting anyone in the bedroom, he had drifted off.

He was awoken by the sound of voices from below.

'Bloody hell, Martyn!' Colette exclaimed.

'What?' said Martyn.

'Did you have to?'

'Have to what?'

'It stinks up here.'

'Don't look at me.'

'Well, somebody's responsible. Open those windows.'

Brogan heard pacing, the window latches being opened.

'Thank God for that,' said Colette. 'It's like someone died in here.'

Martyn laughed. 'I suppose we should get dressed.'

'Well, yes. Don't know about you, but that's why I came up here.'

'Sure. But . . .'

'But what?'

'It's Saturday. There's nothing stopping us going back to bed for a bit.'

'A bit of what?'

'That's the question.'

A silence ensued. One of those awkward silences that said everything that needed to be said.

'I need more time, Martyn. Okay?'

'Of course. It was just a thought. I'm missing you.'

Colette lowered her voice, and Brogan had to strain to hear. 'I know. I'm missing you too. But I'm not in the right place yet. In my head, I mean. I'm confused.'

'I understand.'

'Do you?'

'Yes. I think so. But . . .'

'What?'

'Well, I mean, it's not because you still think that I . . .'

'No. Not that. It's me. Obviously there's something wrong with me. If I'm doing things and then forgetting them, then I can't be right up here, can I? I just don't want to do something I might regret.'

'Regret? Why would you regret going to bed with me?'

'Not regret. That's the wrong word. What I mean is that I need to know it's me, that I'm doing something because it's what I really want to do, and not because my mind is playing games with me. Oh, God, I don't think I'm making any sense here.'

'I'm not sure, either.'

'What I'm trying to say is that I need to get better first. I need to get back to being the woman you married. Do you have any idea what I'm talking about?'

'I think I do. Better get you to that doctor double-quick

then, because I don't know how long I can carry on living like a monk.'

She laughed. 'I'm sure you've got it all in hand.'

'Cheeky.'

The conversation ended as the couple washed and dressed. Brogan could hear them moving about, but chose not to sneak over to his spyhole. He was too damn tired.

Well, that was the biggest load of bollocks I've ever heard.

What was?

All that guff about getting better before she allows him to get his leg over.

You think?

I know. She still doesn't trust him. She can't get turned on by a man who she thinks is trying to dismantle her brain. That's what she was really thinking. She just couldn't come out and say so.

I think you might be right.

I am right. She still has major doubts about him. But a part of her doubts herself too. She needs to see that doctor. But if he confirms she's as sane as she thinks she is, she'll go back to hating Martyn.

And then the fireworks will fly.

Yeah. That's if we don't light the blue touchpaper before then.

The day dragged and the heat mounted relentlessly. Brogan stripped off his sweat-soaked T-shirt, and it was almost as if he were making an invitation to the flies to come and drink from his body. He could hear them buzzing around his ears, and feel the tickle as they landed on his torso and sucked up the beads of perspiration.

This is getting ridiculous. We're baking in here.

Brogan felt for the water bottle in the darkness and took another swig. The bottle felt light, almost empty.

It's beyond a joke. I've never been in conditions as insufferable as this before.

Stop moaning. Think of it as a test of character.

But it was a valid point. It was a hell-hole up here. And yet Brogan could escape at any time. He could open that hatch, descend upon the Fairbrights, subdue them and begin his fun. He could gorge himself on their food, wash in their shower, bathe in their misery.

But the time still wasn't right. Brogan liked to think of himself as self-disciplined. He tended to operate on a reward system. A beer after performing an arduous physical task. A bar of chocolate after working out a clever plan of action. A few slashes of his knife after a particularly devious bit of social engineering of a victim. It added to the satisfaction. Little and often, instead of gorging on one huge banquet.

That was the case here. He was suffering, yes, but it was nothing compared to the torment the Fairbrights would endure. That had to be drip-fed, a steady escalation. He needed to cut slowly into their relationship, needed to see the blame, the recrimination, the self-doubt, followed by fear and loathing. There was still much to accomplish before the grand finale.

But a little respite from this extreme discomfort would make it easier to maintain confidence in his strategy.

He didn't get his wish until just after half past six in the evening.

'You coming, then?' This from Martyn, in the bedroom once more.

'Just getting changed,' Colette said.

'You don't need to change. You look fine.'

'I've been cleaning all day. I look a mess. Where are we going, anyway?'

'I thought Fancy Dan's. I'm in the mood for one of their burgers.'

'Okay.'

'Yeah? Come on, then. I'm starving.'

No, he's not starving. We're starving. It's not long since he had lunch, the greedy bastard.

I don't care. If they're leaving the house, then I don't care.

Brogan heard Colette pottering about, then footsteps. A

few minutes later the closing of the front door. Then came the sound of the car engine being started up.

They've gone! What are we waiting for? Let's get out of here!

Brogan crossed to the hatch, opened it and climbed down. He was still shirtless, and the cooler air down here prickled his skin.

Christ, that feels better!

He closed the hatch behind him to keep the smell and flies contained. On the landing he did some stretching, twisting and toe-touching, then went to the bathroom and splashed cold water on his face.

How long do you think we have?

I don't know. An hour or two, maybe? I don't think we can count on much longer than that.

Food. I need food.

Brogan headed down to the kitchen and began rooting around for food. He didn't have to worry about making a noise now, but he couldn't prepare anything that might leave smells behind. Knowing he couldn't choose anything that might have been bought recently, he pulled out a tin of beans from the back of a cupboard shelf. He ate the contents cold with a slice of bread and butter. After that, he washed the tin and cutlery in the sink.

Where's the water bottle?

I left it in the attic.

Well, don't you think you need to refill it?

I'll do it later.

Get it now. We don't know how much time we'll have later. For all you know, this Fancy Dan's place might be only a couple of minutes away. Or maybe they couldn't get in and had to turn back. Go and get the bottle. And take that tin with you.

Yes, boss.

Brogan started to head out of the kitchen.

When you come back, we'll need some emergency provisions.

I can't take too much. They'll notice.

I don't care if they notice. It'll be their funeral if they do. Fill the bottle, then grab some more food.

All right, all right. Who died and left you in charge?

As Brogan went out into the hall, his mind was on what food he might possibly steal. It would probably have to be cereal again. A couple of Weetabix and a handful of corn-flakes, maybe.

He didn't know why, but he glanced into the front room as he passed its door.

That's when he noticed the flashing blue light.

SATURDAY 15 JUNE, 6.48 PM

Not again! Shit!

Can't be. How could they know about me?

Brogan felt his stomach lurch. He moved towards the open doorway of the front room. The flashing light was subtle but definitely there, pulsing through the bay windows and illuminating the room.

Careful now!

Brogan needed to see what was going on. He stood in the doorway, then quickly bobbed his head into the room. His wide eyes drank up the scene through the window.

Martyn! Martyn was there!

He was standing alongside his car, his concerned gaze focused on something further down the street. Brogan couldn't see any police, but the emergency vehicle had to be very close, its light reflecting off the windows opposite and bathing Martyn in its eerie glow.

What the hell is Martyn doing back here? He's supposed to be having dinner.

They've called the cops. They know!

That's not possible.

Yes! Yes it is! They just pretended to drive away from the house. Don't you see? That discussion in the bedroom about dinner was purely for our benefit. They've rumbled us.

How? How did they—?

Who cares? It doesn't matter now. We need to get out of here.

Brogan looked up the stairwell.

We could hide again.

Where? They know we're in here. They'll search everywhere, including the attic.

Then . . . then what?

We have to leave. Go out the back way.

Don't you think they'll have that covered?

Well, unless you've got any better suggestions . . .

Okay, okay.

He tried to calm his breathing, tried to slip back into the frame of mind of a man on the run. He had done it before; he could do it again now.

The knife. Where's the knife?

I left it in the attic.

Get it. Quickly!

Brogan dashed upstairs, still clutching the empty can. He flew up into the attic, tossed the can aside, grabbed his shirt and knife, rushed down the ladder again.

On the bottom step he paused.

What?

Brogan looked towards the front bedroom.

I need to check.

It's too dangerous. They'll be watching.

If they know, they know. It's a bit late to start getting cautious.

We need to go!

A few seconds, okay?

No. We have to—

But Brogan was already pushing open the door to the bedroom. He stepped quickly to the window and glanced down. He half expected to see a dozen uniformed officers pointing assault rifles at him.

What he saw was Martyn, still next to his car, and . . .

An ambulance!

Jesus.

It's not the cops. It's an ambulance!

Brogan moved to one side of the window and flattened himself against the wall.

What does it mean? Has something happened to Colette?

I don't know. I can't see her. I—

And then it hit him.

Elsie! They're at Elsie's house.

You reckon?

Yes. That's why the Fairbrights didn't leave. They saw the ambulance pull up, and Colette has gone to see what's wrong.

You think Elsie is—

I don't know.

But in his bones, he knew that the signs weren't good. This was what Elsie had predicted.

And all because of him.

What are they doing now?

Brogan risked another quick glance. He could see the front

of the ambulance, but not what was taking place behind it. Martyn was still waiting by his car.

And then he wasn't.

He was coming back into the house.

Hide!

Brogan ran out of the bedroom and up the ladder. Even as he hauled it up and closed the hatch, he was convinced he was taking too long and that Martyn was in the house, aware of the racket upstairs.

Lying across the floorboards, Brogan lifted the hatch cover again, just a fraction. He heard Martyn toss his keys into a bowl on the sideboard in the hall, and then nothing more.

Brogan jammed the hilt of his knife into the gap beneath the cover, keeping it open while he listened. A few minutes later he heard the door open and then Colette's voice.

'Martyn! Martyn, where are you?'

'I'm here, I'm here. What's happening?'

'I'm going with her to the hospital.'

'What? You don't need to do that.'

'She needs someone with her, Martyn. She's got nobody else.'

Martyn paused. 'All right. How's she looking?'

'Not good. She's a terrible colour, poor thing.'

'You could be there a while, you know.'

'I know, but she's always been a good neighbour. I'd hate to think of her going through this alone.'

'Okay, but call me. Have you got your phone?'

'Yes. Listen, I've got to go. Speak to you later.'

'All right. Bye.'

And then she was gone. The front door closed.

Brogan removed his knife and lowered the hatch cover again. He moved back to his position against the wall.

Poor Elsie.

She's ancient. She was never going to last much longer.

No, but . . .

But what?

I'd hate to think this is because of me.

Why? She wouldn't be the only one who's departed because of your efforts.

The others were intentional. I never meant to hurt Elsie.

Not even when you had that knife at her dinner table?

Not even then. Not really.

I still don't get it. Why her? Why do you even care?

You heard what Colette said. Elsie has got nobody else.

So? You've listened to sob stories before. Even the Carters tried it on, with that ridiculous tale about a disabled daughter.

That's the point. They knew exactly what they were doing. They were trying anything they could to save their own skins. They were cowards. Elsie has never had any thought for her own survival.

Elsie doesn't know what she's thinking. She's off her trolley. She believes you're her dead son.

She's deluded, but that doesn't make her crazy.

I beg to differ. Anyway, maybe she'll be okay. The hospital will look after her. And I'm sure it'll help having Colette there with her.

Yeah. That was quite a surprise.

What do you mean?

I mean about Colette getting so involved. I know they're neighbours, but this seems above and beyond the call of duty.

Maybe she's hoping to be included in the old bat's will.

Or maybe . . . maybe she's just a nice human being.

Oh. Oh, wait. This isn't . . . no . . .

What?

You. You're changing your mind about her, aren't you? You're thinking of letting her off the hook.

No. I'm not.

You are. She's being nice to your lovely little old lady, and you're getting all warm and fuzzy because of it.

Don't be stupid.

You can hide your feelings from other people, but not from me. We share the same space, remember. You're going soft.

Shut up. I'm not going soft. I just said I was surprised, that's all. I didn't realise the two of them were so close.

You said she was a nice human being. Whenever have you said that about somebody we're about to kill?

I don't know. I—

Never. That's when. Don't start getting all mushy about Colette, okay? This is a done deal. You can lust after her body all you want, but forget about the lovey-dovey stuff. Her card is marked.

I know.
End of.
Yes, I know. I know.
Good.

Brogan had heard very little since Colette had left the house hours ago. He'd detected the sounds of Martyn cooking, the blaring of the television, a trip to the toilet. What he hadn't heard were any phone conversations.

Brogan climbed into position, pulled away the insulation and put his eye to the hole. Martyn eventually entered the bedroom, huffing and puffing. He looked furious, staring at the mobile phone in his hand. He threw himself down on the bed and stabbed his device with a force that looked like it could crack the screen. He brought the phone to his ear.

'Oh, for fuck's sake!' he said.

He waited a few seconds longer, then began speaking. 'It's me,' he said in a tone that made no attempt to disguise his irritation. 'You said you were going to call. Could you give me a ring at some point and let me know what the hell is going on?'

He stood up again and began to undress. After another short visit to the bathroom, he was sat in bed, propped up and studying a car magazine.

A few minutes later, he picked up his phone again and made a call.

'Hi. It's me.' He was smiling now.

Why the change of tune? A minute ago he was ready to incinerate her.

'She's out,' Martyn said. 'At the hospital . . . No, nothing. She's with an old lady from down the road.'

That's why. It's not Colette.

Then who . . .?

You really need to ask?

'I'm here all alone . . . Yup. A big empty space next to me. You wanna fill it?' His laugh was lascivious. 'Oh, yeah . . . Yeah, I'd love that . . . Really? That's what you're wearing?' He slipped his hand under the duvet.

I swear, if he brings that thing out, I'm going down there to cut it off.

Brogan welcomed the noise of a key being inserted into the front door. Martyn seemed less appreciative.

'Gotta go, Gabs. See you soon.' He ended the call, then swapped his phone for his car magazine and his lecherous expression for a disgruntled one.

Colette looked weary as she came into the room.

'Hi,' she said. 'You're early coming to bed.'

'I got bored. Telly's crap. You didn't ring me.'

'Sorry. It was all a bit . . . fraught.'

'I tried calling you but got no answer. I sent you texts.'

'I switched my phone off, Martyn. There were signs up in the hospital saying that's what you're supposed to do, even though lots of people seemed to be ignoring them.'

'Couldn't you have ignored them too, just for a minute? Even if you had to go outside to make a call?'

'Sorry. I didn't think I'd be gone that long. And I didn't really want to move too far away from Elsie.'

At the mention of their elderly neighbour, Martyn abandoned his righteous indignation act.

'How is she?'

Colette shook her head. 'She's very weak. They're going to keep her in for a few days.'

'Think she'll make it?'

'I hope so. She's the worst I've ever seen her, though. Worse than that time she had pneumonia.'

'What happened? I mean, who called the ambulance?'

'The carer. She found Elsie on the floor. Thought she was dead at first. Apparently it took ages for the ambulance to arrive.'

'Had she tripped or something? A stroke maybe?'

'I don't know. The doctors have got her on a drip and are going to run tests. Hopefully they'll know more in the morning.'

'What about you? Have you had something to eat?'

'A nurse brought me tea and toast. I'm okay.'

'That's not very much. Do you want me to make you something?'

'No. Thank you. I'm not hungry. Just knackered.'

Brogan studied her. There was an absence of energy that was not due merely to tiredness, or emotional strain because of Elsie's condition. There was an air of defeat about her.

She undressed quickly, gave Martyn the fleetest and most

detached of kisses, then turned off her lamp and closed her eyes.

Martyn watched her for a while. Then he put down his magazine and checked his phone. A smile crossed his lips, as though he had found something secretly amusing in a text message. Or perhaps it was simply the memory of his most recent call that was stimulating his pleasure centre.

Enjoy it while you can, you lecherous cheating bastard, Brogan thought. Try smiling like that when I serve you your lips on a plate.

It had been another eternal night. Brogan had spent most of it lying on his back, staring into the blackness, pushing sleep away each time it tried to claim him. He suspected that he had probably dozed off a couple of times, but wasn't certain when or for how long. The local wildlife had continued to disturb him with their buzzing and scratching and rustling and scurrying, and by morning he was itchy all over at the thought that a vast array of tiny beings had taken residence in his hair and clothes.

The heat was building again, along with the smell. Brogan pictured the fumes of morbidity soaking into his skin, tainting him, perhaps even infecting him. Could they carry sickness into his bloodstream, his cells? Would he eventually succumb and add to the death toll?

You're a cheery one this morning.

I'm tired and hungry and thirsty. What's there to be cheerful about?

That's not what's bothering you.

What?

*It's not the sleep and the food and the drink. They're the things
I complain about. For you, it's Elsie. And Colette.*

What do you mean, it's Colette?

*I'm telling you what you already know. I'm applying your
logic. Your – what's it called? – your syllogism.*

My syllogism.

*Yes. You're concerned about Elsie, Colette is concerned about
Elsie, ergo you're concerned about Colette.*

That's the worst logic ever.

I think that too, but it's yours, not mine.

Bullshit. Haven't we already discussed this? Colette's fate is
sealed. As is Martyn's.

Who you happened to be very angry with last night.

So?

Because of his attitude towards your darling Colette.

You know what? Fuck you. I don't need this right now. I've
got enough things to think about.

Brogan thought he heard movement from the bedroom,
and he inched his way across to his peephole. Colette was still
in bed, and Martyn was bringing her a cup of tea.

Colette pulled herself up into a sitting position. 'This is a
nice surprise. To what do I owe this honour?'

A guilty conscience.

'It's by way of an apology. I was a little sharp with you last
night. It was only because I got worried when I hadn't heard
from you.'

Colette smiled. 'It's okay. I should have called. It was just . . .'

'What?'

'I don't know. It's hard to explain. I went into a strange frame of mind. I mean, I don't know Elsie very well, but I really like her. Remember how she kept bringing us home-made apple pies when we first moved in?'

'I remember.'

'And how she always used to check on the house when we went away?'

'Yes.'

'We didn't ask her to do any of that, and now I think maybe we haven't done enough in return and that it's probably too late.'

'We didn't know any of this was going to happen last night, Col.'

'Not last night, no. But we knew it would come one day soon. She's so old. We should have been prepared.'

'Prepared how?'

'Just . . . just been a bit more attentive. Called in to see her more.' Colette gestured towards her mug. 'Had tea and cake with her. Talked to her about her past, her memories. And you know what's really sad about all this? It's that nobody else has bothered either. She has no family, no close friends. If I hadn't gone to the hospital, she would have been there all alone once the carer left.'

'But you did, and I'm sure she'll pull through and that she'll appreciate it. And yes, we can then start to go round to her house more regularly.'

Colette sipped her tea. Brogan could see that Martyn's words hadn't placated her. Her expression was saying, *I don't think she'll be coming home, and even if she does, it'll be me who visits, not you.*

Colette suddenly threw her head back, and for a second Brogan thought she had caught sight of his eye above her.

'Oh, I don't know,' she said. 'Ignore me. I'm just in a funny mood. All the stuff about Jeremy, it's made me think a lot more about what happens when people die.'

Martyn scratched his head. 'Okay. Bit heavy for a Sunday morning, but okay.'

'Some would say that Sunday is the perfect day to think about such things. But that's not my point. I'm talking about the days leading up to death. About how we should make the best of those days, and help others to do the same.'

'I see.'

Colette frowned. 'What do you see?'

'This is more about Jeremy than Elsie, isn't it? You're going on a guilt trip again.'

'No. Well, maybe slightly.'

'Then stop. It's already made you unwell. Don't let Elsie's situation make it any worse.'

Colette flinched at this reminder of her 'sickness'. It told Brogan that she still suspected Martyn of engineering it.

'I'll try,' she said. She took another sip of her tea. 'I'm going to visit Elsie again this afternoon.'

Martyn's response was delayed, as though he objected to being notified of her decision instead of being asked for his approval.

'Yes, of course,' he said, a little too brightly. Then, in an attempt to rescue himself, he said, 'Tell you what, why don't you stay in bed for a bit longer? I'll go out and do the shopping.'

Colette looked surprised. 'What's got into you this morning?'

I already told you. Guilty conscience.

'Nothing,' Martyn said. 'Just trying to help. Bacon butty before I go?'

Colette laughed. 'I'm not sure I can cope. Who are you, anyway?'

Martyn smiled and left the room, but as soon as he was out of sight, Colette's mask of good humour slipped. Brogan studied her body language carefully.

Stop it!

Stop what?

That! Look at her firm body, peer down her wonderful cleavage – anywhere except into her head. You have no idea what's going on in there.

I can guess.

Well don't. Not unless it's something you can use against her.

She thinks a lot about death. She said so.

Yeah, well, don't we all? Hers in particular.

SUNDAY 16 JUNE, 5.11 PM

The day had been nothing but darkness, heat, boredom, hunger, dehydration, sleep deprivation and discomfort. Brogan had been teased mercilessly by the smell of bacon that had managed to penetrate even through the thick, suffocating stench of his flatmate. Martyn had left and returned with the shopping, then Brogan had been teased yet again, this time by what had smelled like soup. After lunch, Colette had driven off to the hospital, leaving Brogan to be entertained by the noise of Martyn hammering sporadically at something in the back yard. The only exertion Brogan managed was some quiet exercise and using one of the empty plastic crates as a makeshift toilet. All in all, a memorable few hours.

He started to long for wide, open spaces again. Out of the city. Back up in Scotland. Watching the changing of the seasons, the beginnings and endings of life. Feeling the sun on his shoulders, the frost on his toes, the rain on his cheeks. It had been wonderful while it lasted. Until she came along and ended it.

Things became more interesting at the Fairbrights' when

Brogan heard a car arriving, followed by the opening and closing of the front door and then the stamp of feet on the staircase.

Brogan moved into position and waited. He heard the toilet being flushed, the whoosh of tap water. Seconds later, Colette appeared in the bedroom. She kicked off her shoes and threw herself onto the bed, face down. She remained there, motionless.

Martyn's voice intruded about five minutes later.

'Col? Where are you? Are you upstairs?'

Colette didn't answer. Didn't even stir.

Martyn came upstairs and put his head around the door. 'Col? Col?'

He moved to the bed and sat down. Put his hand on Colette's shoulder. 'What's up?'

She turned her head towards him. He pushed the hair away from her face, and Brogan caught the glint of wetness on her cheek.

'What's up?' Martyn repeated. 'Is it Elsie? She's not . . .'

'No. She's actually a little stronger today. They've pumped all kinds of drugs and things into her, loaded her up with calories . . .'

'So that's good, isn't it? Why are you so upset?'

Colette rolled over on the bed and sat up. She tucked her hair behind her ears, then found a tissue in her pocket and wiped her eyes. Martyn shuffled closer to her and took her hand.

'I'm upset because it's just such a sad situation. Elsie lives by herself. Her husband died years ago. Her son was killed in a tragic accident. She hardly sees anyone now. But you know what the worst thing about it is?'

'What?'

'She's given up. The doctors told me. They said it's obvious she hasn't been eating or drinking properly. They think she hasn't been taking her medication either.'

'I thought she had a carer?'

'Yes, but you know what it's like. They drop in for five minutes, make her a cup of tea, and then they're gone again. Elsie could have been telling them what they wanted to hear, and then chucking her dinner in the bin and flushing her tablets down the loo.'

'Why? Why would she do that?'

'Because she has nothing to live for. And I think we have to shoulder some of the blame for that.'

'Us? Why us? What have we done?'

'Nothing. That's the point. If we had bothered to check up on her now and again, she might not be in hospital.'

Martyn caressed the back of her hand.

'Did you get to speak to her before you left?'

'Only a little. She was very confused. She opened her eyes, said, "Hello, dear. Is Alex with you?" then drifted off again.'

'Alex?'

'Her son. The one who was killed.'

'Oh. Then she is confused. But at least she'll know you were there. Seeing a friendly face might have done her the world of good.'

Colette frowned. 'I don't think it's a miracle cure, Martyn.'

Martyn lapsed into silence. Colette blew her nose.

'Shall I make you a cup of tea?'

Colette nodded. Martyn kissed her on the side of her head, then stood up and left the room.

Brogan continued to stare.

What's the matter?

Elsie's ill, and because of me. Because I abandoned her.

So?

They'll patch her up, and then she'll go back to that cold, empty house and she'll stop living again.

People get old and then they die. That's just a fact of life. And sometimes before they die they get deluded. Elsie has no feelings for you. She loves her dead son. You need to stop caring about her.

But Brogan *did* care. And before he could stop it, a tear escaped and dropped through the hole in the ceiling. It landed on the duvet next to Colette, but she appeared not to notice.

You okay?

Yeah.

Sure?

Yeah.

Only you're very quiet.

I don't have much to say right now.

So I see. This isn't like you.

These are unusual circumstances.

They are, but we can always change them.

I know.

What I'm saying is—

I know what you're saying. It's what you keep on saying, and the answer is still no. We wait. We stick to the plan. We act when it's the right time.

The plan didn't foresee all this. The plan was supposed to be fun. This isn't fun.

You've heard the news reports. The police are combing the city. This is the safest place right now.

Maybe, maybe not.

What's that supposed to mean?

I don't think dying of starvation or thirst is playing it safe.

We won't die. They'll go to work in the morning, and then we can go down. We can put up with this for another few hours.

Then there's you. I don't think that's very safe either.

What isn't? What do you mean?

You. You've changed.

We change all the time. New experiences change us.

You've never changed this much before. Elsie changed you.

I like Elsie. It's not unusual to be affected by people we like.

And Colette has changed you.

That's not true.

I think it is. I don't think you have what it takes to kill her anymore.

I could kill her. I could kill her in a heartbeat.

Not in the right way.

What do you mean by the right way?

You know exactly what I mean. Yes, you could probably end her life if it came to it, but you couldn't do it properly. You wouldn't take any pleasure in it. She's stolen that from you.

Don't be ridiculous.

It's true. Emotional attachment is dangerous. You of all people should know that by now. Think of all the times you've loved something.

Shut up!

Think about Mitzy. Your parents. And of course—

I said shut up!

Brogan put his hands over his ears, as if to drown out the

285

voice, forgetting that the voice was in his head, forgetting that he could never escape that voice, but also that he would never want to, because that voice was the only thing that kept him going, kept him alive, kept him wanting to exist.

It was a full two minutes before he realised the senselessness of his act and took his hands away.

The voices he heard now were real.

He moved back to the spyhole. Martyn was standing in the doorway, studying his wife as she undressed.

'Another early night,' Martyn said.

'We both have work tomorrow,' Colette answered.

'Even so.'

'Well, I'm drained. What happened to Elsie has taken it out of me.'

She continued to undress, and Martyn continued to stand there watching.

'Look,' she said when she was down to her underwear, 'you stay up for a bit. Watch some telly.'

'We always go to bed together.'

She shrugged. 'I'm not much company. I'll be fine tomorrow.'

Martyn mulled it over, and Brogan noticed that she didn't shed another stitch of clothing while he mused.

'All right,' Martyn said. 'If you're sure.'

'I'm sure. I just need to rest.'

'Okay. I'll be up soon, all right?'

'Fine.'

When Martyn had left, Colette collected her nightie and went for a shower. On her return, she climbed into bed but did not immediately switch off her lamp. Instead, she sat up, staring into space.

I thought she said she was tired.

She was lying.

Why?

To get rid of Martyn. She's shutting him out.

Yes, but why?

I think ... I think she doesn't know him anymore. I think she's reached the conclusion that he's not the man she married. He's a stranger in her house.

Like us.

Yes. Like us.

MONDAY 17 JUNE, 3.15 AM

It began with the usual sounds: the scratching, the crinkling of the bin liners, the scurrying, the buzzing. Brogan did his best to ignore it. He tried to divert his mind onto other, more agreeable things. The vision that was Colette, for example. Her curves, her smile, her—

Damn, that noise is irritating!

He was sure it was increasing in volume. Soon it would even be noticeable down in the bedroom. There had to be thousands of bugs and creepy-crawlies over there. Millions of them! All fat and juicy – filled with the burglar's festering body fluids. Within those bin bags would be one huge seething mass of ugly, obnoxious life-forms. The maggots that had appeared on the Carter corpses as if by magic had been bad enough, but this took things to another level.

Think about nice things. Food. What will we have to eat in the morning? A rasher or two of that mouth-watering bacon? Some of that delicious soup? And tea! Yes. Gallons of the stuff. Dunk a couple of biscuits in it and—

Go away! Go on, fuck off, you greedy little bastards!

But the noise continued to mount. It grew and grew, until Brogan was certain it had to be presaging an eruption of some kind. He could picture the bin liners stretched to bursting point, then a bang as they exploded, showering him with offal and maggots and a thick stew of human remains and oh God, what a stench, what an unbelievably vomit-inducing, gut-wrenching—

He switched on his torch, and it was as if every forager took it as a signal to play possum. The corpse was still shrink-wrapped, lying there like an obsidian-encased mummy awaiting discovery.

Brogan stood and moved closer to the makeshift coffin. He could see now that yes, it was moving slightly, the plastic binding undulating and pulsing along its length. Maggots were escaping from their prison and dropping to the floor.

But the point was that the man was still in there. Whatever he looked like, whatever his structural integrity, he was contained.

Brogan moved away, returned to his spot at the other end of the attic. He lay down on the floorboards and switched off his torch.

He didn't know how much time passed, but something demanded his attention again. Not the insects. Something more sinister.

Footsteps.

Brogan reached a hand out for his torch, but his fingers scrabbled in dust. Where the hell was it? He tried again, fanning his arm across the floor, and still he could not find it, but the footsteps were still there, and he was starting to panic, starting to wonder where his knife was, but there was nothing to save him.

And then he found the torch, and with quivering hands he managed to switch it on. He turned its weakening cone of light towards the body and saw that it looked different somehow. Still black and shiny, yes, but different, and no matter how much he squinted he couldn't work out what it was. He moved slowly towards the bundle, struggling to control his breathing and his fear and wondering why he expected the corpse suddenly to begin writhing and moaning. And it was only when he got within touching distance of the black mass that his brain managed to flip the image his eyes were sending it so that he saw it for what it really was.

He was staring at the *inside* of the bags!

A huge oval-shaped hole had been ripped in the plastic, revealing the interior, but what concerned Brogan most was that he could now see right through to the other side. There was nothing in there. No cadaver, intact or otherwise. Just a shallow pool of pus-coloured, maggot-infested soup. And yet somehow the bin liners had miraculously retained their roughly human shape, refusing to collapse in on themselves. It was as if . . .

It was as if they had turned into some kind of a cocoon.

And the role of a cocoon is—

He whirled at the footstep-like sound behind him, waving his torch in a frantic attempt to identify its origin. It came out of the shadows, rushing towards him, limbs outstretched, fingernails ready, teeth bared, and Brogan saw that it was no longer the man he had killed, that it had metamorphosed inside its cocoon and become—

'ELSIE!'

He awoke with Elsie's sallow face fixed firmly in his head – a mask not of its usual kindliness but instead of undiluted hatred – and his heart was still hammering in his chest at the sight of that apparition.

You were shouting. They'll have heard you!

Brogan got to his hands and knees and carefully manoeuvred himself to the boundary of the boarded area of the floor. He had no time to get to his spyhole: he could already hear voices and needed to know what was going on down there right now. He reached between the joists and tugged away a hunk of the insulating fibres, then lowered his ear to the plaster.

'Are you sure you're okay?' Martyn was saying.

'Yes, I'm fine,' Colette answered. She sounded groggy and slightly annoyed. 'Why do you keep asking?'

'I thought you must have been having a nightmare.'

'I don't think so. Why?'

'I heard something. A loud shout.'

'A shout? From me?'

'I don't know. Who else could it have been?'

'I don't think it was me. Maybe you were the one having the nightmare. Can I get back to sleep now?'

Martyn paused, as if confused. 'Yes. Sorry.'

Drama over.

Brogan let out a slow stream of air in relief. He didn't move for a good fifteen minutes while he reassured himself that the couple had drifted off again, then he retreated cautiously along the floorboards and sat with his perspiration-soaked back against the brick wall.

You had a bad dream.

Yes, I know.

About Elsie.

I know.

Then what you should also know is that you shouldn't be having dreams because you shouldn't be falling asleep.

Thanks for the lecture. That's really helped.

My pleasure. And you know what else you should know?

What else should I know?

That I've never seen you so afraid.

What blessed relief! What pure unadulterated joy!

Both of the Fairbrights had left for work. Ring out the bells!

Or maybe something a little less noisy.

Brogan checked and double-checked before leaving the attic. He was convinced he had heard the cars start up and drive away, but he needed to be certain. He checked at the spyhole, then he raised the hatch cover an inch and watched and listened there too.

Only then did he make his break for freedom.

He was down the ladder in a flash, bringing with him the crate he had been using as a toilet. He washed it out in the bathroom before making use of the facilities himself. On the landing he performed a few exercises to loosen up, then continued on down to the kitchen. At the sink he knocked back several glasses of water, ending with a satisfying burp.

Enough of that. We need food. Rustle up some breakfast, and don't hold back.

Brogan began opening cupboards. It was obvious that Martyn had been shopping yesterday: the shelves looked full enough to last the couple a whole month.

He started with a banana, which he practically inhaled. After that he wolfed down a bowl of cereal with milk and sugar, accompanied by a mug of strong coffee. In the freezer he found what was left of the packet of bacon. Reasoning as he had done before that it would probably be a while before the Fairbrights came looking for it, he defrosted the bacon in the microwave and grilled it, then consumed it with buttered toast and a soft-boiled egg and more coffee.

When he had polished that off, he leaned back in his chair and burped again.

My God, that was good.

Better than sex, right?

That's not funny.

Brogan picked some bacon out of his teeth. It occurred to him that they desperately needed brushing, which acted as a further reminder that his whole body needed a scrub.

I'm going to take a shower. I stink.

The whole house is beginning to stink. But clean up in here first.

Brogan washed his dishes, dried them, then tidied them away. He went back upstairs, whistling softly. When he reached the landing, he could hear that the tradesmen had resumed work on the loft next door.

Makes no difference to us now.

In the bathroom, Brogan stripped and jumped into the shower. He stayed under the water for a good ten minutes, covering every inch of himself in soap. When he stepped out again, he sprayed himself with climate-threatening quantities of deodorant before obtaining great satisfaction from using one of the sonic toothbrushes.

He looked down at his pile of discarded clothes.

They're disgusting. They reek. They look like they could crawl out of here on their own.

Then clean them. There's a washer-dryer downstairs.

You think I should?

I think you need to start realising that you can do whatever the hell you want. You need to stop being so afraid.

I'm not afraid.

You were afraid last night.

That was different. That was a nightmare. Everyone has nightmares.

Okay, then, prove it. Exert some control. Use the damn washing machine.

Brogan put on Martyn's dressing gown, then collected his clothes and took them downstairs. It took him a while to figure out how to operate the washing machine, but he got there in the end. For several minutes he sat watching his clothes spin around. It began to send him into a trance.

I'm very tired.

Then sleep. This is our house now. Sleep. There's a nice big bed upstairs.

Brogan was too drowsy to argue. He trudged upstairs with his eyes half-closed. When he reached the bed, he flopped onto it, pulled the duvet across, and was dead to the world in under a minute.

He got a shock when he opened his eyes and looked at the clock. The day had almost vanished.

He sat up, yawned, rubbed his palms across his face. He felt so much better, so much more alive.

I should get up. Things to do.

Like?

Get dressed. Get some food and drink.

Yeah, all that. You'd better get a move on, then.

You got something else to say?

Not at all. Do what you have to.

Downstairs, Brogan removed his clothes from the washer-dryer and buried his nose in the pile of garments. They smelt of all things homely and fresh. He dressed in the kitchen, relishing the feel of the grease-free fabrics against his skin. After that, he began the job of putting together some provisions for the attic. Opening the cupboards, he came across the litter bin.

Hey, look at this.

What?

Food. Lots of it.

Brogan started pulling items out, setting the edible stuff to one side. It was clear that, having bought lots of fresh produce, Martyn had thrown out anything past its expiry date or no longer looking its best. He found a quarter of a loaf of bread, a bruised pear and two only slightly mouldy oranges, an open packet of crackers, an unopened pack of ham . . .

What's the date on that ham?

It's only three days past its expiry.

It's been out of the fridge for a whole day.

It'll be fine. I'm taking it.

Then it's a good job you cleaned out that crate from the attic. You'll be needing it.

Brogan also found an almost complete cucumber and a jar half-full of jam.

We could have jam butties!

Whoop.

What's the matter with you?

Nothing.

Brogan dropped all the food items into a carrier bag and made a mental note to fill up his water bottle again. He glanced at the kitchen clock.

Not much longer now. I'd better take all this up and do a final check before we disappear.

Aren't you forgetting something?

I don't think so.

Okay, maybe forgetting is the wrong word, because I know it's in your head. You're just choosing to ignore it.

What am I ignoring?

The elephant in the room, my friend. The lame excuse you keep giving for stretching this thing out, for allowing the Fairbrights to live so long.

I don't know what you're talking about.

Of course you do. Your big plan. The mind games. The haunting. Turning the two of them against each other. All of that. Or has it gone out of the window? Is this place just somewhere to hide?

It's never been that. We're here for a reason. We're here because of the Fairbrights.

Well, I'm glad to hear it, because I was starting to think it had all changed.

Why would you think that?

Because of you! I see you like nobody else can. I know what Elsie and Colette have done to you. They've made you soft. Made you care.

Does caring have to be so bad?

Yes, it fucking well does! You know it does. You've experienced the pain that comes when you care, and from others who pretend to care about you. How can you have forgotten all that hurt in just a few days? How can you have stopped wanting to give some of that hurting back to those who deserve it more than you ever did?

I haven't forgotten. My plan hasn't changed.

Really? Because I see little evidence of it. You've been interested in everything else but that today. Food, tick. Drink, tick. Sleep, tick. But the real mission? Still an unticked box as far as I can see.

It's been a tough weekend. We needed the downtime.

No. What we need is to get on with our lives. Our time is

limited – you know that. Make no mistake, they are going to catch us. And when they do, they will lock us up and throw away the key. There is no going back. All we can do now is stay on course.

So what are you asking of me?

Some commitment, some courage, some of the old fire you had when we started this journey. Come on, man. Don't abandon me now. We made a pact. Let's live this to the full, like we promised each other we would.

I . . . I want to. I'm just . . . finding it hard.

I know. I see it. I'll help you fix it.

How?

Come with me.

Where are we going?

The bedroom.

Brogan ascended the stairs in a daze. He did not try to understand how it was possible for his brain to work like this, how each of his two personae seemed sometimes to be able to keep things from the other. He was occasionally aware that the barrier could be breached at any time, that there were no real secrets, but he also knew that there was a security that could only be achieved by pretending otherwise, by pretending he wasn't alone.

Open the wardrobe.

Okay.

There. The wedding dress. Take it out . . . Now remove it from the wrapper . . . Hang it on the picture rail.

Why are we doing this?

You'll see. Like the dress?

Yeah, I suppose. As wedding dresses go.

Pretty, isn't it?

Yes.

Amelia Leavitt's dress was pretty too.

Brogan's expression hardened. His fists clenched, causing his knuckles to crack.

You remember Amelia, don't you? You were at school together. Remember how she wanted to show you her party dress? How she put it on and allowed you to touch it? How she told you she wasn't wearing any underwear?

I remember.

She told you she liked you, didn't she? And you confessed that you'd always fancied her, ever since you first set eyes on her.

Yes.

And when she was standing there in that dress, the pretty dress that was the only thing she was wearing, she told you that she wanted to do it with you.

Yes.

And she kissed you. Started fondling you. But it all got too much, didn't it? You couldn't cope. You ran away.

Yes.

Which should have been the end of it. But it wasn't, was it?

No.

She told on you, didn't she? Told her friends you were impotent. And they laughed. And it turned out that she'd only approached you as a dare, because you were the scary weirdo with no friends. They pointed at you and they giggled and they called you names and they wrote things on the board about you and they stuck pornographic pictures in your locker and they—

Stop. That's enough.

That's what they're like.

Who?

People you trust. People you care about. If you let them in, they will tear their way out. They will break you, rip you apart. That's what they always do.

Yes.

And Colette is no different. She's attractive, and she seems caring, and she has suffered, but don't let that fool you. If you let her, she will laugh at you. She will take advantage of any weakness you show her. You mustn't allow that to happen.

No.

And so what are you going to do? Because here she is in front of you. Here is Colette in her pretty dress. Here is Amelia in her pretty dress. Here is your mother in her pretty dress. Here is the Girl Whose Name We Must Not Mention. Here are all the women who have and will let you down, who will tear another hole in your heart. What are you going to do?

I don't know.

You have your knife?

Yes.

Then you know what to do.

And he did. He took the knife from his waistband and he stepped up to the dress, the beautiful wedding dress, and as the baying and the screaming roared around his skull, as the tears of anguish and humiliation streamed down his cheeks, he slashed and he slashed and he slashed.

As usual, Colette was first home. Listening to her pottering about downstairs, Brogan could barely contain his excitement.

Wait till she sees this. She will freak. She will absolutely blow her top.

She came upstairs. Brogan wanted to giggle like a nervous schoolboy. She entered the bedroom, switched on her bedside lamp. Brogan watched how she fanned a hand in front of her face, clearly disgusted at the increasingly foul air in the room.

Turn around now, Brogan willed. Take a look. See what I've left you.

She turned. Saw it immediately. How could she not?

At first she was simply puzzled, confused. But then she took a step forwards, leaned over for a better look. Got down on her knees.

She picked up the first photograph. Clamped a hand over her mouth. She stared at the photo for a long while, then ran a finger across it in disbelief. Still on her knees, she shuffled forward to look at the next one, then the next.

This time, Brogan had taken a different tack with the

photographs. These pictures were not of Jeremy, but of Colette and Martyn. To be more accurate, they were *originally* of the loving couple; now they contained only Colette, each image of her husband having been carefully scratched out by Brogan with his knife.

Colette continued along the paper trail, picking up and studying each picture in turn. She was crying now.

The trail ended at the wardrobe. It irritated Brogan that he was unable to see the wardrobe from here, but he had ears. He knew that Colette wouldn't let him down.

He heard a click. The squeal of the wardrobe door. And then a huge gasp.

'Noooo!'

A metallic click as the dress was pulled from the rail.

'My dress! Not my dress!'

Brogan almost laughed out loud, not only at Colette's distress but at the realisation he was back in the zone. That phrase 'have a word with yourself' had never been so appropriate.

Colette was suffering. She was meant to suffer. Both the Fairbrights were meant to suffer at his hands, and this was just the tip of the iceberg.

So what do you think?

I think this is genius.

I would humbly agree. A little less subtle than you've been so far, but all the more effective for it.

She's in bits.

Only emotionally. The physical equivalent is still to come. Who do you think she'll blame?

How do you mean?

Somebody's wrecked her photographs and ruined her dress. Far as she's concerned, that someone has to be either Martyn, Jeremy's ghost or herself. What do you think she'll go for?

That's an interesting question. I think she still has enough of a grasp on reality to know that she didn't do this herself and then forget about it. Moving a ring is one thing, but this is in a completely different league.

I'd agree with your analysis.

I was hoping she'd opt for the supernatural explanation. As ghostly revenge acts go, this would make sense. Jeremy would want to destroy anything connected with a marriage to anyone but him.

He'd want Martyn out of the picture!

I see what you did there. Very good. But I still don't think she's buying that theory. It's too pat. She's never actually seen anything spooky taking place: it's all after the fact.

So your money's on her putting the blame on Martyn?

I think it has to be. Naturally, he's going to query her sanity again.

Naturally.

Which means we're in for an evening of great entertainment.

Who needs television?

Brogan watched as Colette came back into view, clutching both the dress and the photographs. Suddenly she tossed them all onto the bed and marched out of the room, wiping away her tears as she went.

Where's she going?

I have no idea. Maybe she's got a gun, and she's going to sit on the bed and wait for Martyn to show his face.

But when she reappeared less than a minute later, she was carrying only a bin bag. She stuffed the dress and the pictures into it, then left the room again.

What the hell is she doing? That's evidence. If she's going to confront Martyn, she needs the evidence.

Brogan had no answers. All he could do was wait.

When Colette returned, it wasn't with the bag. As she began to undress for her shower, Brogan tried to catch sight of her face. He wanted to work out what was going on in her head.

She doesn't seem as upset as we expected.

No. She's more . . . determined.

Colette found some casual clothes in the chest of drawers, then headed out to the bathroom.

Why did she dump the dress and the photos?

I think . . . I think she's going back to her previous strategy. She's going to act dumb. Pretend that she hasn't seen anything while hoping that Martyn will say something to trip himself up.

You think so? You think she can hold it together even after this? If moving her ring sent her over the edge before, how is she going to stay calm when her most personal memories have been destroyed?

I don't know. We'll have to wait and see just how strong this woman is.

Brogan didn't have to wait long. Soon after Colette returned to the bedroom, Martyn arrived home.

'Hiya!' he shouted.

'Hiya!' she echoed. She sounded breezy, cheery even.

Martyn galumphed up the stairs and into the bedroom. He gave his wife a kiss. She responded more positively than she had done for a while, but pulled away from him when it looked like it could easily evolve into something else.

'How are things?' he asked. 'Good day at work?'

'Yes, pretty good. What about yours?'

'Same old same old.' He paused, then ventured, 'You seem a lot better than last night.'

She shrugged. 'I am. Honestly, I don't know why I let it get to me so much. She's just a very old, sick woman.'

Martyn rubbed Colette's shoulder. 'She is. And we don't really know her all that well.'

Colette found a smile. 'Like I said, I think it's because of all the other stuff going on. You know – the way I keep doing weird things and then forgetting I've done them.'

'I understand. But we'll sort that, won't we, eh? Did you get a doctor's appointment?'

'Yes. Earliest I could get was Thursday after work. Not sure how I'm going to explain it.'

'Just tell them the truth.'

She looked doubtful. 'The truth sounds pretty weird. I don't want to be sectioned.'

Martyn laughed. 'You'll just be told it's stress or anxiety. They might refer you for counselling, but that's okay, isn't it?'

'I guess so. I just don't want them to think I'm crazy.'

'You're not crazy. A little wacky, maybe, but not crazy.'

'But what if I am? What if this is the start of early onset dementia or whatever? How can I do something and then not remember it? I don't even know when it's going to happen.

306

There are no warning signs, no headaches or flashing lights or anything. It comes as a massive surprise. I see a message on the mirror in the bathroom, and I'm convinced I've never seen it before in my life. Or I see a photograph on the floor in here, and again I'm wondering how the hell it could've got there.'

She paused then. Stared at Martyn.

She's being tactical. Throwing in that mention of the photo to see how he reacts. Clever.

'I'm sure it's nothing serious, Col. People do weird things when they're stressed.'

'Why am I stressed, though? What's happened to stress me out?'

'Stress can build up over time. Maybe you just reached a breaking point.'

Colette let out a long sigh. 'Yeah, maybe. I don't want to talk about it anymore.'

'That's fine. Let's have dinner. I'll make it.'

'Thanks. I'll be down in a few minutes. I just need to find something to wear for work tomorrow. I thought maybe a dress for a change.'

'Er, okay. Why not?'

Colette moved towards the wardrobe. Brogan heard its door being opened.

'Any thoughts?' Colette asked. 'There must be a dress in here I haven't worn for ages.'

Martyn paused. 'I, er, I'm not exactly an expert on dresses, Col.'

'I'm not asking you to be an expert. I just thought that maybe there's a dress in here you'd like to see me in again.'

'Well . . .'

'Go on.'

'The blue one. I like the blue one.'

'The blue one.'

'Yeah. You know, the one with the little white flowers on it.'

'The one with . . . Martyn, I threw that out over a year ago.'

'Oh. Then I don't know.'

A beat. Then: 'I think you'd better get the meal on.'

'Yes. I think that's a good idea.'

He left the room. Colette came slowly into view. She stood with her arms folded, staring at the door, a thoughtful, distrusting look on her face.

She did well.

She did. I admire her spirit.

But just her spirit, right?

Yes. Just her spirit. The rest is decoration.

MONDAY 17 JUNE, 10.42 PM

He watched her undress, and he watched her climb into bed, and he watched her open her book, and all the while it seemed to Brogan that Colette was still being fuelled by the spirit he had recognised in her earlier. Even in these simple actions she seemed to be acting with more vigour and determination, as though she now had more confidence in her own interpretation of what was happening around her.

Martyn secured the house downstairs. When he came up to undress, then went to the bathroom for his shower, Colette didn't lift her eyes from the page.

But then Martyn reappeared just a couple of minutes later, a towel wrapped around his waist and water still beading his torso. He seemed unsettled. He stood by the bed and stared down at his wife.

Colette lowered her book. 'Are you all right? You look flustered.'

Martyn pushed a hand through his damp hair. 'I, er, I don't know how to say this.'

Colette closed the book. 'You're worrying me now. What's up?'

'There's . . . There's another message. On the mirror.'

'What?'

'A message. I'm serious.'

'What does it say?'

'It says . . . It says, "I know what you did."'

Colette put her book on the bedside table and tossed the duvet aside. 'Let me see.'

She practically ran out of the room, Martyn following. Brogan heard voices in the bathroom, but couldn't make out what they were saying.

The couple returned a few seconds later. 'Now do you believe me?' Colette was saying.

'I believe one of us is writing messages on the mirror, yes.'

'Or somebody else is. I'm telling you, Martyn, this place is haunted.'

'It's not haunted.'

'Well, I didn't write those words. I don't even know what they mean. Do you?'

Martyn hesitated a fraction of a second too long. 'No.'

'So why would I leave a message for you that means nothing to either of us?'

'I . . . I don't know. But we've already agreed that you're not well, haven't we?'

'Yes, but now I'm starting to wonder. The other messages were about Jeremy. I knew what they meant. This one doesn't make any sense. Why would I write a message like that?'

'Who knows? The mind works in mysterious ways.'

Colette shook her head. 'I think this message was meant for

you, not me. Are you sure you haven't done anything you feel guilty about?'

'Like what?'

'I don't know. You tell me.'

Brogan could see the muscles in Martyn's jaw clenching. 'Maybe . . . Maybe you still think I'm trying to mess with your head, and that's what you were referring to.'

Colette climbed back into bed. 'Martyn, you can't keep having things your own way. When I told you about the messages, you said I must have imagined them. And now you've seen the evidence with your own eyes, you insist that I must have written it. Why have I always got to be the one at fault?'

Martyn scratched his head. 'This is getting a bit too confusing for me. I don't know what the hell is going on.'

'I do. We're being haunted. They started with me, and now they're moving on to you. It's not a doctor we need, it's an exorcist.'

'That's ridiculous,' Martyn said, but he didn't seem entirely sure of himself.

Colette picked up her book again. Martyn moved towards the door, but halted for a moment, watching her.

You mind if I ask a question?

Go ahead.

Maybe it's just my memory acting up, but we didn't write that message, did we?

Nope.

Then . . .

Then Colette did. This is her new strategy. She's going on the offensive. She's thinking that two can play at this game.

As Brogan thought this, Colette supplied her own confirmation. As soon as Martyn left the bedroom, she gave a twisted smile of triumph and flipped her middle finger at the door.

Enough.

What?

I'm calling time. We'll end it this evening, when they come home from work. We've played this game long enough, and we're suffering more than they are.

Don't be ridiculous. It's starting to get interesting. Colette—

Colette is stronger than you thought. You saw what she did tonight. She's getting her own back on Martyn. She's not falling apart; she's rising to the challenge.

Then . . . then we'll make it more difficult.

No. It's over. We need to move on.

It's not your decision.

Perhaps. But you know I'm right.

I don't know anything of the kind.

Yes, you do. You know that you've been putting it off. You need to get a grip.

I don't need your advice.

Oh, really?

That's right.

Okay, go ahead. Let them get under your skin. See what happens. See if they're any different from your parents. Or Amelia. Or . . . what was her name now?

Don't.

You're leaving me no choice. That's right. It was—

I said don't.

Began with an L . . .

Stop it!

But it was too late. She was already in his skull, tearing his mind to shreds.

*

Thomas Brogan lost his virginity on his twenty-fifth birthday.

Which was about two months ago.

Happy birthday, Thomas.

Her name was Lola, but she wasn't a showgirl. In fact, her real name was Lily, but for some reason she preferred to be called Lola. Something about it being more exotic and alluring.

Brogan had left home and the loving embrace of his adoptive parents as soon as he was old enough. He had travelled the country, taking on odd jobs whenever and wherever he could. He had little money, few possessions, and even fewer friends. Women sometimes came on to him but he always rejected their advances. His experience with Amelia was still too raw. Intimacy was now an alien concept.

He had spent three years as an assistant gamekeeper in Scotland. He revelled in the vastness, the ruggedness of the land. He basked in the fierce winds, and would stroll untroubled beneath flashing, booming thunderclouds.

He especially enjoyed killing the animals.

The long hours spent stalking never bothered him. They were always worth the eventual kick of the rifle stock into his shoulder, followed by the crazy flip of a rabbit into the air or the crashing of a deer into a bush. He liked to stand over their twitching, thrashing bodies in their death throes, the fevered voice busy in his head.

Lola just appeared one day, high on a hill, like a wild animal. Her blonde hair wafted across her face in the wind as she came directly towards him. It was in his mind to remonstrate with her, to let her know that this was private land and she needed to get off it immediately. But all stern intentions evaporated as she came close.

Her first words to him were, 'You're not going to shoot me, are you?' She accompanied it with a bell-like laugh.

Brogan tried to summon up a witty reply, but instead emitted some sounds that didn't even make sense. She didn't seem to mind, and was happy to do all the talking. She explained to him that her parents had dragged her up here to stay with family for a few weeks, but that she was already bored stiff. She felt an overwhelming desire to get out into the open, away from the prying eyes and ears of gossiping villagers.

The realisation that she was a kindred spirit sent shivers through Brogan's body he had never experienced before. When they shook hands, Brogan was surprised at the softness of her skin. They talked for several minutes, and despite the warnings in his head, Brogan wanted it to continue for hours.

But then the leaden clouds opened, as if to put an end to it.

Her reaction delighted him. She threw her arms wide and tilted her head backwards and greeted the rain. She opened her mouth to catch the huge drops, and he stared at the milky whiteness of her throat and the flutter of her pulse.

He told her that she should probably get out of the rain, and she asked him where he lived, and he told her that he shared a small lodge near to the landowner's house, and then he wondered why she was asking.

He told her about the bothy nearby.

The words just tumbled out. He could feel himself reddening at his own presumptuousness as he talked, but he couldn't stop himself. He told her how cosy it was, and that he used it sometimes when he needed to take a break or escape the weather . . .

He expected her to leave then. He expected her to worry that he might be some kind of pervert or, at the very least, a man not to be trusted.

But she didn't.

She asked him why he hadn't already got the kettle on.

As he led her around the hill, there was a bounce in his step and in his heart. His other voice bombarded him with questions and lewd comments, and he had to fight to suppress it.

The stone bothy was rough and tiny – not much bigger than a shed. The front wall had room only for a wooden door, the windows pushed round to the sides. Brogan started to feel embarrassed by the dimensions of the structure, but Lola trilled at its cuteness. He turned the handle of the unlocked door and opened it, then invited her in. She began picking up trinkets and books and saying how marvellous it all was.

Brogan started up a log fire and made a pot of tea, and they sat talking in front of the roaring flames for well over an hour.

When she left, it was with a promise to return. He asked her when that would be, but she told him she liked to maintain an air of mystery, and that she would seek him out.

Despite the vastness of the land that Brogan was required to cover, he made certain to return to that same hill several times a day, always on the lookout for her long blonde hair suspended in the wind.

He came across her again three days later. And again four days after that. As time went on, Brogan found himself lowering his guard. He told her things he had never told anyone before. When she asked him about girlfriends, he surprised himself in revealing that he had never had one. He half-expected her to laugh and mock him, but she never did.

Brogan felt that he was getting closer to Lola than he had ever been to another human being. The absence of any pattern to her visits frustrated him, but she would never commit herself to definite dates for future liaisons.

Except once.

He told her about his upcoming twenty-fifth birthday, and she seemed sad when he told her he had no special plans to celebrate. She promised to remedy that.

On the day of his birthday, she came running over the hill, yelling, 'Happy Birthday!' with arms flung wide. She gave him a massive hug, and the sensation of it made him want to weep.

In the bothy, he offered her tea as usual, but she turned it down. Instead, she pulled from her backpack a bottle of champagne.

So they sat and they drank and they talked. And Brogan, unused to alcohol, found his head spinning, and when she asked him what would be the best present he could ever receive, he could not come up with a sensible answer.

Lola gave it to him anyway.

On the rug, the wind howling outside and rattling the windows, she made love to him. He was confused and uncertain at first, but she soothed away his fears. The champagne helped, dampening the warnings in his brain and setting him free. He felt like one of the birds that soared and dipped and circled above his kingdom.

When it was over, he started to thank her, but she put a finger to his lips.

She left soon after, and in a way it seemed perfect. Although he had a million things he wanted to say, it was right not to. With the purity of the moment still drifting through his mind, he curled up on the rug and slept.

He returned to the hill many times afterwards, only to be disappointed. A week passed, and then another, and he began to suspect that his birthday gift was also a parting gift. After another month he gave up searching, but he was not unhappy. She had added a piece to him that had always been missing. He began to feel normal again, and even considered giving up this job and going on an adventure in Europe. The world no longer seemed such a frightening place.

But then she returned.

The weather was turbulent again. Storm-force gales blasted him with needles of rain. After many hours without let-up, it drove him to the bothy.

He pushed open the door, which was never locked, and found her there.

With someone else.

The lad was young and gawky, with weak fluff growing on his chin. He was also half-naked. Clearly, he was Lola's new project.

She grinned at Brogan as though this was perfectly normal behaviour. The lad, meanwhile, jumped to his feet and into his trousers and grabbed the rest of his clothes and started to head towards the door.

Brogan fired the shotgun into his legs.

He collapsed to the stone floor and he screamed, and Lola screamed too, but there was nobody around for miles to hear.

Brogan closed the front door and went to work. This time he listened to every word of the voice in his head.

When he was done, he buried the bodies in nearby woods and cleaned up the bothy.

And then he began the journey back to England. Back to the house of his adoptive parents.

*

He spent the next couple of hours rocking gently, his arms wrapped around his knees, his mind consumed by thoughts of Lola and her betrayal.

He was not sure exactly when it happened, but at some point during the dawn, Lola became Colette. And with that change came endless repeats of all that had happened since he had discovered the Fairbrights and their secrets. Everything was so lucid, as if he was reliving it. He saw with fresh eyes Colette's hidden photographs and the engagement ring and the letter. He replayed her actions, but somehow observed them from a different perspective. Neurons in his brain fired to establish previously untried patterns of connections. A new understanding descended, shocking him with its perfection.

By the time the birds had begun chirping and scampering across the roof tiles, he knew exactly how he was going to play this.

Smiling, he made his plans for death.

TUESDAY 18 JUNE, 8.17 AM

Brogan was a little puzzled. It had gone quarter past eight, and Martyn was still in his pyjamas. While Colette dashed around the house getting ready, Martyn seemed to be finding it difficult to get out of bed.

What's the matter with him? Is he ill?

He doesn't look ill.

Then what's he doing? This is a weekday. He should be leaving for work.

I don't know. Something has changed.

What can possibly have changed while they were asleep? He hasn't even checked his phone for messages. Change isn't good.

No.

A change in his plans means a change in our plans, and I don't want to change our plans. I have great expectations for our plans.

Brogan continued to watch and listen. A few minutes later, Colette hurried back into the bedroom, looking as though she'd forgotten something.

'I'll be a bit late getting home tonight,' she said.

Martyn turned bleary eyes on her. 'Why?'

'I'm going to drop in to the hospital after work. Check in on Elsie.'

'Fine.'

Colette went to the wardrobe. Came back with a pair of shoes. She stood looking at Martyn, as if she had only just become aware of his inaction.

'What are you doing? Do you know what time it is? You're going to be late.'

'Didn't I mention it? I'm back at that house just a couple of streets away. The appointment's not till ten, and the boss said I could just go straight there. Gives me an extra hour or so in bed.'

'An extra hour?' she said. 'You can do quite a few things around the house in an hour.'

Martyn groaned. 'I was thinking in terms of a bit more sleep.'

Colette laughed mockingly. 'Oh, you were, were you?'

She walked over to the bed, grasped the duvet and yanked it away. Martyn made a desperate grab for it but was too slow.

'Col!' he complained.

'Come on. Up and at 'em. This house is a tip.'

'What kind of attention?'

'Well, the drains for one thing. It stinks up here. I don't know what you've been putting down that loo, but something must be blocking it.' She fanned at something in front of her face. 'See? Another fly. They're everywhere.'

'It's summer. You get flies in the summer.'

'You don't get smells like this. Not usually. Can't you sort it out?'

'Not in an hour. It could be a big job, no pun intended.'

He grinned, but Colette said, 'I'm not laughing. It can't be healthy. I'm certainly not inviting any friends round until it's fixed.'

Martyn sighed. 'I'll take a look at the weekend, okay? When I've got more time.'

'Promise?'

'I promise.'

Colette nodded stiffly, then left the room. Martyn stared at the door, bemused by her abrupt departure.

Seconds later, she poked her head around the door.

'Right,' she said. 'No excuses this time. This one's a five-minute task, if that.'

'I've heard that one before. Your five-minute tasks usually take at least half an hour.'

'This one won't.'

'Go on, then. What is it?'

Colette came into the room carrying something. 'You can put this away for me.'

Brogan's heart froze.

It was the suitcase. The one that Colette had taken with her to Edinburgh.

The one that belonged in the attic.

'Col!'

'I've been asking you for ages, Martyn.'

'But, Col—'

'I keep tripping over the bloody thing in the spare bedroom.'

'But—'

'No more buts. Put it away.'

'It's filthy up there. I've got work later.'

Colette shook her head in disbelief. 'Then do it *before* your shower, thicko. Flipping heck, Martyn, do I have to do all the thinking around here?'

Martyn blew out a stream of air. He knew there was no point in arguing further.

Colette checked her watch. 'I'm going to be late. Gotta dash.' She pointed at the case. 'I expect to see a nice empty space there when I get home.' She blew him a kiss, then fled the room.

Brogan felt the house vibrate as the front door was slammed shut, but his focus now was entirely on Martyn.

Martyn sighed again. He reached for his phone, turned it

on, stared at the screen for a while. Then he put the phone down and swung his legs off the mattress. Two minutes later, he'd thrown on a T-shirt, shorts and an old pair of trainers.

He's getting ready to come up. He's coming!

Brogan stayed put. He had nowhere to go. He watched as Martyn stood, stretched, scratched his crotch, yawned.

Slowly, reluctantly, Martyn dragged himself towards the bedroom door. He left the room. He would now be on the landing.

Brogan twisted his body again, turned his head towards the hatch. He waited for the noises to begin – the connection of the pole with the hatch, the lifting of the cover.

He heard different sounds. The bathroom door. Another yawn.

He's using the toilet first! Get ready for him!

We should hide.

Where the hell are you going to hide up here?

But Brogan was already moving. Swiftly and quietly, he began stacking boxes, crates and suitcases on the boarded area.

What is the point of this? Don't you think he'll notice?

He might not. He might not even come all the way up. He might just open the hatch and toss the case up without even looking.

Brogan heard the toilet flush. He heard a tap going on, hands being washed, the opening of the bathroom door.

We're out of time. Quick! Get ready.

Brogan took hold of his knife. He crouched down behind his makeshift screen and flicked off his torch. He wondered if it was possible that Martyn might defy his wife, that he might just take the case back to the spare bedroom while making a mental promise to deal with it at the weekend.

But no.

He was coming up.

Brogan heard the hatch cover being raised, the ladder being unfolded. He clutched his knife more tightly.

Footsteps on the ladder. A grunt of exertion as the suitcase was pushed up through the hole and slid along the floor.

Job done, Brogan thought. Go away now.

But then: 'Jesus Christ!'

Brogan realised what had happened. It was the smell. Martyn's head had just been swallowed by a cloud of noxious fumes that made breathing almost impossible.

There was a clatter as Martyn descended the ladder again, emitting guttural declarations of his disgust.

Go after him! Jump him!

He'll hear me. He'll see me. I'll lose the element of surprise.

I don't care. You can take him.

I don't want to take him. Not now. Not like this. We made a plan!

But Martyn was already coming back, this time with a torch. Brogan saw its beam light up the roof tiles.

'Eeeurgh!'

The noise was nasal, as though Martyn was pinching his nostrils, and was immediately followed by a slight retching sound.

The cone of light played across the interior of the attic, zig-zagging like a sniffer dog in search of an intruder.

He's going to find us.

He isn't.

How can you say that? Everything has been moved! He'd have to be blind not to see that.

The workmen!

What?

The men next door. Maybe he'll blame them for moving things around. He might even think that they did something to create the smell.

Yes. That's possible, isn't it? It's a logical assumption. Much more sensible than thinking there must be a serial killer hiding up here.

More creaking of the ladder. Then footsteps: the coarse shuffle of rubber soles on the gritty floor.

He's coming towards us. We can't wait any longer. You have to kill him now!

A halo of light grew in strength around the boxes in front of Brogan. He tensed, held his breath, readied his knife.

Hold your fire. As soon as he moves the first box . . .

And then the halo disappeared.

Martyn's footsteps receded. He was heading in the opposite direction. Towards the dead body.

Brogan raised his head above his parapet. He watched as Martyn was drawn towards the light bouncing off the shiny black bundle. He saw Martyn crouch down and stare in wonderment and revulsion at the shifting bloated cocoon with its coating of maggots and flies.

'What the . . .?'

Brogan wondered what must be going through Martyn's head right now. What does a perfectly normal man think

327

when he pops into his attic and finds a beast like this writhing in the corner?

But then it became clear that Martyn had his suspicions.

'Oh, God!' he said. 'Oh, Jesus!'

He backed away, his hand over his mouth again. When he had enough roof space over his head, he raised himself to his full height.

Then he threw up.

He'd had no breakfast, so all that came up was a small amount of bile.

He knows.

No he doesn't.

Don't be fucking stupid. He's got eyes. The thing is body-shaped. It's decomposing. You've got to take him now.

It'll ruin the plan.

I don't give a shit about the plan. He's found a dead body. He's about to call the cops. You have to stop him now.

I . . . I can't. It's—

KILL HIM!

And then Brogan was exploding through his wall of boxes, leaping towards Martyn with a demonic scream, and Martyn could only freeze, his jaw dropping open as his attacker flew towards him.

But Brogan tripped. Caught his foot on one of the boxes and lost his footing and barrelled towards Martyn in an untidy windmill of arms and legs. The collision was messy, imprecise, the two men connecting and then rebounding, careening in opposite directions. Brogan's head hit a rafter and lights fired across his eyes, and by the time he'd recovered his senses he saw that Martyn was now in control of his own body, that he was now ready and able and willing to fight for his life.

The men ran at each other. Each had dropped his torch. Brogan had also lost his knife somewhere. They clashed again, on more equal footing this time, both fit and strong, one resolute on killing, the other determined to do anything to save himself. But Brogan knew violence, knew how to use it to his advantage. He attacked with savagery while Martyn defended with desperation. The two men grunted in the semi-darkness while they launched punches and kicks at each other, some connecting and some not. They grabbed at clothing, at skin, at hair, at anything that might aid their cause.

And then Brogan suddenly found himself on the defensive as Martyn managed to haul him to the floor. The boards shuddered as he crashed onto them, and Martyn was on top of him, straddling him, landing punch after punch to his face. Brogan tried to twist his body, to protect his face, to drag himself away. He reached out for something, anything, that could be used to help him. His fingernails dug into the wooden floor as he scrabbled for purchase, while Martyn continued to rain blows on him.

And then his fingers found something else.

His knife.

KILL HIM!

He drove the weapon low and hard into Martyn's abdomen. Felt it sink deep into the soft tissues. He pulled it out, emitted an almighty roar, then stabbed it home again.

Martyn stopped punching. He clambered off Brogan and scrambled backwards, staring in disbelief at the knife protruding from his stomach. He brought his hands to the hilt of the weapon, clearly unsure what to do, while whimpering at his lack of success and his pain and his acceptance that all was lost.

As he gathered breath, Brogan kept his gaze fixed on his opponent. The pain of others normally fascinated him, and Martyn was undoubtedly suffering, but this was different. This had not been achieved by design, had not been engineered with the precision and patience and ingenuity that Brogan took great delight in employing. This was crude and spontaneous and it infuriated him.

He approached Martyn slowly, panting, ready for a last-ditch attack. But Martyn had lost interest in him. His focus was wholly on the knife. He continued to retreat, but his options were limited. Brogan could see what was going to happen and did nothing to prevent it. Martyn stepped back off the floorboards and his foot missed the joist and smashed through the plaster. He fell backwards, his upper body crashing through plasterboard too, but on the other side of the joist, his snagged foot holding him fast and preventing him falling all the way into the bedroom.

Brogan raced down the ladder and into the bedroom.

It was an incredible sight. Like a scene from a medieval torture chamber. Martyn was hanging upside down through the ceiling, his arms out to the sides, mouth gaping, the knife still embedded in his abdomen. Blood ran down his chest and across his face and dripped steadily onto the bed below. *Drip, drip, drip.* A countdown to death.

It was unlike her to be so late, and he began to worry that she wasn't coming home. He'd been lucky so far. The fight had created a lot of noise, but if Jack and Pam next door had heard any of it, it didn't seem to have provoked them to take any action, perhaps because the presence of Martyn's car on the street suggested he hadn't left for work. In keeping with that narrative, Brogan had pressed Martyn's thumb onto his mobile phone to open it, then texted his boss to say that he had food poisoning. When the door didn't come crashing in during the hours that followed, it felt to Brogan that the coast was clear.

But what if it wasn't? What if Colette had somehow got wind of what had happened? What if his next visitors were to be the police?

Brogan picked up Martyn's phone from the kitchen table. Martyn was seated here now, his back to the door, all ready for his wife to come home. Brogan used Martyn's thumb to unlock the phone again. He sent a text to Colette.

Martyn: Where are you?

It took a while for her to respond. But then:

Colette: Told you. Visiting Elsie.

Brogan breathed a sigh of relief.

Martyn: Sorry. Forgot.
Colette: And I bet you forgot to put that suitcase away too!
Martyn: Nope. Did that first thing as instructed.
Colette: You know who's boss! See you in about half hour. Get dinner on.
Martyn: Will do!

Brogan stared at the phone for a long time before replacing it on the table.

He resumed his surveillance of the street. When Colette's car pulled up outside at half past seven, he raced back into the kitchen and pressed the play button on the music system. He had already selected the track. 'I'm a Believer' by The Monkees. He ramped up the volume, then hid behind the kitchen door. This room was perfect. As an extension to the main house, it had no shared walls. He could drip-feed the pain, with his victims' cries – and there would be plenty of those – drowned out by the music.

She's coming.

I know.

I'm so excited, I could wet myself.

He couldn't hear the front door being opened, but he heard the subsequent shouts.

'Martyn? Martyn?'

And then her shadow. A glimpse of her through the narrow gap between the door and the jamb as she entered. Her raised voice again.

'Martyn. What the hell are you doing? I can't hear myself think in here!'

He could picture her staring at the back of Martyn's head as he sat in the kitchen chair. She would go straight to the music system and turn it off. Any second . . .

Now.

And then . . .

'MARTYN!'

The scream as she saw her husband from the front. Saw the tape across his mouth, the blood covering his face and torso.

'MARTYN!'

And now she would be going to him, trying to help him . . .

Brogan heard the ripping away of the tape, the rush of air into Martyn's lungs, his voice as he tried to let her know.

'Colette. Get out! GET OUT!'

Brogan pushed on the door. It swung silently. Colette had her back to him, struggling to undo the rope binding Martyn's hands.

'Martyn, who did this to you? What happened?'

'Colette, please! Run while you can!'

And then Brogan's arms coiled around her, a snake's embrace. He clamped one hand over her nose and mouth,

333

cutting off her oxygen supply. She struggled and tried to yell, starting to panic.

'Hush!' he told her. 'I have a knife. Don't make me use it.'

She relaxed a little in his arms, but her chest still heaved. He lowered his hand slightly, allowing her to breathe, then dragged her over to a chair opposite her husband.

'I'm going to tie your hands behind your back. If you yell, I will cut out your tongue. If you try to escape, I will break your legs. Do you understand?'

Colette nodded. Before taking his hand from her mouth, he pulled his knife from his waistband and showed it to her.

'You see this? I will use it if you make me. You will be quiet. Okay?'

She nodded again. He released his grip, then from his pocket he took out a length of string he'd found in one of the kitchen drawers. He pulled Colette's arms through the slats in the back of the chair and began to tie them together. She stared straight at her husband.

'Martyn. What did he do to you? There's . . . there's so much blood.'

Martyn found it difficult to speak. 'He . . . stabbed me.'

'Oh, God.' She turned to Brogan. 'He needs a doctor. Please.'

Brogan touched a finger to her lips. 'Don't worry. I sewed him up myself.'

Colette stared at her husband's blood-soaked shirt. 'Why? I don't understand. What are you going to do to us? Who are you?'

Brogan moved around to stand in front of her. Her eyes were wide with fear.

He smiled. 'I'm the new kid on the block. Don't you recognise me?'

She studied his face. 'N-no. I've never seen you before.'

He leaned down. 'You sure? Take a closer look.'

It dawned on her then. 'Oh, God. Oh, please no . . .'

'Who am I?'

'You're . . . you're . . .'

'Who, Colette?'

'You're the man on the news. The one who . . .'

'Yes?'

'You . . . you killed some people. Your parents . . .'

Brogan clapped his open hand against the fist holding the knife. 'Well done. At last we've been properly introduced. Pleased to meet you, Colette.'

'Why us?'

'I thought it was time I paid you a visit. After all, I am a local resident. I've been living close by.'

She shook her head in confusion. 'What do you mean?'

He laughed. He was beginning to get into his stride. The old Brogan was coming back and it felt good, it felt right.

'I'm the Neighbourhood Watch. By which I mean that I watch the neighbours. I know Elsie, I know Jack and Pam next door, and I know you and Martyn. We're a very close-knit community.'

The mention of her husband's name caused her to snap her attention back to him. 'Martyn. What's he talking about? What does he mean?'

Brogan laughed. 'Tell her, Martyn.'

'The attic,' Martyn croaked. 'He's been living in our attic.'

Brogan saw how Colette's expression transformed from puzzlement to understanding and then horror. She looked up again.

'Our attic? You've been ... It was you! You moved things. The photographs. The ring. You wrote the messages. You slashed my dress. It was you!'

Brogan nodded proudly. 'Yup. The credit is all mine. And you had to go and blame Martyn for messing with your head. Poor guy.'

Tears suddenly spilled from Colette's eyes. 'Oh, Martyn. I'm so sorry.'

'It's all right, Col. It doesn't matter now.'

She turned to Brogan again. 'How did you get into our house? How did you—? Oh, of course. Elsie—' She cut herself off.

The name sent a jolt through Brogan. 'What about Elsie?'

Colette didn't answer, as though sensing a reply would lead to trouble.

Brogan showed her the knife again, then placed its tip beneath her left eyeball. 'What about Elsie?'

'She ... She's not well. I visited her in hospital this evening. There was a news report on the television about you. They were showing what you might look like with glasses or a hat or a ...'

'A beard?'

'Yes. Elsie pointed at the television, said it was her son, Alex. He's been dead for years, but she was convinced it was him. I tried to set her straight, but she wouldn't have it. She said he'd been visiting her. She was right, wasn't she? It was you.'

Brogan nodded. 'She's a nice old lady. I like her a lot.'

Don't be getting all weird now. Stick to the plan.

'And what about us?' Colette asked. 'What are you going to do with us?'

Brogan looked down at her, then at Martyn, then back at her.

'I'm going to play a game.'

'What kind of game?' Colette asked.

'It's like Truth or Consequences,' Brogan said. 'All you have to do is tell the truth. If you don't, there will be consequences. Simple.'

'W-what kind of consequences?'

'The kind that will hurt Martyn. I'm not interested in how much you can take. I want to see how much pain each of you is willing to inflict on your other half.' He paused. 'Right, who wants to go first?'

This is great. I love it. Good to have you back, man.

'No volunteers? Okay, then, I'll decide. How about you, Martyn? Anything you'd like to confess to your beautiful young wife here?'

Martyn squirmed in his chair. His pain was evident. Beads of sweat had formed on his brow and were running down to intermingle with the blood on his cheeks.

'I . . . I . .'

'Come on now, Martyn. Don't be shy. We're all friends here.'

'I can't . . . think of anything.'

'No? Are you sure about that?'

Brogan moved behind Colette. He gathered her hair into a ponytail, then leant forward and inhaled its aroma.

'Ah, that's gorgeous. I used that shampoo when I was in your shower. Bit girly for me, really, but it helped to remind me of you when I was stuck up in that attic.'

He felt the tremor run up Colette's spine.

'You . . . you used our shower?'

'I did. I like it a bit hotter than you do. And I don't hum tunes like you do.'

'How do you . . . ?'

'I've watched you, Colette. I've stood in your bathroom doorway and watched you shower. I've seen lots of things. You know that little hole in your bedroom ceiling?'

Colette's shoulders rolled. 'Oh, God. I think I'm going to be sick.'

'You can be very athletic when you want to be. Martyn, too. Isn't that right, Martyn?'

Martyn coughed, grimaced, but gave no answer.

'I said, isn't that right? Even when Colette isn't there.'

'I . . . I don't know what that means.'

'Of course you do, Martyn. But Colette would probably appreciate some clarification.'

Martyn glared at him. 'You're making things up to hurt us.'

'Am I? What do you think, Colette?'

'Martyn?' she said. 'What's he talking about?'

'Nothing. I don't have anything to say.'

Brogan twisted Colette's makeshift ponytail. He brought the tip of his knife to her ear.

'I will start here,' Brogan said. 'First the right ear, then the left. Then I think the nose.'

'Martyn!' Colette shrieked.

'All right, all right!' Martyn said. 'It's true. I'm guilty, okay?'

'Tell her,' Brogan prompted. 'Before she's unable to hear anything.'

'Oh, God,' Martyn said. He was crying now. 'I'm so sorry, Col.'

'Tell her!'

'I . . . It was when you were away in Edinburgh. I . . . I wasn't alone.'

Colette's mouth dropped open. She shook her head, trying to deny the painful truth. 'Who was with you?'

Martyn swallowed. 'Gabrielle. I was with Gabrielle.'

'Gabrielle? You brought her here, to our house? You . . . you fucked her? In our bed?'

Martyn's features twisted. He lowered his head and sobbed.

'How could you?' Colette cried. 'Why?'

'I don't know,' Martyn whispered. 'I don't know.'

This is incredible. You should feel proud.

And he did feel proud. The old Brogan was back. He'd only just begun and already these two were a wreck.

'It's how it is, Colette,' he said. 'People are selfish. Love is always a mistake. The things I've done are nothing in comparison to what I've seen couples do to each other.'

He moved behind Martyn. Put the tip of his knife to the man's neck.

'Your turn, Colette.'

She sniffed. 'I don't know what you want me to say.'

340

'Come on, Colette. You've heard Martyn's confession. Now let him hear yours.'

She shook her head. 'I haven't been unfaithful.' She practically spat out the last word.

'That's not the only one of the ten commandments it's possible to break. The sin you committed is much more serious.'

She shook her head again, but with less conviction this time. 'Please. I don't know what you're talking about.'

Brogan pressed harder on the knife and a trickle of blood ran down Martyn's neck. 'Do you want me to hurt him? Perhaps you do. After what he's just told you, perhaps there's nothing you'd like better than to see him suffer.'

'No! Don't hurt him. I'm trying. Really, I am. I just don't ...'

'Think!'

'I am! I don't know what to say. Please stop!'

'I'll give you one clue, Colette. Jeremy.'

She stared into his eyes, flames dancing in her pupils. 'Jeremy?'

'Yes. Tell Martyn all about Jeremy.'

'He already knows.'

Do it.

'Not everything.'

'Yes, everything. He knows that Jeremy took his own life.'

Do it.

'Is that all you're going to say?'

'What more is there?'

Do it!

'Last chance, Colette.'

'I've always been honest with—'

DO IT!

Brogan rammed the knife through Martyn's cheek. Then he slit through the flesh from cheek to mouth, sending a geyser of blood spurting onto the table.

Martyn screamed. Colette screamed.

Yes! Yes!

'Stop it!' Colette yelled. 'It's true! Jeremy didn't kill himself. It was me! I killed him!'

You were right.

Yes. I was right.

She's a killer. Just like us.

No. Not like us.

Brogan had taken a gamble, and it had paid off. The insight that had suddenly come to him in the night had been proven correct.

Colette raised her head and looked at him. 'How did you know?'

'I didn't. Not for certain. But you were so afraid that Jeremy might come back to haunt you. And the whole story just seemed odd. A man so depressed that he goes on holiday to kill himself? No witnesses? And then the note.' Brogan pulled it from his pocket, enjoying Colette's look of horror. '"It would be unfair of me to leave without some parting words. I can't carry on like this." And then, "You deserve a future. But it has to be a future without me in it." He wasn't planning to kill himself. He was leaving you.'

Her silence was all the confirmation he needed.

'Why? For another woman?'

Colette nodded. 'That note was just one of many I found. He couldn't even get that right. Couldn't find the appropriate words to put in a note, let alone say them to my face.'

'So what did you do?'

'Does it matter? Does any of this fucking matter now? You're going to kill us anyway. Just get it over with.'

'I want to know what happened. And I'm sure Martyn does too. I think he deserves to know what kind of woman he married.'

Martyn's eyes were closed, his head lolling. The gash in his cheek had turned his mouth into a grotesque one-sided smile. Through the blood could be seen the whiteness of his back teeth. The spectacle was pitiful enough to spur Colette on.

'I couldn't wait any longer for Jeremy to spit it out. We were on the coastal path, there was nobody else around, no eavesdroppers. So I confronted him. And I got angry, really angry. I slapped him, and then I pushed him, and then . . . and then he just disappeared. Over the cliff edge.' She looked pleadingly at Brogan, and then at Martyn. 'I didn't mean to do it. It was an accident. You have to believe that.'

'An accident?' Brogan said. 'Are you sure?'

She stared at him for a long time, as if reassessing her answer. 'No. I'm not sure. I've never been sure. Maybe I intended to do it all along. Maybe that's why I covered it up. I wasn't going to. My first thought was to go back to the cottage and call the police. But it was over a mile walk to get there, and I didn't meet a soul on the way. Nobody had seen me out with Jeremy. And I started to think about the note I'd brought with me, the one I'd waved under Jeremy's nose, and I thought, What if I say he left the cottage alone? What if I tell the police I got out of bed and found this note on the mantelpiece? And now I often wonder whether that had been my plan all along.'

'What about the woman Jeremy had been seeing? Didn't she kick up a fuss?'

'She was married. I don't know whether she really intended to leave her husband, or if that was what she'd promised Jeremy, or even if it was just wishful thinking on Jeremy's part. Whatever, she didn't raise a stink. Sometimes I wish she had. I should have gone to jail. Instead, I get this.'

And then something occurred to Brogan. It seemed that the last piece of a puzzle he was working on during the night suddenly fell into place.

Oh, my God. That can't be true. Can it?

Why not? I was right about the other stuff, wasn't I?

No. Surely not.

'Perhaps Jeremy deserved what he got,' Brogan said. 'He cheated on you.'

Colette shook her head dolefully. 'I'm not sure anyone deserves to die for that.'

'Not even Martyn?'

'I think he's paid enough of a price, don't you?'

'But is that what you thought this morning?'

'What?'

'This morning. When you made him go up into the attic where you knew a serial killer was hiding.'

TUESDAY 18 JUNE, 8.01 PM

Brogan took a step towards Colette, his train of thought gathering steam. 'You knew, didn't you? You'd seen the TV reports, you knew I was in the area. You figured it out. Your things being moved, the messages, the dress. You thought that it had to be either a ghost or Martyn, and you didn't want to believe either of those possibilities. But unless you were going mad, that only left one other solution: somebody else was in your house.'

'No. I didn't—'

'You finally put two and two together, didn't you?'

'No.'

'What was it, Colette? What led you to the answer?' He snapped his fingers. 'Elsie!'

'What about Elsie?'

'She told you she'd seen someone who looked like her son in her house. That's when you realised it was me. You knew there was a way to get from Elsie's house to this one. You knew about the empty house at the end of the row.'

'No. It's not true. Yes, Elsie did say that, but it was only this evening. I had no idea you were here before I came home.' She looked frantically at Martyn. His eyes were open now, bulging as he tried to process this new information.

'I think Elsie probably did say it tonight when she saw me on the television. But I also think it's not the first time she's talked to you about a stranger in her home. She has a habit of doing that. She wants her son back so badly that she just can't help herself. And then it all made sense. Noises coming from the attic, food missing...'

'No, no, no! Martyn, don't listen to him. He's trying to fuck with our heads!'

But Martyn continued to stare at his wife, the veins in his neck distended, his breathing becoming ragged.

'And then the idea came to you, didn't it?'

'No. What idea?'

'You saw the opportunity. Because you knew, didn't you?'

'Knew what?'

'About Gabrielle.'

'No. I had no—'

'You'd suspected for a long time, but then you found out for certain. What was the giveaway, Colette? The smell of her in the bedroom? Did one of the neighbours see her come into the house? Was it Elsie again?'

'I didn't know. Martyn, I swear to you. I had no clue.'

'That was a great act you put on earlier,' Brogan continued. 'But his affair wasn't news to you, was it? The hate was already there. You had a killer in your attic and a husband you wanted to get rid of. All you had to do was bring the two together. That's why you sent Martyn up to me this morning and ran out of the house. You knew exactly what would happen. Or, at least, you thought you did.'

'NO! Martyn, don't listen to him. I couldn't do that to you.'

'Really?' Brogan pressed. 'Why not? You'd done it before.'

'I told you. That was an accident. I didn't mean—'

'That's not what you said a few minutes ago. And it's not me you have to convince. Take a look at your husband. I'm not so sure he believes you either.'

She looked. Saw how Martyn's eyes seemed to be straining to leave their sockets.

'It's not true,' she told him. 'Please. He's making all this up to divide us. We have to stay strong.'

She turned suddenly on Brogan, a fierce challenge in her eyes. 'Why would I come back here? If I knew there was a serial killer in my house, why the hell would I even come through the front door?'

'Why? Because you thought your scheme had failed. You'd spent all day thinking that your husband was probably dead, and then an hour ago you got a text from him. You were shocked, weren't you? So shocked that the only thing you could think to ask about was the suitcase. When the next text told you that the case had been safely put away, you assumed that the man in your attic must have already left. You thought it was safe to come home. And when you entered the house and saw Martyn sitting here at the table listening to music, you were even more sure of it. Isn't that right?'

'No! NO!'

'Colette.' This from Martyn. A croak.

Brogan realised something was wrong. Martyn's eyeballs

348

rolled back in his head and his whole body began trembling.

'No,' Brogan said. He moved towards Martyn, but with no idea what to do. He knew only how to take life, not to safeguard it.

The trembling grew in ferocity. Martyn's teeth clenched, his macabre grin widening and splitting.

'MARTYN!' Colette screamed.

Martyn went suddenly rigid. Eyes and muscles bulged. Breathing halted.

'No!' Brogan cried. 'Not like this!'

As if in reply, Martyn slumped in his chair.

Pain could touch him no longer.

'No!' Brogan said again. 'This isn't right. This isn't fair!'

He went to Martyn. Shook him by the shoulders. Slapped his face.

Shit! Shit, shit, shit!

Colette struggled against her bonds. 'No. He can't be dead. MARTYN!'

'Quiet!' Brogan bounded over to her and clamped his hand across her mouth. 'Shut the fuck up. I need to think.'

He began to pace, tugging at his hair while Colette sobbed.

C'est la vie.

You shut the fuck up, too.

Temper, temper. He's dead. They all die in the end.

In the end. This isn't the end. This is the start.

Exactly. It's the start of what we do to Colette. Now you've got her all to yourself.

You know that's not how it works.

It can still work.

It's not . . . right.

So it's not quite the same as usual. It's not perfect. You can't stop now.

Brogan turned and looked at Colette. Her head was bowed and her shoulders heaved as she cried. She was a pitiful sight.

I can't kill her. Not like this.

Why not?

You know why not. For the same reason I couldn't kill Elsie.

Because you like her.

No, not that. Yes, I like her, but that's not the only reason.

Then what?

Because it's not a couple! You know this. It *has* to be a couple. They have to suffer together, to hurt each other. If Elsie's husband had been with her, I could have done it. I could have done anything to them. But this . . .

'Are you going to kill me now?'

He looked at Colette again. Looked into her large sorrowful eyes.

'Do you want me to kill you?'

'I think . . . I think it's probably what I deserve.'

'So you admit it, then? Your plan to kill Martyn.'

'No. But he died because of me, because of my actions. That's what I do. Whether I intend to or not, I kill the men who cheat on me. So I guess this is karma.'

You heard her. She's gagging for it.

She's not supposed to do that.

The others did.

Yes, at the end. When it was the only way of escaping the pain. Before that, they would do anything, promise anything, to be spared. Colette isn't doing that.

Who gives a shit? Let's party.

I . . . I don't know where to start.

Jeez. I'll help you. Don't I always help you?

Yes.

Right. Good. Put the music back on. Loud as possible.

Brogan started playing 'I'm a Believer' from the beginning. Colette's head was bowed again, as if awaiting the kiss of a guillotine. He turned the volume right up, and still she didn't move.

Excellent. Go to her.

He stood in front of her. She didn't look up.

The clothes. Start with the clothes.

He reached down and grabbed her sleeveless top. He inserted his knife between two of the buttons and sliced quickly upwards, neatly severing the top button. He continued until every button was lying at his feet. Then he slid the knife under the shoulder straps and cut through those too. The fabric fell away.

Wonderful. Now step away for a minute. Take in the sights.

He stepped back. He stared.

Look at that! Gorgeous, isn't she? So sexy.

Brogan forced himself to focus on Colette's chest, but all he could see were the tears running down her cleavage.

You're not relaxed. Feel the music. Look at that soft skin, those luscious curves. You've waited a long time for this. All those days spent in the attic, watching from a distance. Now she's yours. All yours. You can do whatever you want with her.

Yes. Anything.

Remember how she teased you? How she tormented you? They

all do it. Amelia did exactly the same. Lola betrayed you. You need to show them. Prove that they can't get away with it.

Yes.

Go back to her now.

All right.

He took a few steps forward again. He raised his knife. The music filled his ears and his mind.

She lifted her head. Mouthed something he couldn't quite hear above the song.

'What?'

'Make it quick.'

Ha! Who does she think she is, trying to order you around? Show her who's boss. Cut her. Go on, cut her.

Colette's eyes flickered to the blade and then back to Brogan. 'Please,' she said.

Go on. Cut her. She needs to know you're serious about this.

Brogan moved the knife closer to Colette's face.

That's it. Think about Lola and Amelia. About your adoptive parents. The kids at school. They can't treat you like that. They all need to be taught a lesson.

And then Brogan was moving. Away from Colette.

Where the fuck are you going?

He turned off the music system. The silence seemed immense.

And then he felt the pain.

Like a crick in his neck to begin with, but then suddenly mounting in intensity. He reached up, felt the hot wetness gushing onto his fingers. He looked at his hand, saw the alarming redness running down his palm and onto his wrist.

He whirled around. Colette was still in her chair, several feet away.

But much closer, a kitchen knife clutched in her trembling fingers, was the deceptively frail and insubstantial figure of Elsie.

An astonishing cocktail of emotions engulfed him. Fear, confusion, anger and self-preservation all jockeyed for position in his mind.

You have your knife! Use it!

He moved towards Elsie, but she slashed wildly at him, slicing his fingers. His knife clattered to the floor and he staggered backwards.

Forget her! You're bleeding everywhere. Stop the bleeding!

He clamped his hands over his neck wound, but still the blood seemed to find a way to spurt through his fingers. His back hit the wall and then his legs gave way and he sank to the floor.

Elsie stood over him. She was breathing heavily, rasping, and her face was a mask of pain. Her whole body was shaking. He saw that she was wearing a dressing gown and slippers, now spattered with his blood. Below the gown, her ankles were painfully swollen, the paper-thin mottled skin seemingly on the verge of bursting open.

'YOU'RE NOT ALEX!' she screamed. 'You're not Alex!'

Brogan tried to say something, but all that came out was a croak.

Elsie pointed a quivering index finger at Colette. 'She said you were a killer, and I didn't believe her. You were my son, and you couldn't hurt a fly. When she left, I couldn't stop thinking about it. I had to come and ask her why she said those horrible things. I had to come and find my Alex. He's the only thing I live for. I left the hospital. I walked straight out and got a taxi.'

She paused for breath. For a second, Brogan thought she was about to keel over.

'Elsie,' said Colette. 'Get me out of here. Please!'

Elsie seemed not to hear her. 'I thought she would tell me the truth if I came here. I thought she might know what happened to my Alex. I rang the bell, but nobody came. I could hear the music. I have my hearing aid in and my glasses.' She said this so proudly it almost made Brogan smile. 'I looked through the letterbox and I could see all the way into the kitchen. I saw you. Saw what you were doing to her. My Alex wouldn't do that.'

Brogan felt his heart speeding up, his breathing becoming ragged. He knew his body was being starved of oxygen.

Colette continued to plead to be released, but Elsie reached into the pocket of her dressing gown and took out a bunch of keys.

'I have a key,' she said triumphantly. 'I look after the house when they're away. I make them apple pies. I help them. Not like you. You weren't helping. You were hurting her. It's not right. You told me that life is precious. You lied. You lied.'

She was wheezing now. She dropped her knife, then

clutched at her chest and swayed. She dragged out a chair and collapsed onto it, oblivious to Colette's frantic appeals.

'Elsie,' Brogan began, but it was a whisper that drained him. It was becoming hard to see. Pinpoints of light were sparking in his vision. All sound in the room seemed to fade and then disappear completely.

Has she . . . has she killed us?

I think so. We've had our nine lives.

Like Mitzy.

Yes. Like Mitzy.

I don't want to die.

No.

Will you stay with me?

Of course. I'll always be by your side.

That's good. I was right, wasn't I?

What about?

About the ones we care for. They always hurt us. I tried to tell you.

Yes. You did. I should have listened.

Too late now. It is late, isn't it? It's getting cold and dark.

Yes. Close your eyes. We can sleep properly now. The pain will be gone soon.

I love you.

I know. I love you too. Hush now. Go to sleep.

Brogan took one last look at the two women who had somehow managed to touch his soul.

And then he stopped.

ACKNOWLEDGEMENTS

This is the start of a new journey for me. Not only is this my first standalone novel, it also heralds the beginning of what I hope will be a long and fruitful relationship with a new publisher. I'm incredibly excited to be in the vanguard of authors being published under the Viper imprint, and for that I owe a huge debt of gratitude to Miranda Jewess, my editor. She had faith in me where others didn't, and her editing skills are second to none. She is a joy to work with, and has without a shadow of a doubt moulded this into a much better book.

Thanks also to the rest of the team at Serpent's Tail for getting behind the book and lavishing it with much-needed love and attention. I know they will continue to nurture it long after it takes its first steps into the world.

As ever, my heartfelt gratitude to Oli Munson and the team at A M Heath. This publishing deal and the others around the world would not have been possible without them, and I'm still over the moon about the introductions that led to my being represented by the United Talent Agency in New York and Los Angeles.

A massive shout-out to the authors and bloggers who agreed to read early copies and provide quotes and reviews. I am truly touched by the level of support.

And, of course, the biggest thank you of all to Lisa, Bethany and Eden. I do it all for them.

ABOUT THE AUTHOR

DAVID JACKSON is the author of nine crime novels, including the bestseller *Cry Baby* and the DS Nathan Cody series. A latecomer to fiction writing, after years of writing academic papers, he submitted the first few chapters of a novel to the Crime Writers Association Debut Dagger Awards. He was very surprised when it was both short-listed and Highly Commended, leading to the publication of *Pariah* in 2011. When not murdering fictional people, David spends his days as a university academic in his birth city of Liverpool. He lives on the Wirral with his wife and two daughters. He does have an attic, but there's nothing interesting up there. He's checked.

Find him on Twitter @Author_Dave or see his website at www.davidjacksonbooks.com